ELSEWHERE, CALIFORNIA

✳ ✳ ✳

ELSEWHERE, CALIFORNIA

DANA JOHNSON

COUNTERPOINT
BERKELEY

Library of Congress Cataloging-in-Publication Data is available.

ISBN: 978-1-58243-784-2

Printed in the United States of America

COUNTERPOINT
1919 Fifth Street
Berkeley, CA 94710

www.counterpointpress.com

Interior design by Tabitha Lahr
Cover design by Debbie Berne
Distributed by Publishers Group West

10 9 8 7 6 5 4 3 2 1

For Leo and Hattie Johnson

Now I face home again very pleas'd and joyous;
(But where is what I started for, so long ago?
And why is it yet unfound?)
—Walt Whitman, "Facing West from California's Shores"

"Let's make an alliance! I'll look out for you, and you look
out for me! I'm good at catching and I've got a damn good
pitching arm!"
—Ralph Ellison, *Invisible Man*

This ain't fun. But you watch me, I'll get it done.
—Jackie Robinson

PROLOGUE

MY PARENTS WERE not playful people. They did not tell jokes or laugh a lot. When I try to remember how they were when I was a child, I only remember them working very hard. And fighting. But once, when I was five, my mother and father played this game with me. I asked, Where am I from?

My father listed all the possible places. He started with my mother. That's where you came from, he said.

Where else! I asked. Where else!

Watts, he said. That is where I was conceived. Then 80th Street, he said, the place I first knew as my home. Then Los Angeles. Then California. All the way from Tennessee. All the way from Africa, my father said.

Where else, I cried. From kings and queens?

No, he would say. Kings and queens had buckets of gold, and we never had any of that. Yes! I said. No! he said, and we went back and forth. To prove it, he tried to tell me serious stories about hard times and sacrifices and how far we've come and how far we have to go. Boring, sad stories. And so I said, I'm not from any of those places. I'm just from California.

Where in California then? he asked me. California is big, he said. I couldn't pick Los Angeles, because I was already here. So I picked a name I really liked, all by myself, with the help of television. A crazy, complicated name. Supercalifragilisticexpialidocious. Hmm, my mother said. She frowned. Supercali who?

Who lives there, then? she asked. Anybody who wants to, I said. How you get to this place you talking about? she asked. I was stuck then. I didn't know. How was everybody going to get there? I hadn't thought that far ahead. I loved where I was already, in Los Angeles. But I still loved my invented place in California even better because it sounded like confetti and long streamers coming down from the sky, caressing my face—this other place in California, like glitter and myriad pieces of confetti, the beautiful Blue Chip Stamps my mother and I used to save, and all kinds of other images and words and ideas I couldn't put a name to at the time.

THE FIRST TIME my father told me my mother was crazy was after one of their fights. She had tried to stab him with the butcher knife. He had said that he'd be home by eleven that night, but he came home at eleven thirty. Half an hour. She was waiting for him when he came through the door. My brother grabbed for the knife, but she slipped away from him and chased my father down the narrow hallway of our small apartment. He made it to their bedroom and slammed the door just in time. My mother stuck the knife in the door and pried it out. Stuck it in and pried it out. My brother and I stayed away until she was done, had tired herself out. Later that night my father sat me on his knee while I cried in the living room of our five-room apartment on 80th Street and my mother cooked his dinner. Your mother, he said in low, soothing tones. Something is not right. Her brother is crazy. Her sister. I told her eleven and I came home at eleven thirty. All she had to do was wait one more half hour, he said. What difference does thirty minutes make?

I told this story when I first met the therapist. At first, I didn't tell anyone I went to a hypnotherapist. Massimo rolled his eyes and shook his head. But I went anyway, though I had to wrap my mind around the idea of hypnosis. My first attempts at therapy did not do me any good. I was defensive and could not submit to the idea of giving myself up to someone I didn't know, someone who thought they knew what and who I was. I thought it would be true what my family and Massimo said, if I were to go to therapy. I was weak. I was self-indulgent. And there was this: Therapy was for people with real problems. Terrible loss. Trauma. My brother Owen said that my main trauma was that the house I was living in was too big for me to clean all by myself. Me, throwing good money away in Massimo's big house on the hill. White folks. *Rich* folks, and they doctors, Mom said when I told her. But I needed help. I couldn't get it together on my own. I needed someone who would listen, yes, but also hear. The first two therapists didn't have a chance. I did not respect their earnestness, their kindness, their gentleness. They looked at me and this is what I thought they saw. A success story. A bright and articulate woman. An affirmative action baby. A bourgeois snob. A hard worker. A whiner. A well-dressed woman. A whore. A woman who spread her legs for a nice place to live. A woman who wanted to be an artist, who was not really an artist. A charming, smiling, elegant liar. They didn't tell me that this is what they saw. I already knew. I already thought I knew. I was already negotiating the twists and turns of the people and personalities I could be to anyone at any given time, so, kindness and gentleness, what good were those things to me?

But the moment I saw him, I liked the hypnotist.

He was handsome, patient, and paying attention—and I thought I was in trouble, even though I knew he wasn't what he appeared to be. I thought I should pick another doctor, someone else who looked different, who didn't have sandy hair and turquoise eyes. A man who looked like that, who looked at me.

Dr. Harrington. He was a hypnotist, after all. He was going to hypnotize me. He hypnotized me.

I told him all kinds of stories when he said, Good. Let's start from the beginning.

WE CAINT GO tricka treating. The Crips went and shot some-body and the Bloods done shot em back. Me and Mama stan-din out front the partment building with all the other mamas and they kids. We pirates and princesses and witches. My cousin Keith got on glasses with no glass in em, a black tie with green stripes and a blue vest with his jeans. He a lawyer. I aint never heard of no lawyer before, but I guess he look awright to have no money for no real costume. And Im happy to see him because he come all the way from the desert to come tricka treating. Thats where he live.

Auntie Janice holding Keiths hand. She say, Aint no need a walking around, up and down the street getting shot up for no candy, not with these niggas running the streets and carrying on.

You right, Cassandras mama, Miss Channey, gree with Aun-tie Janice. She run her hand over the part of Cassandras hair sticking up in the front so it lie back down. Cassandra got pretty hair, almost straight but still kind of nappy and the color gold like her eyes. Cassandra try to fix the crown on her head and mess up what her mama just fix.

I got a princess outfit too, from Newberrys. Mine just a mask with blonde hair painted on the sides and a plastic dress you slip into. Itty bitty red lips with a hole you posed to breathe out of. I beg and beg Mama for the costume and a baton. I want to twirl and throw it up in the air like I seen girls on TV do. Majorettes, Mama say. She say, No, I caint get no baton, neither, but she get it for me later. But its hot inside the mask right now. I pull the mask back so its sitting on top my head so I can breathe.

Mama wearing a patch like she a pirate, but she and Daddy fight and now she wearing the patch cause he hit her in the eye. Mama say, Lets go on over to Miss Maxies house, and Howard and nems. I know they got some candy for yall. We go to a couple houses, Avery, she say to me. Then we gone get on in the house.

Mamas afro is orange this week. She look like a lion, the way it stick out all around, with her eyebrows painted on dark black. Mama make me feel like we may as well go tricka treatin. Caint no bullets hurt us. She wont let em. I ask Mama can we go to the liquor store after the houses cause last year and the year before that they give out candy. But she say, Not now, not tonight. Maybe tomorrow.

We all go to the same four houses right next door to our partment building and then we go to each others partments. And then, thats it.

Later Mama dump all my candy on the bed and pick out all the ones that look like might be something wrong with em. And the apple. My brother Owen pick it up and shake his head. When he do that, his eyes got extra light in em. They light brown eyes and he the only one in the whole family got light brown eyes like that. Dont nobody know where them eyes come from, but he look different because he so dark and them eyes so light. Look like somebody color them eyes.

He say, Who this stupid gone put a dang apple in the bag? He pretend to bite it and Mama snatch it out his hand.

Quit playing boy, she say, and throw the apple in the trash. And dont call Miss Shepard stupid, Mama say. She old and dont know how mean the world done got, thats all, bless her heart.

I get to eat bout five pieces of the candy Mama aint throwed out, and then I take my costume and fold it up neat for next year.

Girl, that thang aint gone fit next year, Mama say. May as well throw it out.

It barely fit now, fatty, Owen say. He sitting on his bed on his side of the room, trying do his school work. Owen tall and skinny like JJ on Good Times. He tall and skinny like a rail, Mama say. He always calling me whale and fatty, and I call him bean pole back, but he never care that he skinny. And I dont care they calling me fat.

I stick my tongue out. I dont care. Ima keep it.

Suit yourself, Mama say. Owen just laugh at me.

When Daddy come home, I listen for cussing and fighting but I dont hear nothing but Marvin Gaye and Mama and Daddys words sound far away and soft until Daddy say, Goddamn. Kids caint even go tricka treating no more without getting a bullet in they ass. We getting out of L.A.

I

MASSIMO IS IN the air. Due home from Rome very soon. He will be here to support me in this little show that I'm doing with a few other artists. He has always been on my side, though we come from completely different worlds. "Different worlds, yes," Massimo always says, "and yet we came from the same places, places where people have no money. Nothing and nowhere." And so my goal is to show something that will make people think about different worlds, to look at the same old thing they've been looking at in a new way. Maybe they will say, *I never saw it that way before.* "Your show will be fantastic," Massimo has been saying, and I have always been so unappreciative of this support in the past. He doesn't understand the source of my inspiration and, yet, he thinks understanding isn't necessary, as long as he lets me be and do whatever I want. I don't know. Maybe he is right about this.

The show is small, just like the only other one I've had. In just a few hours. A box of a gallery on La Brea, owned by a friend of Massimo's.

I have gotten used to thinking that Massimo, with all his Roman grace and European credentials, makes me more—to those who value such commodities. I'm not just another person trying to be an artist showing work that nobody will buy, let alone understand, but a sophisticate. Not just another hard-luck story who "transcended her humble beginnings, who may fulfill her potential," according to a recent, scant mention in the *Sentinel,*

L.A.'s black newspaper. A paper I don't ordinarily read. Potential, always there is potential lurking around like a mandate. It had one paragraph, this mention. But it was still a mention. Now, though, because of our struggles throughout the years, Massimo and I have arrived at the same oxymoronic conclusion. I am, and am not, the ideal American, African-American, and any other identification one wishes to project.

"How can you let them put that shit, that American boot string bullshit—" Massimo said when I showed him the article one morning. He had toast crumbs in the corners of his mouth, and I had reached across the table and brushed them off.

"Straps," I said. Boot *straps*."

Massimo lit a cigarette and considered me through the smoke. We were in yet another argument, the one about something being wrong with me. "What does it matter? You are here. You do what you do. That is all," he said, turning up the palms of his hand.

But today I'm really missing Massimo, fights and all. Massimo, with his perpetual cigarette which is either bouncing off his lips as he talks or dangerously close to burning someone as it sweeps the air with grand, elegant gestures. He is the best publicist I could have. He works a room, Massimo, making everyone fall in love with his accent and malapropisms, elevating us both at the same time, yet with another elevation through language that I can't achieve. I'm only American.

"That is because you have no accent, my love," Massimo says, and he's right. I'm flat. I sound as though I come from no particular place at all. My flatness started out as a costume, a disguise—hand-me-down words accessorized with various inflections until at last, without even realizing it, I'd settled on the voice I now have, a voice that goes anywhere with anything. Flat. But my lack of accent is only half of it; the other half of it is that one must have the right kind of accent, phrasing and diction, the kind that opens a door and lets you in. Massimo knows this because he uses language whenever he takes me by the elbow at gatherings and says, "I'd like you to meet my wife, Avery. She is an extraordinary painter who seduced me in Piazza Navona." He knows this line with words like "piazza," "painter," and "seduced" is much more charming, sounds much better than: "This is my wife, Avery, from West Covina. The suburbs. She is trying to make art." And anyway, painters don't come from West Covina. They come from Italy, France—New York, Los Angeles—but never West Covina. Massimo reminds me that I was born in L.A. and only moved to West Covina when I was a girl, but L.A. feels like the before of who I am, who I turned out to be. I can hardly remember before. And anyway, he picked me up in a bar. In Hollywood. Less romantic. So as it turns out, the past does matter, whether it is invented or not.

Massimo likes to tell half-truths, and the half-truth about us is that he picked me up at the Formosa, worlds away from Rome, where I was out with Brenna and he was out trying to get laid, wagging his accent around like a big cock. After he bought me many drinks and spoke to me with so much Italian charm that I now understand to be nothing more than leg-spreading rhetoric, I gave him my number. Later, much later, after Massimo and I were already living together and I had blended into his life, there was the Piazza Navona, me sitting at a café sketching, waiting for Massimo. Still, Massimo insists that everything he says is the full truth—at least emotionally—and that I'm always the one with the caveats and qualifiers, with a tendency to diminish. He's a struggler, a fighter. He knows how to win. He says that I am too, but what drives him crazy is that I won't struggle. I won't fight, and so how am I going to win?

I was a child then. Twenty-one years old. "Massimo's little girl," he used to say with affection. Now, in my forties, I am too old for such a term of endearment to be endearing. This is the struggle between us now, the struggle with myself. Wanting someone, usually Massimo, to do all the things I need to do on my own, like a teenager who insists, "I know. I *know*. I can fix everything I need to fix by *myself*," thinking, *but would somebody just help me?*

My art doesn't sell, except to people close to Massimo. Almost every painting or every installation I've sold has been to friends of Massimo, and friends of Massimo's friends who have wandered through my workspace and/or came to the other show and purchased a piece or two. The people I know, my friends and family, they spend money on rent, on food, on gas. And if they had the money, they wouldn't spend it on most of the things I make now: found objects or random pieces of things that put together a story. Old shoes with holes I have repaired with red thread; piles of candy—Pop Rocks, Now and Laters, candy cigarettes, Pixie Stix, and jawbreakers—formed in the shape of a heart within which I have typed the name of every teen idol I have ever loved.

Before that, I had to paint away the reactionary anger of my youth. It was as if I had discovered racism all on my own, made a record album of it, and let it skip and skip and skip. I wasn't remembering the nuances of other recordings, a record or song, a piece of art that goes all over the place and back to the place it started, like John Coltrane, like David Bowie. Before, I'd painted portraits which were, I've been told by the few people who have seen them, offensive, racist, and, according to the mention in the *Sentinel,* "unsettled in their critique of iconic negrobilia images."

Racist. I was twenty.

I read that word over and over and could not process it. Some woman had gone to a coffee shop that let me hang my portraits on the wall. The owner was a young man, his hair dyed jet-black and arranged in carefully messy spikes. He rubbed his arms, both covered in lavish tattoos before people started covering themselves in tattoos en masse. He bent his noodle of a torso over my portfolio. "Badass," he said. "Fuck yeah." But the woman who had seen my portraits hanging had been so disturbed, so *offended*, that she wrote me a long, hateful letter and e-mailed it to the owner of the coffee shop, but it was addressed to me, Averygoodbyeain'tgone, a name I'd made up by combining my name with a saying of my mother's. She says, all the time, "Every shut eye ain't sleep and every goodbye ain't gone," and I've carried that phrase with me my whole life, like a warning, a threat. The woman's e-mail said that I "obviously hated white people" and that I had some kind of hysteria about white people. I had inappropriate, misplaced anger, which she didn't want to be subjected to while she sat and drank her coffee. She closed with the almost-funny question, What did I have against June Cleaver?

I laughed. And later I cried.

I deleted the e-mail because I wanted it out of my world. Once, I told Massimo about it, this letter from so long ago. He asked me a very simple question: "Why are you still telling this story from almost twenty years ago?" In Massimo's world, Americans and their constant discussion of race was a nag, as inconsequential as a gnat I was supposed to swat away. My blackness had me on a string, he said, in his way. "One idiot talks and that is the only one you hear. Always, there will be some asshole. Sometimes you think they are truly asshole, and sometimes you think they are asshole and they are not. You want to cry over both of them." I wasn't sure why I cried, this was true. Massimo likes to remind me of the president, who is always so calm. "Do you realize, Avie, what he had to do to get elected? What he puts up with now? He's Muslim, he's racist, he's socialist, he's fascist, he's not even an American? Do you see him crying?" I had to agree. But still.

I look at our president closely, looking for that slight bend in his straight spine, the strained grin, the loose string that may unravel, because I know it is there somewhere. Tucked away.

My portraits, the ones that so incensed the anonymous woman, weren't that complicated or that incendiary. I'm not even original. Other artists, famous artists like Kara Walker with her silhouettes of white masters fucking their male slaves, are much more audacious. But these artists, they were in galleries, not in coffee shops hanging over people's heads while they tried to go about their lives and drink their lattes. I simply painted portraits of Shirley Temple's cherubic face, Elizabeth Taylor circa her thinnest, most luminous days, June Cleaver in her crispest dress and most elegant pearls, and Sandra Dee during her sweetest, just-learning-how-to-surf phase. All of them in blackface. I used four portraits for each woman. The first frame is the original, how they looked as we saw them on film, on television, in pictures. The second frame looks as though someone has flung mud on their faces. Or shit. Cadmium Red and black, thick, thick oil paint, and I put one dollop somewhere on their faces—the forehead, the cheek, the chin. I wanted the viewer to be surprised, to wonder what was that muck ruining sweet Shirley's dimpled cheeks? The third portrait is full blackface. I put rags on their heads, made their skin completely brown, and fattened them all, desexualized them, gave them big clown lips stretched in magnificent smiles so that they all looked like they just walked off a box of pancake mix. In the last portraits all the faces are scratched up, as if someone else or the subjects themselves had tried to scratch all that dirt off their faces. I was trying to collapse time, layer irony. My intent was not to infuriate anybody. I was hoping to simply arouse thought, discussion, and consideration. I didn't realize how someone could get furious just by seeing Sandra Dee with big, doughy tits, a rag on her head. Shirley Temple's face, not altered in the least, a replica of an original photo of her in blackface, except I painted her sitting on the steps of a dilapidated apartment building, broken wine bottles all around her.

There were more portraits. Reagan eating a big piece of watermelon. Leif Garrett, one of my several girlhood crushes, eyes popping out of charcoal face, fishing off a riverbank in tattered trousers. George H.W. Bush stealing across a burning field with two chickens under his arms.

Massimo doesn't quite get this phase of my work. I've shown him images from the past, none of them with layers of irony, all the mammies and uncles I could find on film, on toothpaste packages, selling detergent. Little Shirley Temple in blackface, just a normal scene in a Hollywood movie. He sees what I'm doing, but doesn't appreciate it, not really. He's told me this, himself. But I've told him that he's not my audience, the European who's been in the States for only fifteen years. And anyway, I'm past that now. The art I do now comes from any and all things that don't seem to go together because this is what I appreciate about life and living. There is race, but there are also lots of other things. Things that aren't supposed to fit and go together but nevertheless do. I'm not very good, putting together all my pieces of discarded things. But it is also who I am.

❋ ❋ ❋

MAMA WAS RIGHT. It aint been but one year and my princess costume dont fit no more. Mama was finna throw it away cause we moving but I thought I might could still fit it. When I tried to put the mask on the rubber band snapped out the staple on the side, and the sleeve split when I tried to put my arm in it. Thats when Mama throwed it in the trash. I didnt care, not really. I was looking at all our stuff packed in boxes and happy to be moving, going somewhere. To a better place, Daddy say.

A while back, after Daddy had done already decided we was moving, Owen came home with blood dripping down his arm. The Crips had done cut him up because he wasnt gone join they gang, not cause he didnt want to, but because Mama say Daddy would beat his ass if he did.

After Owen come through the door bleeding trying to make it not look bad, Mama called Daddy at the car factory and told him all about it. He musta ask how Owen look cause I hear Mama say, He bleeding, but he look awright. Ima call the ambalance, though. Then she say, Um hum, un hunh. Nod, say, Okay then, I wont. And hang up the phone. Your daddy coming home to run you to the doctor hisself, she tell Owen, and he stand there squeezing his arm with a towel Mama gave him. Mama dont know how to drive, and we only got one car anyway.

Daddy got home, took Owen to General Hospital, and got him thirty-two stitches. But when they got home, Daddy was mad. He stand with one hand on his hip, quiet. He take his cap off and turn it around in his hand some, then he put it back on. He say, Take me to the mothafuckas that cut you up. I got some-thing to tell em.

They was gone but a little while before Owen come back grin-ning and calling Daddy Shaft, but Daddy wasnt grinning. Owen say Daddy walk down to 83rd Street, found two of the boys that cut Owen, and told them if they ever touch his boy again, he was gone kill they black asses. They aint bothered Owen since. Good thing there was Daddy. I dont think them boys would of listened to Mama like they did Daddy.

Now we moving to a place that aint got no gangs, so it dont matter to us no how.

ALL OUR STUFF in the van, and Mama hugging folks and Daddy shaking hands. We packed and ready to go. Me and Cassandra sit on the steps, and I think I want to remember what she look like, but I dont know why since Im gone see her again. We both got Baby Alives that pee and boo boo and eat and drink. When Mama holler at me to come on, lets go, me and Cassandra trade dolls at the last minute and say we gone trade em back next time we see each other. We gone babysit each others kids. I trade my black Baby Alive for her white one, even though Cassandra done washed her hair too much and made it hard. Its different than what I had all the time at least. But still, I hold my black baby one more time and kiss it. I say, Goodbye, Baby Alive. Then Mama say she aint gone tell me again to come on here, and we get in Daddys Buick Wildcat and drive away from 932 West 80th Street, partment 8. I want to be prepared for my long journey, I tell Daddy.

Journey? he say. It aint but thirty minutes up the road.

I dont care. I take all kinds of books with me for the trip to the valley. Daddy say its the San Gabriel Valley and I never heard of that before, San Gabriel. But it sound pretty to me. I never been to where we going but I been to the desert and down South. It aint as far as all them places, but its far enough to read for a long time. I been reading Little House in the Big Woods, about traveling far from where you from.

Owen seen the house before. Daddy took him to see it, and

Mama too, but I aint never seen where we going. Mama just say the house nice. Theres gone be grass in the front yard and the back yard. And no guns.

I look out the window before I read some more of my book. And after while L.A. start looking different. Dont see no trash in the street, no liquor stores, no Church's Chicken. We driving on a long highway. The sign say 60 with Pomona next to it. I see hills on both sides of the freeway, green and yellow, thats the color of the hills, and theres flowers in patches, yellow, white, and purple. And cows way off in the fields. Not a whole bunch, but cows anyway! Big and brown. I get happy to see the cows and I say, Look, cows. They make me happy cause I never see no animals never, not where I lived, not even hardly cats and dogs, except at the zoo. Got to be down South to see animals. But how can this be so close to L.A. and be so different? How come I never seen this before if its so close?

So what, cows? Owen say, and slouch down in the seat and put his cap over his face to take a nap. But Daddy say they got dairies around here and they need the cows for the dairies. But a couple cows aint dairy cows they farm cows cause they brown. Just because the cow is brown it does different work? Ima ask Daddy about this later.

But its not just the cows. They got a big ol shopping center out here, Puente Hills Mall, they call it. Mall, I say to myself. Mall, with a water slide and little cars you can drive with bumpers. A big place for walk in movies where they play a whole lot of different movies all in one place, not just the drive in where we used to go when I was real little. They got more stuff to do out here. More places to go. It smell different and look different and everythings gone be different. We headed west, to West Covina in San Gabriel Valley. I say it to myself over and over again, WestCovinainSanGabrielValley, and it sound like a song.

JUST WHEN I was getting to the part in the book where Laura and them might drown in they covered wagon trying to cross a river, Daddy say Look, we here. We turn a corner and in the middle of the street that take us to our house there a tall white pole with a ball and points coming out of it, like a planet. Under it, it say, Welcome to Galaxy Homes and stellar living.

What stellar mean Mama? I ask. She move her shoulder up.

Darnelle? Mama pull on her hoop earring and look at Daddy.

It mean something to do with the stars, Daddy say. He driving the car going up and up a long street to the new house. Stellar mean up there with the stars, Ave.

I can understand that part, but what do stars and houses mean to each other?

Daddy seem to know I dont understand. So he add, They built these houses in the 1950s, Ave. Long time before you was born. When space and progress was on everybodys mind.

Now I dont understand what progress mean, though. I want to ask what it got to do with houses and planets and stars. But then Owen say, Well, its 1976 now, and that little ball on top the pole look stupid.

Our house look like a barn, not a star or nothing I thought it supposed to look like. Its a dark red almost the color of chocolate and the garage door is the part that look like a barn. Two Xs in white, and white all around the edges. But then, the barn make me think of Laura Ingalls, even though she wasnt living in no barn. I dont care. If this was a house on TV there would be hay and chickens and horses, and I would be milking my cows and pitching my hay with a giant fork. Chores. I always like the sound of that word, so many chores to do with Pa getting the lay of the land, they say. Chores to get your house in order. But this is just a garage that got a water heater and dirty paint cans left from the people who used to live there so I aint no pioneer. I feel happy because we got grass in the front and in the back, too, Daddy say. When we get out the car and walk to the door, everybody quiet. Daddy put the key in the door and turn around before he unlock the door. He smiling at everybody. Yall want to go in?

Quit playin, Darnelle, Mama say. Its hot out here, but she smiling too.

And when we go in, I run straight to the room thats mine and lay down in the middle of the floor. Its mine. I got my own room. Dont have to share with Owen. Its the smallest room in the whole house, only my bed and one dresser gone fit into it, but I dont care. All around the house everything make me feel happy and silly. I get up and run around, trying everything out. We got a glass door in the kitchen that supposed to slide back and forth but when Mama try it, she caint open it. I tell Mama, Let me do it! Let me do it! And then I open it easy. It must be broke, Mama say. She look at me like Im playing a trick on her, like I made it hard for her. But Mama, I say. It aint broke. You just have to know how to do it. And I open that door easy. I slide it back and forth until Mama tell me to quit it. You smart, I can see that, she say. You know how to do it. Good for you, she say and tug my hair and pat me on the back. And then theres a tree, a big, big tree I can climb up until I get scared to go higher. Rubber, Mama say. A rubber tree. We got three bedrooms and one bathroom with a tub, and one bathroom with a shower. A living room. A kitchen more than two people can stand in. I feel like we rich. When I tell Daddy it feel like we rich, he laugh. Naw Ave, we a long, long way from rich, but we doing better than we was. Thats what progress mean.

2

THE HOUSE WE live in is much too big for just Massimo and me. This house has embarrassed me with my family, miles and miles away from the suburbs and 932 West 80ᵗʰ Street, where I lived as a young child. My mother calls it the crazy house, but it's just modern architecture, a knockoff of Frank Gehry's Schnabel house built in the late '80s. Even though it's too big for the two of us, this is not a very large house compared to some of the other houses on the hill. But it is the one that's the most unique, even if it copies another style. Stucco, cinderblock, copper, wood, glass, and lead all come together to make a house the shape of cubes, pillars, and trapezoids. This is not what houses are supposed to look like. Houses are supposed to be recognizable as places to live and work, where children are supposed to play. Like my beloved barn house. But I delighted in the puzzle when Massimo first brought me here. The playfulness of it, the oddness of it, reminded me of Miro's *Peinture Collage.* I was so relieved. I thought that Massimo did not take houses seriously, the having them and getting them and holding on to them. Why else would one live in a house that didn't seem to make sense? But I was wrong. Everybody still cares about having and holding on to everything they have, even if it doesn't make sense.

Mom and Owen were the first family to come see me. I like to think of this first time because it was the beginning, when I did not think much about anything and suddenly did. The past came pushing through to remind me of so much that I forgot. Like now, sitting on my bed, I see her. Mom is here, wearing jeans and sneakers. She's at the door, hesitating at the threshold, as though she doesn't know how to enter. And then, Massimo is pulling her through, kissing her cheek, turning his head to kiss the other cheek. Mom does not know what to do with that. "Okay," Mom says, nodding, looking at the puzzle all around her. "This is a house," she says. "No lawn or nothing, front or back, all right?" she says, as if convincing herself. And Owen says, "Shit, Massimo, man. This is nice." But Mom is suspicious. "Any black folks live around here?" she asks. Massimo slips his arm through Mom's, waiting for me to answer because this is not a question he cares about, either way. "What you think, Mama," Owen asks. "What do you think?"

Mom turns up the corner of her mouth and levels her eyes at me like she's about to tell me something that's funny, but something that I've got to know nevertheless. "One or two," she says. "One or two of us might be around here. Got three of us now, in this house, don't we?"

And there, that day, the question sat next to me, quietly, waiting for me to consider it. Not, What do you think the answer is, Avery, but, Remember why the answer is so.

Still, when Massimo's friends and acquaintances visit, I am grateful to have this house as an accessory to hide behind. I can fade away into the house, serving cocktails in fancy glasses and dishing out Massimo's complicated meals on gorgeous bright dishes that call to mind Kenneth Noland color fields, vibrant concentric circles, inviting and mesmerizing.

Now, I lay out two dresses on our large antique bed, my favorite thing about the whole house. Boxy and plain, with distressed wood that looks as though it was retrieved from a shack. I can sleep for hours and days in this bed. I have.

✳ ✳ ✳

DONT NOBODY ELSE lie down in they yard, but I like to. I get a towel and lay out in the yard with books and the radio like Im at the beach. I like that song that go Fight it! Fight the power, and thats been playing all the time, and Oh girl Ill be in trouble if you leave me now. We been here just one week, but I do it almost every day. Owen say I better watch it else the white folks gone call the police about niggas laying in the yard in they neighborhood, but Daddy tell Owen not to say nigga, and he tell him, this our neighborhood now, not just theirs. If Avie want to lay in the yard and read books, then she ought to. So thats what I do cause I dont know nobody.

One day Im reading in the front yard. The book is Trixie Belden that Daddy got me because he says its time to move on from Laura. He ask me, Aint I about tired of her yet? Because he surely is. Im reading about how Trixie having trouble figuring out the math, just like I do, when all of a sudden I got a shadow over me and when I look up, theres a white lady. I think Im in trouble, that she gone tell me not to lay in the yard. She have white hair all over her head like cotton, and big blue eyes. The lines around the circle of the eyes are extra blue, like somebody traced them with a crayon over and over again. They kind of scary eyes with all that blue trace. But when she smile, I aint that scared no more. Them eyes change and I dont look away.

Hello, she say. I am your neighbor, Joan, and then she brush the front of her pants. They the color of orange ice cream. She put her hand out and I stare at it. She say, I would like to welcome you to the neighborhood. Her voice sound sharp to me. Clean at the end of each word like when you snap your fingers. After each snap, the sound end, aint nothing coming after it like when we talk. When we talk, its like you humming at the end of every word you say. I just stare at her big hands because I dont know what to do. Grown people I know dont really shake my hand. They just nod at me. And Joan more than grown. She old. Its okay, Joan say. Whats your name? She wiggle her fingers at me like come on, take my hand.

Avery, I say. But I say it in a low, quiet voice. I feel funny, like she gone take my name and do something with it, now that she know what it is. Where is Mama? Dont she hear somebody talking to me? Why aint she coming so Joan can talk to her instead of me?

Avery, she say. What a pretty name. She finally, finally put her hand down, so I know I dont have to shake it no more, but now I want to. She still smiling at me and she said my name is pretty. Is your mother home? she say. I think about this for a little bit. No, I say. She aint home. But Mama is home, and I dont know why I say she aint.

Im sorry to hear that, Joan say. Please tell her that I stopped by and give her my regards. But I dont know what regards is. I'll give them to her, I say. Where they at? Joan laugh at me. Just tell her I said hello. Thank you, Avery, she say, and then she walk down the driveway and disappear around the palm tree. Regards, I say to myself. Regards. I shine it up around the edges. That day, the day with Joan, thats the first day that I really start to pay tention to the sound of white people when they be talking.

ONE DAY BEFORE school start Joan came over and ask Mama if I can go swimming in her backyard. She ring the doorbell, and Mama walk over to the door with Pine Sol in her hand cause she mopping the floor. Im watching TV in the living room, so I can see her talking to somebody at the door. I can hear its Joan. Joan say, Hello, Addie Mae. How are you today?

Mama say Fine, Miss Cooper, and you? but dont open the screen door. I turn off Lucy pretending to Ricky that she caint remember who she is because I already know how its gone end.

She gone get a spanking from Ricky, and anyway, she remember. She just faking. I walk to the door and stand next to Mama. I like Joan, I like the way she sound. I like how nice she be whenever she see me in the yard or trying to roller skate on our dead end street, a cool the sack, Daddy call it. When I stand next to Mama, she look down at me and her eyes say I bet not say nothing until she tell me to.

Joan look down at me and smile. Then she look at Mama. Weve got a pool in the backyard. Its so hot. I thought Avery might like to go swimming, she say.

I want to go to Joans. I want Mama to open the door and say come on in and tell me something good, like she always did on 80th Street. But she dont. She say, Avery dont know how to swim. And I dont. I aint never been to no pool. Only to the beach sometime and a river in Tennessee. I swallowed a bunch of water and then cried all about it.

Oh, its only a wading pool, Joan say. It wont come any higher than her chest.

Avery aint got no swimsuit, Mama say.

I have one she can wear, Joan say.

Then Mama put her hand on the screen door like she gone finally let Joan in. Avery got her lunch to eat and then she can come over. I bounce up and down cause Im happy to leave the house. Im bored. Dont know nobody. School aint started yet. And all I do is sit in the yard reading Trixie.

Hows that? Mama say, looking at Joan. When I look at Mama, one corner of her mouth smile, not the whole mouth.

Wonderful, Joan say. She pull on the side of her head and move some of her hair out the way. Put in behind her ear. Her hair white and fluffy like a cloud. She older than Mama. Ill take good care of her. Please. Dont worry, she say, and then she turn around and leave. She got on purple pants that stretch across her behind. Tight. Me and Mama watch her walk down the driveway and across the cool the sack to her house.

Nosey, Mama say. She take her hand off the screen door, look at her hand, frown and then wipe it on her shorts. She nice, Mama say, but she too much in our business already.

But I like Joan. When Mama make me a fried baloney sandwich and give me a bowl of turnip greens from last night, I eat it so fast I dont taste it. Wonderful. Wonderful. Wonderful, I sing to myself and wiggle in my chair. I try to sound like Joan, like a TV lady. Wonderful. Joan.

Quit playing and eat your food, Mama say at the kitchen sink. Washing dishes.

But in a minute, Im already through. Im ready to go, Mama. I wipe my face and hands with a paper towel.

Go on then, she say. She frown like when she mad at me, but I aint done nothing wrong. Go on then, Mama say, squeezing the towel in her hand. Leave. And dont stay too long, wearing people out.

And I run out the door. Slam it.

WE DONT KNOW nobody here, but Mama done already signed me up for school. It didnt take but ten minutes to walk there, and when we got to Westdale a white lady helped us find the office. There white people everywhere in West Covina; Mexicans and Chinese people too. I never saw that where I was living. Only white people sometimes down South. And at my old school, there was only Maria. She only spoke Spanish and got tired of me playing with her long brown hair.

Before we leave, Mama make me dress nice. She put out a yellow Easter dress thats too dressy for school. Aint even started yet. She grease my hair real good and make two plaits. Put ribbons in them. I feel like I want to die. Its too dressy, Mama. People gone laugh.

Nobody laugh at you if you look good. If you look neat and put together. They only laugh at you if you look dirty and sloppy.

I dont believe that because if I was in a school and a nine years old girl come in looking like me, looking like a baby doll in a box, I would laugh at her. But I dont say nothin else to Mama. Do, and Ill be in trouble.

When we get to the office at school, everybody look up and they all white, too. I look up at Mama and ask her if everybody here is white. Her eyes tell me I best be quiet.

May I be of some assistance? the lady say. She pretty, with long black hair down her back. She have blue eyes like one of the dolls I used to have where the eyelids flip up if you pick her up. I stare at the lady cause she sound funny to me. Different.

Um, yes, Mama say. Her voice light and soft, not Mamas voice at all. Heavy and hard. I think something all of a sudden. I think, *Mama is trying to sound like the lady*. I want to enroll my daughter in this school, Mama say. I got some a the papers you gone need with me.

The lady smile at me, nod at Mama, and I look back and forth between them. I think about how the lady sound and how Mama sound. Not like our peoples in Tennessee that got voices sound like long slow singing. The way the lady talk be the other side of that. Short fast talking. Like night to the day. Like TV.

I KEEP THINKING bout the way that white lady talk at school. When she and Mama finish the papers, she say to Mama, Welcome to the neighborhood, Mrs Arlington. Im sure Avery will do very well here. Then she look at me. Avery? she say. You are going to like it here. Youll fit right in. She bend over the counter in the office and touch my face. Then she smile at me. I look at Mama when the lady touch me. I feel funny. Mama never touch me like that and sometimes when other people be really nice to me and talking to me like a baby, Mama dont like it. She say whenever that happen that aint nobody gone always be around to hug you and kiss all on you. Better be ready when that day come Avery. And when I look at Mama after the lady touch me, I see Mamas eyes move all over the ladys face. She looking at her long brown hair parted down the middle. Straight. Straight. She looking at all the other people in the office. Nobody in there looking like us. There two men, one tall, one short and blond. One other lady and she old with tight curly gray hair. They all look different, but they still aint looking like us.

Thank you, Mama say. She pull me away from the counter. I know Avery gone fit in, Mama say. Why wouldnt she? And when Mama say why wouldnt she it sound hard like when Mama aint playing. And the lady smile get a little small. This dress, Mama, I want to say. Thats why I aint gone fit in. This hair. Two braids with yellow ribbons on the end. How bout that? But Mama already walking out the office.

FIRST DAY OF school. I beg I beg I beg. Mama please not the two braids. Please. I want to wear a afro. We in the kitchen. Im sitting at our table that is round and glass with placemats stacked up across the table so we dont get hair all over them. Mama got the Afro Sheen out on the table and I love the glass jar it come in. I love that the grease be blue and I love how smooth the grease is in a new jar before you put your finger in it and mess it up. I love the way it smell too. Clean but with a little bit of perfume in it. But Afro Sheen is for the hot comb on the stove in the fire turning red hot. And I dont want my hair pressed. I want a afro.

Please Mama. Mama look at the clock on the wall. White with yellow and orange flowers. The 1, 3, 6, 9, 12 are big and the other numbers small. Its 7:30. I have to be at school by 8:15. All right, she say and turn off the stove. She say, We aint got time no how. So I get a afro. Mama pick my hair out and then she put a red scarf on my head and pat all around it to make my fro good and round. She lift the scarf slow so she dont mess it up. I pat it and she slap my hand. Leave it alone, now. You gone mess it up. And she walk me to school like Im a baby and I hope nobody see me walking with my mama. Its so quiet on the big streets. No cars and noise like on Vermont in L.A. This look like the streets on TV with they lawns and nothing else. Mama say I can walk home by myself and I want to tell her I could have walked to school by myself. Im nine years old.

I WAS SO HAPPY about the afro. And I had on Toughskins and I had on a yellow T-shirt and white tennis shoes. Mama drop me off at the playground and I watch everybody play tetherball, handball, and I just stand alone by the steps that go inside the classroom until the bell ring. I see a black boy look like my cousin Keith. But his hair is cut short. Its not big like mine. Too bad for him. I dont think nobody look as good as me. Im looking sharp as a tack, like Daddy always say.

3

TO GET TO our house, Massimo's house, there's a direct way, but you can also take a more scenic route. You can start at the beginning, in east L.A., at Cesar Chavez in downtown, drive until it becomes Sunset, and drive all the way down Sunset Boulevard, past the panaderias and taco stands of east L.A., as far west as you can before running into the ocean and drowning, I like to say. But Massimo thinks that sounds ungrateful. "Drown yourself, then. Shit," Massimo said one time when we fought. I said I was unhappy. I said it was his fault. "You act as if you are special to be unhappy," he said. But right away he said he hadn't meant it. And I lied. It wasn't his fault at all.

Hank Williams's voice floats down to me from the house. I've left the door open so I can hear him explaining to me, "I'm so lonesome I could cry." Up here the houses are close together, crowded in so that as many people as possible can own pieces of the hill. Within the enclave of houses, most pieces of the hill look the same, houses nearly up under each other with no lawns or with minimal lawns, turf grasses or ornamental grasses, succulents and bamboo, some spiraled. There is always a potted palm here and there. The landscape of the neighborhood, the various textures of house and greenery, reminds me of the patchwork quilts my grandmother made from scraps. Nothing matches, not exactly. And yet. All the textures and pieces are having conversations with each other. Only in the distant hills does it still look like the wild, unclaimed West.

Our backyard is not a yard, but a small concrete space with a living wall of succulents. The front has no lawn either. Just a pool, but with all the chairs and tables and potted plants for entertaining. Massimo has, of course, a system for outside, so that the music is so loud and confrontational all you can hear is the noise. Hardly anything that gets said between people is heard. That's why I leave the door open, so that I can hear. The last time I was in the pool, Massimo was in the pool with me, and we fucked. It was two months ago, December, but it was so hot. I wasn't teaching that day and Massimo didn't work. The quality of the air was bad. The sky was hazy, a heavy brownish gray, and our eyes were burning from the pollution, but the sun that penetrated the haze shined on the distant hills like a Sergio Leone film, as though Clint Eastwood would be coming through any moment on his horse, taking off his poncho, his boots and socks, dipping his feet in our pool.

That afternoon, the music that was too loud was Paolo Conte, and I loved his gravelly voice and the style in which he sang, delivery reminiscent of French cabaret but with the power of the blues. Maurice Chevalier mixed with Howlin' Wolf. It was one of the few CDs that Massimo and I both liked, and it was a happy combination; the Wild West, Italian, French, the blues. Ordinarily Massimo was very narrow about his music. Anything by black people was good—jazz, rhythm and blues, hip hop—and it was my music too, but I also had inclinations that pained Massimo. Patsy Cline. Merle Haggard. The Partridges. They were banned. Whenever Massimo was home he screamed like a knife had just been plunged into his back if ever he had to hear Keith Partridge's honey voice telling the world, "I woke up in love this morning! I woke up in love this morning!" "I will puke my guts," Massimo said, the first time he heard Keith. "You cannot possibly be serious." He was spooning pasta into our dishes and his cigarette dangled from his lips, as always, and he tightened the muscles in his face so that he could smoke and complain at the same time.

"I am serious," I said. "I love this song." And I still do. Massimo had put the wooden spoon down and stared at me. He looked concerned. The ash from his cigarette was long and in danger of falling into our pasta. But then he grinned at me. "You are a very funny girl," he said. "Now. Enough." And he took out my CD.

Moments like these are the moments that used to disappoint Massimo. He did not find them endearing then, but rather he found them indicative of something that was terribly amiss with the black American woman he thought he bargained for. When he picked me up at the Formosa years ago, I'm certain he had visions of the black girls on sitcoms, black girls full of sass, with singsongy voices and playful gyrations of the neck for making their points. "Oh no you *didn't*," Massimo prompted me. He was pleased with himself that he was relating to me, the black woman he was just getting to know, and I stared at him as though he were speaking to me in Italian.

When we were last in the pool together, I clung to him and he pumped into me and we laughed because it was not the kind of thing we usually did, but Paolo Conte was singing to us and the heat felt good on our bodies and our skin felt good, slippery and light, and Massimo rubbed my head which is shaved close to my scalp like a man's and the water felt cool, trickling down my neck and down my eyes, and even though we had only been out for a little while and the smog was obscuring the sun, I was browner than I was thirty minutes before. My skin soaked up the sun. Massimo especially liked me in the summertime when I was three shades darker than in the winter.

❋ ❋ ❋

DONT NOBODY PAY tention to me when Im in the school yard, but when I get inside the class and sit down, the kids look at me. They stare. I stare back. I dont care. Im bad. We sitting in rows and Im in the front where I like. That black boy sitting in the back. Its only me and him thats the same. The teacher stand at the door until everybody in and then she close the door, slow, so the sunlight coming in gets less and less and then aint no more. Just the bright light in the ceiling. This girl sitting next to me. Im Brenna. Whats your name, she whisper.

I tell her and stare back. Her face got a bunch of brown dots on it. She look like Pippi Longstockin and I love Pippi Longstockin. Her orange hair is straight like Barbie. But when she smile she got a gap in her two front teeth like me. I like Brenna.

But then the teacher say, Class settle down. She roll up the sleeve of her yellow blouse and push her glasses up her nose. Before we start, I want you to welcome your new classmate Avery. Avery, wont you please stand?

Hi Avery, everybody say at the same time. And that was it, until later. Mrs Campbell give us art to do. She tell us to pick up our own box of crayons and draw whatever we want on the page. She say, Just use layers of color. Just scribble a bunch of yellow on the page, a bunch of orange, maybe even some red, if we want to. I dont want to just scribble so I take the colors and make a real picture. I draw Mama, Daddy, and Owen. I draw our new house too and I mix up the color to make other colors. I know how to do that. I know that blue and yellow can make green. Yellow and red can make orange. I got a orange crayon but I dont like that color orange. Its too bright for what I want to do, make Mamas afro, which is brown and orange, not just bright orange like a clown. Then I make our palm tree in the front yard with a brown trunk but make the green part of the tree purple. I like what I done. I stare at it, happy. Then Mrs Campbell say, Kids are you all done?

Yes, we say all at the same time. Good, she say. Now I want you to take your black crayons and cover up your pictures.

We look at her. Dont know what she talking about. I worked hard on my picture. I raise my hand. Mrs Campbell, I say, I dont want to mess up my picture. Here, she say. Let me show you. She come to my desk and she pick up the black crayon and she start to color all over my picture. She dont stop until its all covered up. Its shiny because of the black crayon and I cry. She messed it up. Why she mess it up? Avery why are you cryin, she say. But my eyes just watering. No tears running down. Look, Mrs Campbell say. And then she take a pencil and draw a heart in the corner, small, just to show me, she say. I like it. I like all the colors underneath. I see colors and all the things I love, that are good. Mama, Daddy, and most of the time, Owen. And even though I like it, I like what I started out with best, before she put all that crayon on top and covered up everybody. When she go help other people, Brenna touch my arm. Its okay, Avery. I think it looks good both ways, she say. But I liked your way the best.

This fat boy sitting in the row in front of me turn around. He look at my picture and then at my hair and then he take a crayon and throw it in my hair. I dont know what to do cause Im surprised. He just laugh and turn back around. Anh hah, he say. Stupid Harry, Brenna say. You dumbass. I try to find the crayon but its stuck in my hair somewhere. Brenna put her hands in my hair and then she pull her hand back real fast like something bite her hand. Eww, she say. Your hair feels funny. And I dont know what she talking about. I dont know what to say. What she mean my hair feel funny? It feel like it always feel but she make me feel bad. I look back at the black boy but he bent over his paper, coloring. He dont say nothing to nobody and his hair too short to get a crayon stuck in it.

Brenna and me walk home halfway together. She live up the street from me. But on the way home we stop at 7-Eleven and she buy a Slurpee and a magazine. I dont have no money so I dont buy nothing and she let me drink some of hers. Go ahead, she say. At first, I dont want to drink after she do. Mama say thats nasty, drinking after people. But I dont care. I want some blueberry Slurpee. When we walking she show me the pictures in the magazine. Look, she say. Donny Osmond. Hes totally decent. She show me his picture and I like Donny Osmond all right. I watch him all the time on the Donny and Marie show. It say above his picture Can You Turn On His Love-Power? Whats love power, I ask Brenna. She hand me the Slurpee. You know, she say, smiling big. Can you make him do it til youre satisfied? She turn the page. Robbie Benson! She scream. What a fox. She pass me the magazine and point to him. He got dark wavy hair and blue eyes and I like the way he look. Foxy, I say, trying Brennas word. He foxy. When we come to the corner to my house, I stop. Well, Brenna. See you tomorrow. Im finna go home now. Brenna frown. Whats finna, she ask me, and I dont understand. What you mean, whats finna?

What does that word *mean*, spaz. Brenna scratch her elbow, waiting on me.

Whats spaz, Im thinking. Then I say, It mean Im gone go home.

Brenna say, Then why dont you just say that? That youre going to go home.

But Im thinking, That aint what I said, that I was go-eng to go home. I said gone. But from now on Im gone think about how I say it. Im gone make it sound how Brenna say it whenever I can remember to. Eng, she say. Not *in*.

Brenna and me just look at each other. Then she shrug. You want to take the magazine home? You can just bring it back to school tomorrow. And I think it again. Brenna nice. Yeah, I say, and Im glad I get to take Robbie Benson home. He foxy. He totally decent.

Mama dont understand why Robbie is foxy. When I show her his picture in Tiger Beat the next morning after she get home from work, she drinking Folgers and I always like that smell, like burnt dirt and sugar mixed together. She stare at him and say, And *who* is this supposed to be? *Mama*, I say. Thats Robbie *Benson*. He a babe. Mama look at me. Babe, she say. You coming up with all kinds of language. She look at him again. She say, He dont look like all that much to me. Then she pick up the magazine and flip through it, drinking her coffee. Aint no black boys in here? She put the magazine down and put another spoon of sugar in her cup. I hum and tilt back in my chair. Sit in that chair right, Mama say. Aint no toy. And she look at me but I caint figure out the look. She not mad, but she not happy either. I say, Why you ask that about black boys? Mama put her cup down. You dont ask me why about nothing, you hear? *Im* the mama. I ask the questions, she say, and hand me the magazine. And Robbie aint all that cute, she say. To me, she say. And then she go to the sink and pour out her coffee.

MORREY HAVE THEM dimples in both cheeks. If he smile you can see them good but he hardly smile. Except today. There are some days when you can bring stuff from home that you want to show people at school. Morrey brought in a record. The Commodores. Mrs Campbell say he can play it at the very end of class. Morrey wait and wait. He look at the clock again and again. I watch him. I ask permission to sharpen my pencil cause the sharpener is next to Morreys desk. I say, Hey. We only got two more hours to Brick House. And thats when Morrey smile and I see the dimples. The door is open to the classroom and Mrs

Campbell only got some of the lights on so we can mellow out. Thats what Brenna say. Mellow. Mellow, I say, quiet, to myself. Mellow. Brenna tell me it mean kick back. Relax. But I dont want to mellow out. I want to dance to Brick House.

And finally, finally three o clock come and Mrs Campbell call Morrey up to the front of the room where she roll out the record player. She hold out her hand and Morrey give it to her careful. She say, Morrey is sharing a record called Brick House, class. By the Commodores. And when she say Commodores I wonder all of a sudden what are Commodores anyway? I will ask her later. Morrey stand next to the record player, when the song start, I jump up and start to dance and then Morrey start dancing too. Other kids move in they seats but only Brenna get up and dance with us. Morrey looking happy. Them dimples. And then Mrs Campbell start to frown. Then in a minute, right after the part that say about her ways make an old man wish for younger days she built and know how to please, she take off the record but she scratch it on accident and it make a loud sound like scriiiiitch. Morrey look at her with big eyes like she just smack him across his face. Im sorry, Morrey, Mrs Campbell say. I dont think this song is appropriate for class. She give Morrey back his record and tell him to sit down.

After school, I walk home with Morrey. He quiet, so I say, My cousin Keith got a shirt like yours. Red with a zero on the back like football players. He say, My mama got it from Zodys. A whole bunch of kids are walking home. I see Brenna up ahead and then I ask, You want to go to 7-Eleven and look at some magazines? Morrey walking real slow up the hill. I dont know, he say. What kind?

Like Teen Beat or something, I say.

Nah, Morrey say. I dont think so. Why I want to look at that? Them magazines for white girls. I say Oh, but I dont believe

Morrey. Then Brenna call me. Avery! she call out. Catch up! And so I tell Morrey, Later days dude. Dont worry, the Commodores rocked. He look at me like I say a cuss word. No they didnt *rock*, he say, They aint rock. But I dont see why that matter. I dont know whats wrong with Morrey. Mellow out dude, I say, and run off to Brenna.

4

MASSIMO IS CHARMING. When he decides to seduce you, man or woman, child or pet, he looks at you as though you are the rarest of finds. His eyes tell you that he cannot believe his good fortune. Here you are, so close to him. Grace has brought you in his life and you are a treasure. You are more beautiful than anyone else, anything else. He showed me off the first time I met his friends. Even though I lived only thirty minutes from his home in the hills, Massimo drove in the opposite direction down Franklin, and then made a right on Vermont where, he likes to say, he rescued me from the top of my shabby storefront apartment on the corner of Vermont and Melbourne. He joked that I was an unfortunate creature, trapped in a tower and held prisoner above a musty-smelling vintage clothing store because no one understood that I was, in fact, a princess. "Queen," I said. "I hate princesses." "Whatever you want," he said. "Whoever and whatever you want to be," he said. He smiled broadly and he drove us back to the hills, but now we both know that whoever and whatever I want to be isn't exactly what he meant at the time, before he learned who I was. Within reason. Within his reason, is what he meant.

The distance between my apartment and Massimo's house and his friend's house was not that far. What is thirty minutes? But I had never before driven up iconic Beachwood Street. Beachwood. At first it looks like nothing, a school yard on the corner. Nothing special. But then, something happens as you drive up the narrow streets. Apartments and houses can emerge or hide away; there are bungalows and cottages, modern and classic, trying to be Spanish, English, Mediterranean, or French. Shabby complexes and elegant ones, too, clustered together like the guests of an extraordinary host. Cantilevered cliffhangers. A beautiful and ordered confusion. We drove up, up, up the hill, and the Hollywood sign was very close, it seemed. We were almost there. So close. But then we made a turn down a narrow street and I didn't see it anymore.

We arrived at Massimo's friend's house and I stared at it from inside Massimo's black Mercedes. I had been intimidated by the car when I first climbed into it, and now there was this house. It was a new house, all concrete and angles and glass. There was no lawn like the one I grew up lying on, only sharp-edged rocks and human-sized cactuses that stood like thorny, deformed guards. Massimo had come around to my side of the car and opened the door, and it was a gesture that I had only seen on television, when Wally Cleaver or Richie Cunningham took their girls on dates. I had always hoped that one day, a boy would take me out on a date and treat me that way, the way Massimo was treating me, and yet when he opened the door and reached for my hand, I was embarrassed. I thought he was making fun of me. When I hesitated, he leaned into the car and tenderly pried apart my hands that were clasped on my thighs. Gently, he pulled me out of the car. He closed the door, held my hands in his, and stared at me. "Bellisima," he said, and ran the back of his hand against my cheek. "Do you know who is behind that door? The people who are inside?" He tilted his curly head toward the entrance of the gray house. I shook my head and began to feel dread.

"Who?" I asked.

"Nobody," Massimo said, grinning. "Nobody matters but you."

✳ ✳ ✳

ME AND MY cousin Keith the same age. Me and Keith the only ones in the family thats born in California. They say me and Keith the same because we always got to be told to pay tention, always got to be told what to do and what not to do. We got the same eyes thats shaped like cats eyes, same afros, everything. Only our color is different. We both brown, but brown dont really describe it. His skin be red looking all the time, like that red in Popsicle, red like he just finished running from somewhere. Not me, though. Everybody say my brown is yellow underneath. Im the good one, though but we get whipped together anyhow if Im with him when he get in trouble. We fight bad, but then he my favorite cousin. Sometimes Ill rub his dingaling or he will kiss me on my titties. We dont like kissing though because it feel like we got little rocks on our tongue. Right now he make me sick because he showing off in front of John.

John has a Playboy in the back of his pants and is covering it with his shirt. At first I say Im going to tell, but Keith say he let me be with them if I dont. We stand around sweating because its so hot in Victorville. Keith look at me trying to decide if Im going to tell. Bet not, he say. Bet not get me in trouble. And I wont. I wont tell because I dont like it when Keith get in trouble. Come on, John say. Take all fucking day, why dont you, and Keith pull the neck of my T-shirt. Come on, then, he say.

John is twelve. I like him. He looks like Shaun Cassidy. Johns hair is blonde and parted on the side. Feathered, thats what they call it. He wears corduroys and shirts that say Hang Ten and he puts a cigarette behind his ear when nobody looking. He and Keith smoke all the time but I dont tell nobody. If I dont say nothing they let me hang with them, so I never say anything.

We walk across dirt lots to get to Johns school. He in junior high. Its Saturday, and its like a hundred degrees. It feel like summer, and in two weeks Ill be done with the fifth grade. I already done turned ten in October, the same as Keith, but he act like Im younger than him. John and Keith take off running when they see the dugout and I yell Wait for me, but they dont. By the time I get to them, John already taking out the Playboy. I run up to them, and I make it more dusty. Goddamn, Keith say. Get dirt all over a nigga. You not supposed to say that, I say, and then John say to me, Nigga please. Keith and John laugh. They laughing at me. I dont like it. I want them to be nice to me. I know boys like sports and I like baseball and Im like the only girl I know who care about baseball so I say, Dodgers going all the way this year. Don Sutton got a good arm this year and Ron Cey already got seven home runs.

Fuck baseball, John say. Nows the time for titties. Him and Keith scooch together and open the magazine. They pull out a long page from the middle. John whistle. Choice, he says. Thats some choice pussy right there. To the *bone*.

I lean in next to Keith so I can see what they looking at. Her skin look creamy, like somebody painted it. She got long straight black hair and green eyes, but they kind of rolled up in her head like a dolls so you can hardly see them. Her titties a lot bigger than mine and got pink nipples that look like teeny drops of icing. I stare and stare. I never seen nothing like that before. I stare at her mouth. Its half open.

Look at *that*, John say. *Man*.

John lick his lips and I stare at his mouth. Its shaped nice, like Shaun Cassidys. It look soft and wet and I want to rub my lips on his. Do John think Im choice? I say to John, Keith saw my titties before, didn't you? Shut up, Keith say. He look like he shy and I get mad. They looking at her titties. Whats wrong with mine?

Ah hah, John say. You saw Averys black titties. I bet she look like Aunt Esther on Sanford and Son.

I like Aunt Esther. She makes me laugh, but she dont look like the lady in the magazine. I want to be choice like the lady in the magazine. I dont want to look like Aunt Esther.

Why dont you kiss Aunt Esther right now, man, John say. You probably already felt her up.

Shut up, Keith say. Why dont *you* kiss her he say, and he kick some dirt on my tennis shoes.

Ill fucking kiss her dude. Like I care, John say. He put the magazine down on the bench and walk over to me. I get scared and happy. Im going to get to feel his lips. He grab me hard. He kiss me but he kiss me too hard and our teeth bang up against each other. He grab the back of my head, pull on my cornrows, and hold my head tight so I cant breathe. Then he squeeze my tittie. I push him away. Fuckin asshole, I say, like Brenna always do. He just laugh and then he wipe his hands on his cords. Afro Sheen all over my *hands*, he say and his mouth curl up in the corners like he smell something bad.

Yeah, nappy, Keith say, and when I look at him, he smiling but he look away. I feel like Im going to cry but I dont let myself. I just walk away. Come on Avery, John call out. We were just playing. For reals!

But Im tough. I say, Later days fuckers, and then I give them the middle finger like Brenna showed me.

SCHOOL IS OUT but the Hardy Boys are reruns. I make a collage out of all my old Tiger Beats and Teen Beats. I find all the Shaun Cassidy pictures. I got tons of them. I paste together all the shades that kind of look the same so I can make a big face out of little Shaun Cassidy faces. I want it to be like, from far away, it just kind of look like anybodys face, but when you get up close, you see that all the little pieces that make up the face are all pictures of Shaun Cassidy. Im making it all on a big piece of white cardboard.

Daddy come in the living room with a drink. He look down at me on the floor with my stuff all spread out. He say, What you doing, Ave? I tell him Im making a big face out of all the little faces. Daddy take another drink. What you watching, he ask. Hardy Boys, Daddy, I say. Daddy look at my collage and then at the TV. Aint nothing else on?

I dont know, I say. I want to watch this. Daddy stand there like he got more to say, but then he just leave me. It take me three hours to do my Shaun Cassidy. I finish it in my room because Owen kick me out of the living room. He want to watch TV but he dont want to watch all that white shit, he say.

In my room, I tape my Shaun Cassidy on the wall. Then on the floor underneath him I spread out some Now and Laters, Pop Rocks, Pixie Stix, and Red Hots. I like how the candy look mixed up all together, and maybe Shaun Cassidy like all that kind of candy. To me, John dont look like him anymore. He *wish*. Shaun Cassidy is a total babe and John is a total dog. Like I even care about that doofus, anyway. Before I go to bed tonight Im going to get on my knees and say my prayers in front of Shaun Cassidy. Dear God Now I lay me down to sleep I pray the Lord my soul to keep if I should die before I wake I pray the Lord my soul to take God bless everybody amen Dear Shaun Cassidy I love you I love you Shaun Cassidy when you sing Hey Deanie wont you come out tonight I pretend youre singing it to me Shaun Cassidy. Shaun Cassidy, *please*.

5

THE NIGHT I met Massimo at the Formosa, he was suddenly at the bar, standing next to me. I saw him in the mirror that reflected our images. I was playing with my hoop earrings, and my silver bangles gleamed in the moody light. My lips were covered in a waxy, blaring red lipstick I never would have worn years before. I would have avoided drawing attention to my lips in any way when I was younger, because everyone always told me they were so big. But that night, because Brenna thought I looked better with it, I wore lipstick. I leaned on the bar, my nearly smooth head in my hands, listening to Brenna make some poor man in a pink oxford shirt suffer. I had dragged her out to Los Angeles, when she simply wanted be sitting in her living room in West Covina, watching television. Watching Massimo in the mirror, I saw that he was standing too close to me, but that his copper skin and wavy hair were striking. He was looking at me. Appraising me. He didn't know that I was watching him in the mirror. It was only when he glanced in the mirror that our eyes met. They were light eyes, contrasting with his skin. I expected him to look away in embarrassment, but instead he held my gaze for a very long time. *You,* his eyes said. *You.* And I was the one who looked away.

He said, "Please excuse me. May I buy you a drink?" I heard his accent then. Italian. Rich and heavy, and he leaned into me and spoke with a delivery and physicality that was both confident and halting, like a cobra that rears back its head before it strikes. It was late and a weeknight, and so we didn't have to shout over noise.

He asked me to sit in a booth after Brenna asked me many, many times if I was okay alone with this charmer. She left me behind, long ago having disposed of the pink oxford shirt. We sat in the booth and talked about art because, I had said, he came from the most beautiful place in the world. I had never been to Italy or anywhere else outside of the United States to know it was the most beautiful, but I believed it when everyone who had been there said it was so. We fought. We fought over subjects I only knew by reading about them. Which was the best contrapposto: da Bracciano's *Orpheus* or Michelangelo's *David*? He picked da Bracciano and I picked *David*. He smiled at me and reached across the table, lightly touching my arm with his warm fingertips. He said, "But that is too easy, Avery. Americans pick always the thing that is easy. But anyway," he said, a slow grin forming, "neither sculpture is as beautiful as you." It was a line, but I still fell. Even now, to this day, when we are hurting each other and fighting, he may call me stupid, silly, or idiotic, but he will also always look at me with such longing, such bewildered hurt, as though all he wants to do is adore me, if I would just let him.

That night, in the train car of the Formosa, he talked about my skin. Lucille Ball, Lauren Bacall, and Doris Day looked down on us as he told me that the color of my skin was perfect. "What colors do you mix together to get that color?" Massimo asked. I laughed. "I don't know," I said. "I never have thought about it." But that was a lie. He leaned back, and the red leather of the booth was a nice contrast to the dark blue cotton of his shirt. He leaned back with his glass of whiskey, and whenever he drank from it, he peered at me over the rim. His eyes moved all over my face and not once did he look at anyone else. At the end of the evening, he walked me to my car. He took a card out of his wallet and pressed it into my palm. He released my hand before the gesture became too insinuating. He said, "I would be lucky if you would call me. Please, Avery," he said. "Please."

6

MASSIMO CLAIMS THAT he buys white sheets especially
for me, because I look like art, like a sculpture, all twisted up in
them, my ass barely concealed by bunched-up cotton, a brown
thigh protruding from a white shroud. Massimo loves crisp
white sheets; he chose the heavy, cool duvet, which has main-
tained its perfect whiteness and bluish hue. The black dress that
I've laid on our bed in consideration for tonight looks dramatic
against the sheets. It's expensive because someone's name is on it.
The other outfit is jeans and a black turtleneck. I will be uncomfortable in the jeans because I will know that I am supposed to
look like something else. But I will also be uncomfortable in the
dress, because I don't like black dresses; they are too somber and
formal, no matter how they cling to the body. It's always difficult
to choose which will be the least crazy making. In the jeans, I
won't look the part, won't look elegant and sophisticated. But in
the dress I will feel as though I am in costume. I want to feel as
though I am only wearing my skin.

Skin.

Sometimes Massimo pulls me close and runs his fingers all
over my skin, and sometimes over my scalp, until he gets drowsy.
He likes it when my hair is just a little longer, so that he can feel
the kinks and waves of the texture. He likes my hair nappy, he
says, and he makes me laugh, the way he says it, stressing the first
syllable and holding it much too long. "Nahh-py," he says slowly,

as though he's making love to the words, and I can feel his hardness against my ass. Hard because of me. My skin. My hair. My ass. My lips. "Nahh-py," he whispers in my ear and caresses my breasts, and his hot breath makes me shiver.

Early on, when Massimo and I were first dating, I asked him, "What else do you see in me?" Was he just trying to get me in bed? "Of course," he had said, "don't waste my time on the obvious." But also, he said he saw someone trying to say something and do something, just like him. He saw someone trying to put one foot in front of the other. Sometimes, though, he saw that I stood completely still, which he hated. And I moved sideways, back and forth, and diagonally. I had many steps that Massimo had to learn. It was difficult for both of us, but he learned them. And that's how I grew to love Massimo. He loves my skin, yes, but that is the least of it. He finally stopped trying to tell me who I was. He simply let me show him. For better and for worse, for everyone involved.

The colors and textures of such basic things—skin, hair, eyes—or even the color of black and the color of white is what I am always trying to get to. There is always something underneath the name. To name something, say, gray, is to name it nothing. The human eye can distinguish nearly five hundred shades of gray. If gray is this complicated, so are all the colors. When Massimo says "black" and he's talking about me, I hear in his voice all the things he is trying to name for what he sees. Me, though, I painted and painted, but at some point I got tired of color, of trying to define it perfectly. That's when I started collage and also began to create pieces, messages, from whatever I could modify, interpret, adapt. Found bits of things for the distinctions that are so hard to explain.

There's something else I tried to explain to Massimo, something about him that I love. He doesn't see it in himself, but he has a center that is immovable in the middle of motion. He's impatient. He can be volatile, emotional, impulsive. Hair-trigger. "You stereotype me!" he always cries. "You are not being PC! Just because I am Italian," he says, whenever I go on about his temper. But his stillness in the middle of motion is extraordinary. You don't travel as far as he has without having it. I told him that he reminded me of Fernando Valenzuela, lifting his right leg high and looking up to the sky before he pitches. It looks messy; it looks like he's not keeping his eye on what he's supposed to be focused on. But then, at the last minute, he pulls it together and has changed speeds on you, or that screwball he has just thrown, strange like a reverse curve, is already a memory.

"Don't you see it?" I had asked, more convinced of my theory the more I thought it through.

"No," Massimo had said, running out of patience. He thinks baseball has nothing to do with him. "Avery," he said. "Enough. Don't be silly."

❋ ❋ ❋

I WANT THE Dodgers to win for Mama May. Daddys mama. She visiting from Tennessee and she wants to see as many Dodger games as she can. She love Dodger Stadium like I do. The sun so bright and the palm trees on the hills far off look like a picture, like they sitting on top a sheet of blue thats supposed to be sky. I always love the organ playing between innings and at bat. Plus I got to catch a bag of peanuts from the man that sells them and throws them from far away and somehow even though hes far away if you send a five dollar bill down the row of people, you always get your change back. And I got some Carnation ice cream and a Dodger dog, even though Daddy never usually lets me eat that much because he says Im fat.

We sitting at the third base line and its the top of the ninth. Its their last chance to do something. Its zero/one, Padres. Cey got three hits, Lopes got two hits, but Mama Mays man let her down. She keep pulling on her baseball cap and pushing her glasses up her nose. Dusty Baker had five at bats, but only got one hit. Come on now Dusty Baker, she yell. Dusty now I know you gone do better than what you doing! You call yourself playing baseball! Shit Dusty Baker!

Im sitting next to her and on her other side is Daddy and Daddys friend. He got a lot of new friends since we moved. Her name Angeline. Angeline is white, has long black hair down her back. She skinny with pale, pale skin and light brown eyes, and she dont say much. She dont scream like me and Mama May. She just sit back and drink her beer. Me and Mama May didnt know she was coming. Daddy just tell us he was gone pick up a friend on the way to the game. He say all this after he drop Mama off at work, at the motel cleaning rooms. Mama May speak to Angeline when she get in the car, but after she dont say much sitting in the back of the car with me. When we got to Angelines house Mama May got out the car and sat in the back seat. Daddy got mad and told her that Angeline would sit in the back with me. You got arthritis, Mama. You need to stretch out your legs up front. But Mama May say, No Darnelle. Me and Avery is right fine back here, aint we Ave? I have a bad feeling, had it since Mama May sat in back with me and pretend not to hear anything Daddy say to her all day. And now the Dodgers done lost the game. Thats the end of that, I guess, Daddy say. He pull on his cap and it look like he looking at me and Mama May but he got on shades so I cant see his eyes. I can only see myself.

Daddy drives us back home and drop us off. Then he take Angeline home. Later Im in my room playing eight-tracks when Mama get home. I got the K-tel Music Magic one and my favorite songs are Brick House, for sure, then it has Crystal Gayle Dont It Make My Brown Eyes Blue and Bay City Rollers who are just so foxy. I love that song they sing, that Saturday Night song, but I turn it down when I hear Mama and Mama May talking. Mama May say, I thought I raised him better than that but he thought his daddy hung the moon and we dont need to say nothing else about his sorry ass. But *anyway*. You got to do something about it.

I can smell cigarette smoke through my door, so I know that Mama is smoking her Kools. Must be the one calling my house and hanging up, Mama say. Cook his shit and wash his draws, motherfucker. Mama May say, He my son, but. Mama say, Taking Avery around that heifa.

And then I dont hear anything until later. At night. Mama May is sleeping with me and Owen is in his room. I hear Mama screaming, What the fuck you gone do, huh? What the fuck you gone do? And I know her face is close to Daddys, pointing her finger in his face, like a dare fight at school when somebody says, Cmon, man. Do it. Ill kick your ass.

Stop it Mama. Stop it. Hes going to hit you.

You caint treat me like Im the maid. I aint the maid, hear? I aint gone clean this house, other peoples nasty hotel rooms, wash your shit and fix you dinner and you out running the streets taking Avery around just any old kind of tail.

I get out of bed and walk to the door because I dont want Mama to get hit. She always gets hit. Or maybe it would be better if she get hit and then the fight would be over soon. Or maybe she deserve to get hit because everything was fine until she caused problems with Daddy. She hit Daddy too, but she can never get him good like he gets her. Shut up Mama. Shut up. Shut up stupid. Leave Daddy alone. You gone get another patch on your eye and its gone be all purple and swollen. You gone have to wear your arm in that sling again. I walk to the door because Im gone go out and stop it. Me and Owen, we always go out and stop it. And thats when Mama May sit up and say, Avery come here. Its too late anyway. When I open the door Daddy is hitting Mama and Owen is getting in the middle of it. He pulls Mama away and says, Thats enough. I cry and cry and we all stand around in the kitchen. Finally Mama say, Come here, Avery, its all right. Daddy say, Come here Avery, its over. Avery, Mama May say, and Owen look at me. Stop cryin, he say. Stop it. So I stop. I dont go to anybody. I stare at the blood on the wall from Mamas nose, spots of blood with little tails on the end that make me think of space, of comets, of Mars and Jupiter far, far away. Or tadpoles like the ones I swallowed, the ones we see in the ponds in Tennessee, four days on the Greyhound from here. Or two days if Daddy driving. Tennessee, Mars, Jupiter. Stellar living. Far away from where we are or ever gone be. I walk to the wall and put my finger on the end of one of the tails. I drag my finger so that the color gets light and you can see the light of the wall coming through the color that went purplish red to reddish brown to light red, already turning back to brown. Everybody is talking and saying something but I dont hear. I keep painting with the colors, make up my designs on the wall, and I keep thinking about how one color can turn into so many others. One color is a lot of things.

Avery! And Daddys voice make me jump. No, he say, and it sounds like when people tell their dogs no. When I look up at him, everybody else staring at me like they dont know who I am. What are you doing? he say, looking at me funny.

Changing colors, I say. He stare at me for a minute and then look down at his feet. Mama gets a paper towel and holds it to her nose. She say, Quit it. Thats blood, Avery. You dont play with blood.

7

I LOVED BASEBALL when I was a child. And I do now. But more than the statistics of baseball, the endless facts, I loved the ceremony of baseball. I loved Vin Scully's reassuring voice on the radio—calm, matter-of-fact, full of possibility or resigned deference: *And the 3/2 pitch? Foul ball.* No matter what was going on, I had a place to be in baseball. Then and now, always, Vin Scully. I loved Dodger Stadium because you never met a stranger. The people in our section, wherever we sat, we were happy together when the Dodgers were winning and in steadfast denial when they were losing, but it was always okay because there would always be another game, another year. And anything was possible in baseball. In baseball, everybody was the same because we all bled Dodger blue. Who was this person giving me a high five? There was no way to tell, except we were all on the same team.

Keith, the older he got, decided that baseball was not the sport for him. Too slow. Too white. "Ain't nothing happening," he'd say, whenever I forced him to watch or listen. He was turning toward the money and flash of the Lakers. So glamorous, glittery, and Hollywood. The only Laker I ever liked was Kurt Rambis, which Keith said figured. But sometimes, still, my father would take Keith to games too, since Keith had no father and no other man to do such things with, no other man to show him how to be. My father tried.

The sun has gotten too hot, and Hank Williams has stopped singing, and so I get out of the pool for a hat and to change my music. My favorite hat to wear is a tattered Dodgers cap. Massimo hates the hat, mainly because it's tattered and because whenever I wear it, I look like a man. My face, free of dangly earrings and makeup, looks like it couldn't possibly belong to a woman, couldn't possibly be the face of the woman that Massimo is fucking. I have heavy eyebrows and a strong chin. And my lips can belong to any gender until they are covered in color. The enormous breasts of my body don't match what I am told is the masculinity of my face. A delicate and fine-featured masculinity, but still. Once, driving in the car with Massimo, I got pulled over when I ran a red light. The cop looked me squarely in the face and called me sir. Massimo looked at the officer and then at me with wide eyes, as if horrified to suddenly find himself with a black man. "Avie," Massimo says now whenever we're out and about and I'm wearing my Dodger blue. "Lipstick at least. I don't want people to think I'm a fagoni."

In the entrance of our hallway, hanging against an otherwise stark white wall, is a portrait of me and Keith. Whenever Massimo stayed the night and was made miserable by the sparseness of my apartment, the thing that made him the most miserable was this portrait. In the portrait, Keith and I are naked from the shoulders up, and we are kissing in what I have always thought to be an innocent way, both of our lips puckered and stuck way out so that our lips are barely touching. We are both wearing Dodger caps, which Keith would no doubt protest. I am looking at Keith and Keith looks out of the corner of his eye with a hint of fear, as though someone or something is about to be upon us. In my apartment, the portrait was positioned so that as I lay in bed, alone or with someone, Keith was watching. I liked that about the painting, but I was also most proud of the colors I managed to get right. I am darker than Keith with yellow undertones and a hint of gold. Keith is light skinned, with a pinkish cinnamon undertone I always used to call red. Keith was not a "black guy," painted in nondescript brown or literal black, as I had seen time and time again. He was cinnamon and saffron and I was burgundy. The Dodger caps were, of course, the true blue.

"It's creepy," Massimo said one night as we lay in bed in my apartment. He had finally eased up on his relentless charm and allowed me to see him irritated.

"Why?" I looked at the portrait and smiled. "Don't you like it?"

Massimo rubbed his belly, pulled on the coarse black hair. Then he stroked himself absently while he looked at the portrait. He was almost hard again. "I don't like looking at you kissing some guy. Some black guy," he said.

"Aww." I propped myself up on my elbows and winked at him. "Jealous. It's not some black guy," I said. "It's my cousin."

"Oh," Massimo said. "Okay. That's normal."

Now the portrait hangs in the hallway because Massimo refused to hang it in our bedroom. He finally consented to the entrance hallway after I yelled and yelled that I was bringing nothing to his house that I owned except my clothes, a few books, and my paintings, and couldn't he see that I had to try to make this place something of my own or else I would disappear?

When I pass the portrait on the way to the stereo, I lift the bottom left corner to straighten it out, and as I walk away, Keith's fearful eye follows me down the hall.

✻ ✻ ✻

SCHOOL IS OUT in a week and we are all going to Tennessee later this summer to see our people, but for now Aunt Janice said to Mama can you and Darnelle take Keith for the rest of the summer because I am about through with him. She say Keiths daddy came around to see him, aint seen him for five years before this, and Keith is just acting a fool for no reason. Say his daddy took him out to eat and bought him some clothes but then he was gone again. Keith done stole a bike, money from Aunt Janice, and run the streets when he should be at home. His mama is through with him. She tired, she say. That boy aint but eleven. She tell Mama she work two jobs and between making pancakes at the International House of Pancakes and working at her factory, she cant keep up with him running wild. Im tired, she keep saying to Mama. Im just so damn tired.

He a smart boy and he think he slick, Aunt Janice say. Maybe Darnelle can snatch a knot in his ass, make him act like he got some sense, Aunt Janice say. She say, He running around with that white boy John getting into shit, but he aint like John with a lawyer for a daddy.

But I know that sometimes Daddy gone too but he always come back and Keith act like he dont care about anybody making him do anything. Only once did Daddy tell Keith to watch himself, and that he wasnt going to tell him again, that he didnt talk back to Daddy. Not ever. But still, Daddy has taken us to three Dodger games, the zoo, and Huntington Beach. Owen came too, except for the zoo because he said he was too old for all that. And the Dodgers. He say hes too old for them too. Plus hes got all his new friends from high school who think hes cool because hes tall and acts like he the king of everything.

Today Keith and Brenna and me cant find stuff to do. Schools been out for a week but we feel like its boring already. We walk up and down the streets of the neighborhood playing my K-tel

Disco Dazzler eight-track. Its hot and the sun is so bright and none of us have sunglasses on. We just squint and hold our hands over our eyes all day. We all like that song Float On. Float float on. Float float float on. We pick the parts of all the guys who sing in the song. Everybody wants to be Larry because his voice sound the best and he gets to say the best lines. We all sing, Cancer and my name is Larry, and I like a woman that loves everything and everybody.

We already been down to the school on the swings but it got too hot, and anyway, Brenna say, What a bunch of dumbasses we are. Back at school. Keith laugh at everything Brenna say and he tries to get her to laugh at everything he say. I can tell he likes her even though she tells him stuff like, Shut the fuck up man. Or Fuck off, dude. Youre a fuckin liar. Brenna dont ever think about what she saying. But at my house she do. She dont say stuff like that around my house because Mama heard her once when we was in my room playing music. She open my bedroom door and she ask Brenna, What did you say? Mama looked at me like I said it. Mama say again, What did you say? Nothing, Brenna say after a minute and look down at the floor. We dont speak like that here, Mama say. But I wanted to say that she do, Daddy do, and Owen do. Just not me. Im the only one who would get into trouble. Thats why I like Brenna too. She gets to do and say whatever she wants. Just not at Mamas house.

We decide to go back home and be bored at my house because its too hot to keep walking around. I can see Joan watering her lawn. Her lawn is the kind of grass thats hard and tough feeling under your feet. Hey Joan, I call out, and wave real big. She wave back big, like me. When we get to her, she smiling. You kids look hot, she say. Brenna and Keith just look at her, but I say, Yes, yes, Joan. We are hot.

Brenna and Keith look at me funny.

Would you and your friends like to swim? Joan stick her thumb in the water hose to make it spread over more grass and some of the water get on us. It feel real good, even though I usually hate water.

Yeah, Keith say. I want to get in the water.

Me too, Brenna say. She pull all her red hair to the back and then hold it up, away from her neck.

This my cousin, Keith, I say, but I forgot a word. So I say it again. This *is* my cousin Keith and this *is* Brenna. I talk slow and concentrate on every word I say. Joan still smiling at us. Nice to meet you both, she say. You kids come over whenever you like. Now, even.

Thank you very much, Joan, I say.

Brenna tell us that she gone be back in five minutes. She got to go home and get her swimsuit. When we get to my house to put swimming clothes on, Keith say, Yes, yes, Joan, we are hot, and he make a face at me. You sound stupid, Keith say. All retarded.

I tell him, Thats how you speak right.

LOVELY IS A word she use. I never known or seen anyone who say lovely in real life. But lovely is the right word to describe Joans house. It smell new. The dark green carpet smell new. The furniture is nice colors like light brown and pink. It smell sweet like flowers every time I been over. It never smell like my house, like grease and collard greens and ham hocks and cigarette smoke. And I like her backyard. It got a picnic table and a garden with roses. Our yard got roses but they all tangled up and got a bunch of weeds and bugs in them. Because nobody has the time to pay attention to the outside of the house. Caint nobody see it nohow, Mama say. But I wish they were like Joans roses that are perfect like fake ones.

Joan left us in the yard by ourselves to make us a bite, she say. So we float in the water and just play around in the pool. She

dont have the big kind, the real kind you see on TV. She got the
kind thats on top of the ground and all of us can touch the bottom
and still not get our heads wet. Im glad because I dont really like
being in the water that much and I dont want to get my hair wet.
Mama pressed it two days ago and if I get it wet its going to get
hard and nappy and be hard to comb and Mama wont do nothing
to it until the weekend.

Brenna wearing a bikini. I never seen her almost naked before. I seen the freckles on her arms and face and on her legs, too,
but all together with just a bikini on all them freckles look strange
like Brenna got polka dots all over. Im not sure what Im thinking
about them polka dots. I dont think they look bad. But they dont
look good, neither.

After a while, Keith say, Lets play something, yall. Lets close
our eyes to find each other in the pool. If you touch somebody,
see if you can guess who it is without opening your eyes.

I look at Brenna to see what she says. I dont want to be in the
water with my eyes closed and feel like Im drowning. I say, I dont
want to play that. Keith say, What about Brenna though. She want
to play maybe.

I dont even care, Brenna say. She lean back and float across
to the other end of the pool. Her hair float out around her like
orange ribbons, and I wish I could do that, just lay my head back
and float and not worry about my hair turning hard and nappy.

Awright, then, Keith say. Everybody close your eyes.

After he say that I watch Brenna close her eyes. But me and
Keith, we dont close our eyes. He moving over to where Brenna is
floating and he move quiet and slow with his hands like claws and
high in the air like he playing boogie man. When he get to Brenna,
he stand over her and wait, and then he put his hands under the
water like he helping her to float. Brenna smile and open one eye.
They cant see that Joan is standing behind them looking through

her sliding door. I wave at Joan and smile but she dont smile back. Thats when Keith put both hands on Brennas titties. Boo, he say. Youre a dumbass, Brenna say, but she laughing. Thats when Joan open the door. She look at Keith for a long time. Kids, she say, and her voice sound different than usual. Like she worried. Come out of the pool, kids. Have some lunch, she say. Ill bring it out to you.

When she bring out the lunch, we dont know what all it is. I know a tuna sandwich and the little bowls of tomato soup, but she also got three little plates with something on them that look like little hard green plants. She give all of us one with our sandwich and soup and put a bowl of yellow cream or something in the middle of the table. We just stare at everything and look at each other.

I know, Joan says. All kids hate vegetables. But I thought you might like to try. These are going to go bad if I dont get rid of them. Eat, kids, Joan say, and sit with us at the little picnic table and drink her coffee.

Im thinking and thinking. How you eat this?

I aint eating that green thing, Keith say.

Joan put her coffee down on the table. Thats an artichoke. Youve not had an artichoke?

Keith shake his head and make a face like something stink. Joan say, Avery?

No, Joan, I say quiet. I have not had an artichoke.

Joans face get red. She looks at Brenna. Well, she say, I know Brenna has. She can tell you. Its good, isnt it?

Brenna make the same face Keith make. No way, she say. We have normal food at my house. Good food, she say. Out of a can. Like Spaghetti Os.

But I pick up my artichoke because Joan look like she feel bad. I bite into it. Avery! Joan shout, and I drop it back on the plate. Spit the rest out.

Kids, Joan say and she frown, but she laughs too. For heavens sake. You pull out a leaf and then you dip it in this butter. Here. Look. She pull one off, dip it in the sauce, and eat a little bit off the bottom. She dont eat the rest of the green part. Mama and Daddy yell at me if I dont eat all the food on my plate like that. Try it, Avery, Joan say. I do what she tell me and its not nasty but it dont taste like food. It taste like you have to eat a hundred artichokes to be full and it still only taste like the sauce anyway. Like butter. I'm not going to ever eat another artichoke if I can help it. I decide I do not like them. I say, Its really good Joan. I like it. Thank you very much.

Keith and Brenna laugh and then Joan face turn pink. She laughing too. Honest to goodness, she say. Eat your soup and salad then. You dont have to eat this if youd rather not. Youre right, arent you? Of course you wouldnt like this. Then she snatch up the artichokes and walk into the house.

You a lie, Keith say. You know it takes like dookie. I like it very much, he say, trying to sound like me. Yeah, Brenna say. Kiss her big ass, why dont you. And I dont know why they getting mad at me. I didnt do nothing. They the ones being rude to Joan. Shut up you guys, I tell them.

Avery eat anything anyway, Keith say. Porky Pig.

Brenna laugh at Keith again. He been trying all day and now he made her laugh twice. I sit and stare at my sandwich. They make me feel bad about eating it. I put it down. Brenna eat her sandwich with a big smile on her face and Keith eat his sandwich, just staring at her like he want to eat her up. Im the only one not eating and I get so mad. Both of you assholes can eat shit and die, I say. Nappy headed nigger. Polka-dotted honkey.

Avery! Joan say. Shes standing at her door again and the way she look at me make me feel like I want to die. She look at me like Im ugly. She say, You talk like that? Brenna and Keith put their faces down in their soup. Joan look at all of us like she dont like anything she see. I think you kids better leave, she say after a while.

I tell Joan Im sorry and she say its okay but I can tell that its not really okay. We all walk through her house and Im looking at all her matching furniture and all I can think about is please Joan dont tell Mama and Daddy because they will be so mad. Mama will beat me for sure and Daddy will look at me for a long time like he figuring out a punishment but then he wont punish me because he never does. He will just probably say, Avery. You know. You know better than that. We taught you better. But when he say the we, it don't sound like he just talking about him and Mama. It sound like theres a whole bunch a people somewhere that I have never even met and they watching me. They disappointed in me because they all taught me better than what Im doing.

OWEN HATES SCHOOL but he likes West Covina all right. He always say that he glad he only had to do one more year of high school when we moved because he wants to go out and make some dollars. School cant do nothing for him, he say. Daddy aint happy that Owen aint going to college. *Isnt* going to college. Daddy say he and Mama work like dogs cause thats the choice they had. Work like a dog and lie down and die. Daddy say Owen and me got more choices than being dogs and dying, but Owen head hard, Daddy say.

But Daddy let Owen have a graduation party at the house, make Owen pay for it with his own money he saved from his job at the market down by the high school. Im glad about the party because I get to spend the night at Brennas house so I can be out of the way. Mama have rules about me going over there, though. Dont go over there being loud and tearing up anything, Mama says. Eat what they put on your plate but dont be eatin up all they food. Clean up after yourself and do everything that Brennas mama tell you to do. She and Daddys main rules for Owen is they dont want people tearing up they house but even Owen isnt that crazy that hes going to let somebody do that. Even if he eighteen and taller than Daddy, he would get whupped for sure. There are going to be people from L.A. that we have not seen in so long. Owens old friends from L.A. High coming too.

But Id rather be at Brennas, just down the street from my house. We got the same house, too, shaped like a barn, but it doesnt feel anything like my house. Brennas mama and daddy look young, not like my mama and daddy. Brennas mama look like a sister, same size and everything. Same freckles. She always got a cigarette in her mouth and she let Brenna light them for her sometimes. She says, Do me a solid, kiddo, and hand Brenna a cigarette, that Brenna light up on the stove or with matches. Then she take a puff and pass it to her mama. She dont even care.

Now she got a cigarette hanging in her mouth while she open a can of beans. She let Brenna and me make hamburger patties that Brennas daddys cooking outside.

Like this Ma? Brenna hold up one.

Too small, kid, Colleen say. She hate being called Mrs Kiersted. I called her that when I first got here. She say, I dont care what else you call me, kid, but Mrs Kiersted sound like a fucking old lady, dont you think? I said, Yes maam, and she looked over at Brenna and told her, Maam. Manners, kid. Those are manners. And she bumped me on the hips with her butt and smiled at me.

I hold my hamburger up. What about this one? Perfect, Colleen say. Beautiful Ave.

When we done we sit in the backyard and watch Brennas daddy grill our hamburgers. He plays the radio loud and sings to it. He looks like a high school guy to me, like Brennas brother

Tate. His hair is blonde and long down his back. He looks like a surfer. He always wear a baseball cap. Angels. Wear his pants low like they falling off. I stare and stare at him because he kind of look like a rock star to me. Like Robert Plant who is a stone fox. He dont ever see me staring because he hardly pays attention to us when were around. He hardly ever home because he drive a truck all the time. He open up another beer, turn over our hamburgers, and sing about how your cheating heart is going to tell on you. He point to them with his big fork. You girls ready to eat? Got you some killer burgers over here. Tell your mom, he say to Brenna. Its ready. And then he wink at me, and it make me feel like he and me got a secret.

Sometimes the way Mama and Daddy talk about white people make me think all white people be practically the same, but here its not like at Joans house where she set the table and put everything out nice. At Joans house she take things out of the boxes and plastic they come in and then she put it on another plate so it look good on the table. Here its more like my house. Brenna and me get our paper plates and then just get us some beans out the pot. We get everything ourselves and go to Brennas room.

In Brennas room, we can do whatever we want. It looks like Brenna spill trash all over the place. Shoes on the floor. Bowls with dried up Cheerios on her desk. Clothes on the floor and not hanging in the closet. Papers and books inside the closet, on the floor in the closet, and not on her desk. I think its a good thing that my mama is not Brennas mama. Brenna can have John Travolta and Lorenzo Lamas posters everywhere. Daddy wont let me put up nothing, wont let me put up anything, because he says it mess up the walls, but what if I could stare at Lorenzo Lamas all day? How sweet man. But the last time I had tried, Daddy made me take Lorenzo down. Daddy passed my door, saw Leif Garrett and Lorenzo and Shaun Cassidy. Avery, he say, Who in the hell are all these white boys? Get that shit down off those walls right now, Daddy say. So I did.

Brenna turns on her radio and Disco Inferno is on. This song sucks, she says. But I like it. I like to dance to it in my room like Im on Soul Train. Ugh, Brenna say. She say, Rock and roll is here to stay, throw that disco shit away. She turn the station. You light up my life, Debbie Boone sing. Brenna can sing the whole song in pig latin but now she says, This song makes me want to barf. She needs a stiffy for reals. When Queen comes on, Brenna is happy. We are the champions, my friend! she scream and hug me so tight she make me drop my hamburger on the carpet. I pick it up and its got stuff on it now, look like lint. Look what you did, Brenna. She say, God made dirt and dirt dont hurt. Kiss it up to God, she say, hold her burger up after she kiss it. I cant eat mine, though. I just cant and I can hear Mama. You did what? Ate a hamburger off the *floor*? Now you know you know better.

We should be at your house, she say. Tates there. We could be spying on some babes right now.

Like who?

Brenna shrug and put her burger down and leave it lying there. She never finishes her food. I want it, but I dont want to ask for it. I dont know, she says. Maybe theres a guy who looks like Leif Garrett.

Owen never ever went to school with anybody who looked like Leif Garrett, but I dont tell Brenna that.

We stay up late because nobody tells us we have to go to bed. Nobody tells us anything. We hear Tate talking, so we come out and pretend to get some soda.

How was it, Colleen say. She on the couch in the living room, watching TV and drinking a beer. Youre home early, kid, she say.

Tate take the beer from Colleen and drink some. Some asshole called the cops, he say. Brenna and me look at each other and

Colleen frown. Why? What happened? Tate rub his eyes. Theyre red because hes a stoner. Thats what Brenna say. Tate take off his Vans and pull his T-shirt over his head. I try not to look at his back, but it looks soft and I wish I could touch him. Dont even ask me, he tells Colleen. I dont know why. They said we were too loud but we werent. It was kind of lame, he said. Owen kept telling people not to mess stuff up and not party too hard. And there were a lot of brothers there, too. Like a lot of black dudes. Colleen look at me and say Tate! Goddamn it. Watch it. Sorry, Tate say to me, and go to his room. He didn't mean anything by that Avery, she say. That kids got a big mouth. But Im not even sure what he said that was bad. If there were a lot of black people there, then thats the truth, isnt it?

When Im home the next day I ask Owen what happened, and he say that the cops say that his party was disturbing the peace. Yeah, Owen say. He was taking down trash to the curb. Member that, Ave, he say laughing. Too many niggas always disturb the peace. But I dont know why hes laughing. Thats not funny to me.

MAMA AND DADDY have a party too. Well, not a real party. Just people that used to live in our building in L.A. Four people. Mr Channey and his wife Bonnie, her brother named Dash and their daughter Cassandra. But its not the same like when we lived on 80th Street and we used to just walk into each others apartments like normal. Like first, they walk into the house all quiet and keep saying, Dang Darnelle! Dang Vicky! This nice! Miss Bonnie look down at the floor when she first come in the house. This floor wet? It look like its wet. We supposed to be walking on this floor like this?

Mama say, Bonnie, girl, now you know this floor aint wet. Its just shiny. Got two coats of that Mop n Glo on it.

Sheeiit, Mr Channey say when he standing in the kitchen. He go to the sliding glass door and look out at the yard. This real nice.

We gone get some more furniture in here when we can, Daddy say.

Cassandra stand by her mama like she shy of me. Hey, I say. Hey Cassandra.

Hi, she say, but thats all she say.

Come on, I say. Come to my room and look at my magazines.

Go head on, her mama say. Stop hanging all on me. Miss Bonnie push her away and run her hands over her bun like she checking if a hair out of place. She still pretty. Light brown hair like Cassandras. I see how her fingernails match her lipstick. Bright red like orange. So Cassandra come to my room. We sit on the floor and I show her Robbie Benson and Leif Garrett pictures, but she dont like them. She say, They ugly. I say, What else you want to do then? Nothing, she say. She get off the floor and then sit on my bed. She sit perfect and straighten out her yellow dress.

Lets go outside and run around then, I say. Come on. Lets go. I grab her hand. We can run around in my yard. Its big.

I cant, Cassandra say. She smooth her hair just like her mama. I cant get dirty.

Why is she being so boring? I dont know what else to do so I just tell her, Im going back out to the kitchen.

But everybodys outside sitting on the patio, they not in the house anymore. I get a chair and pull it over to Cassandra's mama. Come on over here, Miss Cassandra, Mama say. Sit next to me. And Cassandra does. She sit and kick her legs back and forth, and I stare at the shiny dress shoes she wearing. Cute, Mama says. Aint you looking cute? She looks alright to me. Not all that cute.

The grown folks are drinking and Mr Channey and Dash keep getting louder and louder. Dash got on a lot a jewelry. Lots of chains and a shiny red dress shirt. Its not orange red, though. Its red, red. He keep cussing real loud and Daddy say, Dash we got to keep it down out here, they real particular bout noise around here.

Oh, alright. Thats why you got Aretha playing so low we caint even hear her. Man, Dash say real loud. Fuck these white folks, and Mama look at Daddy and Mr Channey look at Miss Bonnie, like you better tell him something. Plus, Aretha is not playing low if you ask me. She loud. She sound mad. Some people want! she holler. But they dont want to give!

Dash, she say. Come on now. You done had enough I think.

And Ima have some more! he say. Why yall leave the bottle in-side? He gets up and almost fall. He walk to the sliding glass door but when he get to it he dont stop. He walk right into it. Goddamn! he say. I thought this shit was open. Thought I was just gone walk through it. He rub his forehead and then Daddy standing right next to him. I didnt even see Daddy get up, but he there.

You all right man? Daddy put his face close to Dash face. Look like you already getting a knot above your eye.

What you a doctor now nigga? You gone diagnose some shit?

All right, now. All right, Mr Channey say. He get up too.

Yall leave me alone. Im cool, Dash say. Ima get me another drink, though. I know that much. He pull on the door but its locked.

Let me show you, Daddy say. You got to switch this latch thing right here.

I know, man. I know, Dash say. You think I dont know how to open a door negro? But he try it and it dont work for him. He keep trying but that door stay closed.

Here, Daddy say. He flip the lock real quick and slide the door open. Dash walk in but Mr Channey right behind him telling him he aint getting no more to drink and right after that, everybody else get up and they leaving.

Im glad, though. Dash scary. He make too much noise. And Cassandra is boring anyhow.

Mama says, Well. Dash crazy but I wish they could have stayed longer than what they did.

Maybe Jonathan and Bonnie could have stayed, Daddy say. He pour himself some more J&B. He take a sip. But, uh uh. Daddy shake his head. Dash need to stay his ass on 80th Street.

8

BRENNA IS COMING over, even though Massimo will be home later in the day. I didn't tell her he would be back today because I'm tired of being referee. Let them figure each other out. I am trying not to make that my job anymore. She does not like him. They were enemies from the start. Her big American mouth full of confrontation and opinions offends Massimo's expectations of sophistication and femininity. "She's common," he has said. Once I pointed out to him that when we met, I was not sophisticated nor easily feminine. I'm common, too. I had big gaps in what I knew and what I should know. I didn't know what words like "al dente" meant. Or what grappa was. I liked to drink cheap wine with Twinkies, chase my Mountain Dew with a shot of vodka. "Still," Massimo said. "I have a jeweler's eye. Rough diamonds, I can see. And anyway, you are too strange to be common." In Brenna, he sees roughness only. No diamonds. Sometimes, even trash. He's just a little classist, I once told Brenna. "What?" she said. "That's like saying someone's just a little bit of an asshole."

After that very first time she saw him at the Formosa, she had already dismissed him. The next morning she asked, "How did money bags turn out?" She was eating a bowl of Cap'n Crunch for breakfast, the kind of food that I have tried to outgrow, living with Massimo, aside from the covert Twinkie or fried Spam I still love every now and then. Such food is what Massimo calls plastic. Everything I ate was plastic to Massimo. Now I eat food that

Brenna mocks. Poached eggs. Veal. English tea with milk and honey. Expensive pastries from the gourmet shop down the hill.

"How do you know he has money?" I had asked, though this is something that I now know easily and clearly by looking and listening to a person. Still, that night, the possibility of a man with real money, interested in me, oddly had never occurred to me. If you never experienced something in the flesh, how can it possibly exist? How could it be possible? It was something I had heard of but never seen.

"Please," Brenna said. "Those clothes. The way he talked to you."

"You didn't hear anything he said to me." I was lying in bed, staring at the portrait of me and Keith. It was crooked, and so I got up off my futon and cradled the phone while I straightened it.

Brenna said something that was muffled and then I heard a bowl hit the table. "You just drank milk out of the bowl," I said.

"It's Cap'n Crunch," she said. "The milk's the best part. And I didn't have to hear him say anything to you," she said. "I *saw* him talking to you. The way he moved in, leaned into you and touched you while he was talking to you. He was *handling* you," Brenna said. "People like that, these fuckers with money, they're always handling somebody."

"Pink Oxford Shirt looked like he had money," I said. "You should have been a lot nicer."

Brenna snorted. "I'd rather suck ten dicks for free than have to sit through his bullshit over some fancy meal."

I laughed. This was the kind of talk that made Massimo crazy. But all our lives, this has been the source of my admiration for Brenna. She is never, has never been, handled. As for me, she says she likes my malleability, though she doesn't call it that. It's my blendability. My ability to play it straight. Play dead. Whatever is necessary. Brenna calls me her mellow bud. Awesome Pay, she took to calling me in junior high. Possum in pig latin, and this name has stuck through high school and even college, when I went off to USC and Brenna stayed home because she made choices that no one understood. I have always known Brenna and she knows me as best as anyone could.

JOAN HEARD ME say some things I never, ever say. When we leave Joans house we stand in the middle of the cul de sac and it got to be one hundred degrees and nobody wearing sunglasses so we squint at each other. I think cool the sack, cool the sack, and it sound better than the real word that I learned it is. Cool the sack, cool the sack. I let my mouth make the words but I dont say them. I think about what Joan hear me say, and I think about the way she look at me. I think, Asshole. Shit. Nigger. Honkey. But I dont even let my mouth make those words. My lips are closed but my mouth feel full like I need to swallow so thats what I do. I swallow them words. My house is just three houses away from Joans, right in the middle of the cul de sac, and I wonder why they build a house on a dead end where there be only one way to get in and one way to get out. Not like the corner houses where you can go up and down the streets to your left, to your right, too. It is good to think about something else, not about being at Joans. But I dont want to be at home, and I dont want to be at Joans. I just want to stand still and practice words in my head.

Are you talking to yourself you spaz? Brenna say.

Yeah, she is, Keith say. She always do that. Pardon me, Keith say. He tilt his head back so his nose is high in the air. Will you pass the Gray Poo Poo? He makes the Ps sound hard like he spitting something out of his mouth, like polly seeds. Brenna thinks this is funny, and I dont like when they always do two against one on me. Here come the words. Fuckers. You fuckers. But I swallow that too and change my face like Mama tell me to when I get mad at her and show it on accident. Better straighten up that face before I smack it straight, Mama always say. So I fix it. My face is straight. Just like Im playing dead. And the sun is so hot but we just still standing around.

Uncle Darnelle is gone beat your ass when he find out what you said to Joan, Keith say.

You a lie. My face change just a little bit because Keith scare me. I didnt say nothing to Joan. I said it to you. And to Brenna.

Still, Keith say. Still.

Why do he have to find out? I make my face as straight as possible like I dont care. I dont even say what I want to say to Keith to mode him: My daddy dont hit me. He never hit me. Only Mama, and thats because she make him, because she starts the fights. If she would just be quiet and not yell and scream at Daddy, she wouldnt get hit. I say it again. Why do he have to find out?

Brenna look back and forth between us like something gone happen. Some sweat roll down the side of my face but I dont even wipe it. Cool. Im cool the sack and them words make me smile because I think they sound funny right now and so Keith smile too. Awright, he say. Nobody have to know nothing. He stand next to me and kick his leg behind him so his foot hit me in the butt.

How bout this? Brenna say. Anybody got to know bout this? She pull a watch out of her pocket. Its small and silver with a teeny tiny face. Keith lean in to look at it and take it out of Brennas hand. We all knock heads trying to look at it. Where you get this old ass watch? Aint even digital, Keith say.

Brenna snatch the watch back. I got it just now, she say, when we left. It was on the kitchen counter so I swiped it.

I stare at the watch in Brennas hand. We are gone get in trouble. I already know this. Why she mix me up in this? Now I have to worry about what I said in Joans house plus this. She push it around with her finger like she playing with a worm and it shine in the sun. I thought it was pretty, she say. And its better than digital, dumbass, she say to Keith. Any moron knows that old stuff is better, she say. But me and Keith look at each other. Anybody know that new stuff is better. Nobody that we know want old stuff. Everybody we know want new things that are clean and work and look nice. Keith shrug and do his eyebrow at me like,

Dont even try to figure out crazy Brenna. We too busy checking out the watch to know that Joan aint but two steps from us. She grab Brennas arm so hard the watch drop on the ground. She pick it up and look at us hard like she making a memory. She look at us like she counting careful, like one—thats me. Two—thats Brenna. And three—thats Keith, and she look at him the longest before her eyes pass over all of us again. We one, two, and three.

Okay, she say. Who did it.

I knew it. God Brenna is stupid. Nobody answer but we look at each other trying to figure out a story. What is the story?

No, Joan say. Look at me. And she make that word *me* sound hard like when she say No. She say. Im asking you, Avery. Who. Took. The watch. She has a scarf in her white hair. A blue scarf that match her eyes, and I look past her at her house that has orange roses in the front looking like frosting roses and her grass is green green green. Not like ours thats part yellow because water cost money, Daddy always say, and our yard is up high off the driveway so cant nobody see it no how.

And I think, Fucking Brenna Goddammit You Dumbass! Now look. But I say nothing for a long time until I say, Keith, and I say Keith because he steals all the time and nobody will care if its him, but if I say Brenna then maybe we wont get to play with each other again, and shes the only friend I have here, but Keith and I will always be together because. Because we family and you cant really keep no family apart.

Keith dont say anything, and I knew that was gone be how he did it because he stubborn. He dont care what people say about him. He steal and his mama beat him and he steal and his mama beat him and he steal.

Joan say to Keith, Is this true?

Keith stare through Joan like she clear, like a window. She stare at him, and what she thinking be in her eyes that look down, her mouth that turn into a white line across her face, and her fist that squeeze that watch in her hand, but I still dont know what it is she is thinking, exactly.

She look at Keith and then she say, If you are going to steal from me, you cant come to my house. But if you dont steal from me, you are welcome, and she say it like she struggling. Im surprised at you, she say soft, but it sound like she dont really mean what she say, like she not surprised at all.

I ask Joan, Are you gone tell?

She slip the watch on her wrist and turn her wrist back and forth. I dont know. Maybe. She talk to Brenna. Who is your mother? she ask. Brenna look serious. Shirley, she say. Shirley Jones.

What street?

This one, Brenna say. Down the other end.

And Joan satisfied with that. Dont know nothing about the Partridge family. She wipe her face with the back of her hand and give us the one, two, three. But she done. She just turn around and walk away.

Dude, Brenna say to Keith. Avery seriously dogged you out. Sorry, she say, and hit him on the shoulder.

Fuck you, Keith say. You didnt stick up for me neither, and because Keith have a point, Brenna shut up. Im tired. Tired of standing in the hot street. Tired of Brenna and Keith. Keith scratch his head and say hes going to go watch TV. Brenna say she going home, and I dont want to go home or to Joans or to Brennas. I dont know what to do except stand in the middle of the street.

9

I SIT IN a lawn chair and watch Brenna swim the pool end to end. She has the matter-of-fact physical beauty that, for a long time, I learned to prefer. Her legs are long, her breasts are large, but, because she has a narrow waist, her yellow bikini and red hair make her look like she should be on the cover of a Beach Boys album. I used to think her big breasts didn't desexualize her and mammy-fy her in the ways that I assumed mine did whenever I got heavy. That's what I used to think, that the difference between getting fucked and being the shoulder to cry on, the ears to listen on and on, was about thirty pounds.

We play Led Zeppelin and it always makes us nostalgic for junior high, the hours we would spend in each other's bedrooms, talking about how foxy Robert Plant was—even though I was becoming even wilder for David Bowie. To me, Bowie sounded black when he sang a song, which made him like me. And when he was Ziggy Stardust, he seemed to be something I couldn't name. He wasn't a man or a woman. He wasn't even from this planet. Because he was anything that we wanted him to be, he could be with anything and anyone he wanted to be with, with someone who was whatever she wanted to be, somebody like me, so many things rolled into one. With Avery. He'd be with Avery. Robert Plant, tight jeans and cock trailing halfway down his legs, he wasn't for nerdy little nappy-headed girls like me, though I wanted him to be. Longed for him to be. The irony of Plant singing the blues—and my feeling excluded from the blues—was lost on me then, but not now.

Keith loved Zeppelin, and Bowie too, because his friend John liked them. When we first saw Bowie, we got the shock of our lives. He was on *Soul Train,* and my family was visiting Keith's family in Victorville. We watched *Soul Train* like it was church. We *needed* to dance like those people going down the line. We just knew we were black swans that were going to look like them one day. Faith. We had it. "People all over the world," we sang along with the theme song. "People all over the world!" But we didn't know what that meant until we saw something that made us think our eyes were lying. Everybody loved Bowie's "Golden Years." But when we saw him on *Soul Train,* we freaked out. "Avie!" Keith called out. He was adjusting the hanger, which served as an antenna, on his black-and-white television set in his bedroom. "Look!" Keith said. "Trip out!" I ran to his room and looked at the thin white man singing on *Soul Train.* Bowie was wearing a dark suit with a light shirt. He was moving very slowly, as though he were high or drunk or too cool to sweat. "He sing 'Fame'?" I said. We loved that song. "I thought he was black." We stared at the television as though we didn't know whether to laugh or cry. "I'm trippin'," Keith kept saying. "I am really trippin'." "Me too," I said. "He *white*?" "I don't care," Keith said. "He bad. He a bad dude." We were traumatized and amazed. Who was this man who wasn't anything close to what he looked and sounded like? Who let him do that? Who let him be white and weird and on *Soul Train*?

Brenna climbs out of the pool and lies next to me in a chair. She says, "You got any booze? We should go get some if you don't." We don't have any alcohol in the house since Massimo has gone. It's my way of policing myself, since I have taken to drinking much more than I should. But now I would like to have a drink. It seems appropriate today.

We leave the music playing and go get vodka for Brenna and Chardonnay for me. I have to back out of the driveway and then turn carefully so that the car doesn't get too close to the edge of the hill and roll down it. Then, we have to drive very carefully down the hill, which is very narrow and barely allows for two cars. Brenna vigilantly looks for cars coming around the bend, even though I am always careful up here.

"Why," Brenna says. "Why come way up a hill like this? It's crazy."

"I don't know." I hunt for a CD and put it in while I'm driving with one hand. After a moment, Michael Jackson sings about making pacts and bringing salvation back.

"Bummer," Brenna says. "Poor bastard. Do we have to listen to this now?"

But I love when he sings, "Let me fill your heart with joy and laughter. Togetherness, that's all I'm after." So I let him sing his song. Maybe, if he hadn't hated himself for looking the way he did. Maybe if he had someone telling him before, earlier, before he ever got on a stage, something different about himself. Maybe then he wouldn't have tried to move bone and skin and hair into shapes and textures and colors that he thought made him better. Or maybe, if he just could have been all of that, mixed up, in peace, weird and black in the first place. I tell Brenna all of this as we're driving down the hill.

"Maybe," Brenna says. She reaches over and turns down the volume. "But too much money—and little boys—I think that's what did him in. Be careful," Brenna keeps saying whenever I hug a curve. "Jesus. Pay attention. Why live way up here? And he's dead now, anyway."

Because it's beautiful, because not that many people live up here, get to live up here, and because we can. But I say, instead, "I don't know why Massimo lives up here," thinking Michael shouldn't be dead, that he's not really dead, making people sad when they hear a song, like he's in the car with us, reminding us of so many things we can't articulate.

In the Gelson's we split up and get the things we need. We meet again and wait in line, making fun of celebrities on the covers of magazines and of some of the people in the market, like the alarmingly tan, middle-aged man desperately trying to look boyish, hunks of muscle straining under a T-shirt several sizes too small. "I hope that one right there takes a dump in that big bag of hers," Brenna says. She nods at a black woman with long dreadlocks who is cooing to her Chihuahua. We laugh, but then I see something else that makes me stop. It's a book, for sale, bargain bin, and Brenna is telling me to hurry up because the woman at the checkout is scanning our groceries. But the name on the cover, I recognize. John. John Etherton. I turn the book over, and there is John, the John of *Playboy* magazines and summertime. I scan the book, a memoir entitled *Where I Used to Be*. About his days lost to drugs and addiction. It's all so interesting and book worthy, now that the devastation is behind him and touches no one but himself. I'm thinking, Of course this is how it has ended up, you and your book, famous for running around and doing drugs with a black man. What an edgy life you've led, John. I turn over the book, and the image staring back at me is a pleasant one, a smiling man with gray temples, who lives in Santa Barbara with his wife and son, the book says.

"Avery!" Brenna says. "Stop making this woman wait."

"I'm sorry." I put the book back on the metal rack and pay in a daze, wondering about John and how long I've made the checkout woman wait. I watch her bony wrinkled arm scan our things, thinking that she's too old to be working, to be waiting for people.

"What the hell were you reading back there?" Brenna takes the bag from my hand and pulls out an apple she bought. She pulls the tiny sticker off it, flicks it on the ground, and takes a bite.

"You should wash that," I say, not really thinking of the apple.

"Fuck it. What were you looking at?"

"This kid that I knew. That Keith used to know. He wrote a book about his addiction. They got in a lot of trouble together, and now he's got some book."

"Good for him," Brenna says, disinterested, though I've talked about John before, of course. Why would she remember anything about some kid I used to know from a long time ago? And anyway, she would only care about Keith, the one who is still lost.

We are gone just for a half hour, but when we walk up to the front door, the house feels different. Bowie is singing to me about my face, my race, the way that I talk. "I kiss you, you're beautiful," he says, and I feel something dark and heavy. "Brenna." I grab her arm and stare at the front door that is wide open. "Did we leave this open?" And the open door feels like a dark hole I'm falling down.

"Shit." Brenna pulls me back from the door and we take a few steps back. She says, "Stay here." She takes a few steps, crosses the threshold of the door, and then comes back to me.

We stand together, paralyzed for a moment, and then Brenna says, "Fuck it. I don't hear anything. Let's go in."

She walks in slowly, her head cocked to listen more carefully. Her hair is still damp from the pool and is sticking to her back. I place my palm there and grab her hand, expecting that I will have to pull her back and that we will have to run away from the house. But no one is there. It takes me a while to notice that things have been moved. A rug is missing. A camera that was sitting on the dining room table is gone. A few drawers are open in the living room, empty. Food is sitting on the kitchen counter that wasn't there before. Some crackers. Cheese. Croissants with pieces missing from them like the shape of a mouth. "Hello?" I ask. "Hello?" When I don't hear anything, I walk into the bedroom and see that my bed, which used to be smoothly made, is messy. There are two spots of blood on the end of the comforter and two tiny vials lying in one of the comforter's indentations.

Brenna is standing behind me, her breath hot on my neck. "Let's go back in the living room," she says. "It's too weird back here." She pulls me back into the living room and we both stand there, thinking. Something else about the living room feels strange. Two walls are blank, paintings missing. When I glance back at the entry, I see what else. My portrait of Keith and me is gone.

10

THE PORTRAIT ISN'T the only thing that's missing, but it's the thing that worries me the most. In addition to the camera and one of Massimo's Rolexes that he left in a tiny bowl full of coins, the Persian rug—one that Massimo got in Tehran during one of his trips without me—a camel-bone mirror from Morocco, and some cigars are missing. The cigars are Cohibas, Genios Maduros, that cost "hundreds of dollars for just ten of them," Massimo is always reciting. He loves his cigars, puffing on them after dinner, and I have to admit that I'm drawn to him, sitting in our garden in one of his crisp shirts, a cigar held between his brown, elegant fingers and smoke obscuring his green eyes. He looks like power, smoking his cigars. But as always, Brenna is not impressed by Massimo or his cigars. She rolls her eyes at me when I say, "Massimo is going to lose it. I'm half afraid to let him know."

"Fuck him," Brenna says. She walks to the stereo and turns Bowie down. "Can't believe they left *this*," she says, tapping the stereo. "Call the cops. That's who we really need right now." She is stiff and alert, her skin shiny from the sunscreen she slathered on to protect herself from even more freckles.

I feel a flash of loyalty to Massimo when Brenna disparages him this way, and yet he would say the same about her. And, no, he is not the priority right now, this is true. Brenna is still standing near the doorway, but when I hesitate, she blows air out of her mouth and takes three steps to the phone propped up on my bookshelf. Her finger stabs at numbers until I take the phone out of her hand.

"What the hell, Ave?" She puts one hand on her narrow hips and throws the other hand up in the air. She is all action, always. If there is something to do, Brenna does it—that is all. But me, I am always thinking that there are too many ways to do things, and so as a result, I do nothing.

I stare around the house, my eyes scanning the walls, the floors, the tables, looking for anything else that might be gone, and there's not that much missing, not really. "Just wait a minute," I say. She waits with a frown on her face, and I almost don't tell her the truth of what I'm thinking. What if it's Keith. It might be Keith. It is Keith. Brenna is waiting. She tries not to think of Keith in the ways I do. She does not want to be in a headlock or an embrace with him. She has tried to discard him, though she has not been successful. He is just a sad memory, a reminder of her teenage transgressions, of what her life could have been.

"Wait a minute," I say. *Just wait.*

❋ ❋ ❋

ALL DAY AND all night Im scared. Mama is home from work and boiling a ham hock for greens, and me and Keith in the backyard kicking around a ball. Its dark in the backyard even though theres a light on, and Keith keep kicking it hard on purpose so it end up in the cactus in the corner of the yard. The cactus look like a giant spider like in the scary movies—its bigger than me and Keith and even Mama, Daddy, and Owen. The pieces of it grow up and out, like green giant spider legs coming out of the ground, and on the sides of the pieces it got sharp stickers like teeth. I already got the ball once and got stuck on my legs and scratched up on my arms. I make Keith get the ball after that because its his fault it end up in the cactus anyway. Dude! I say, Stop being so lame, but he just shine me on and ignore me. He keep running in the dark getting stuck by needles, and it look like he dont even care. But he got to care. It hurt.

Mama slide open the patio door. She say, Avery come here, and I know she talk to Joan. Keith, she say. Get in here. Keith face dont look scared, dont look worried, dont look nothing. I cant make my face that way right now. We walk through the door, and Joan standing in our kitchen. Inside. In our house. Mama never ask Joan in the house since we been living here. Joan looking all around her. She can see the living room, Jesus on the wall and our white leather couch that have black cracks all on it, my bedroom with my bed and nothing else but a Raggedy Ann blanket, nothing on the walls, no desk no chairs, just my bed. She can smell our food, and Mama looking at Joan looking around, and I know she mad about Joan being in our house on top of the watch that Brenna took. But Mama dont have speeches like Daddy. She say, Joan told me all about it and you need to tell her you sorry. I did not do nothing. *Anything*. Neither did Keith, but I say sorry before Mama even done telling me to say it. I just want it to be done. I say, Im sorry for cussing. And Mama say, For what? And

Joan say, I did not mention that, Avery. Im thinking, You moron Avery. You moron. Keith dont say sorry fast. He stand there for a little bit. I am waiting for him to tell it. Avery a lie. I didnt take nothing. Brenna did it. This lady at the wrong house. But he more scared of Mama than his own mama. He know that Mama might hit him if he make her mad enough, and Daddy too. He mumble that he sorry.

Mama say, Okay Miss Cooper? She say this slow. She say this like she dont remember how to talk. She say, Avery and Keith know better. I am very sorry, and they just caint come over to your house no more, worrying you to death. She say that like she done talking, and she look at the front door and then back at Joan and then back at the door again.

I didnt mean that, Joan say. Her eyes catch mine, and then she look at Keith. I didnt mean that, she say again. Avery is still welcome anytime. These are just lessons that kids have to learn. Im sure you agree, she say, but Mama dont answer that question. She say, She welcome, but I have to see about all that. Well, Joan say after Mama dont say anything else. Ill let you get back to your din-ner. It smells wonderful, she say, and turn around and walk out the kitchen and out the door. I remember wonderful, wonderful like the first time I met Joan, but it dont feel the same, and I feel more scared watching Joan walk out the door than I did when I saw her standing in the kitchen. Me and Keith are going to get it.

Joan is gone. Mama standing in front of me and Keith. She slap me hard across the face. She slap Keith harder, and slap him two times. The water from the ham hocks is boiling over in the fire on the stove, making sounds like on cowboy movies when they burn letters on cows. Sizzle. It sizzle. But Mama dont move. She hit me again. Cussing, she say, like she getting used to the word. She hit Keith. She say, That woman will never come in this house again telling me what kind of lesson I need to teach you.

Keith look straight ahead, aint even crying. But I keep wiping at my face and I say, Brenna really took the watch, not Keith. But Mama dont want to hear it. She say, Its too late for all that who shot John. If you run with bad folks, you bad, and if they took something aint theirs, you might as well been the one that took it now. She say, Look at me Keith, Im talking to you. Got me burning my food, Mama say. She all of a sudden hear the sizzle, but its been sizzling for such a long time now. She say, Get out of my face. You need to go and sit down somewhere. Keith go lay down on the couch where he sleep when he come here, and I go to my room. Close the door. Then I breathe.

In the middle of the night, I wake up and my bedroom light is on. Its so bright I cant open my eyes all the way. Daddy on his knees in front of me, and Im scared because Daddy dont come in my room for nothing. Never. Most he do is stand in the doorway, and now he is on his knees. What Daddy? What is it?

He put his face in mine. Close. I want to lean back but I know Im not supposed to lean back. Hes talking in a very low voice that I almost cant hear. Very quiet. He say, Im waking you up to tell you this one time. Are you awake? Are you listening to me? I bet not ever hear a story like the one your Mama told me tonight. He aint looking me in the face like Mama do, he is looking past my face at the blank wall next to my bed. He is very still and his hands make a fist. His jaw move like something crawling underneath his skin. He is trying, trying to stay calm. He talking to me like Mama do. He dont say much. He say, Do you hear me?

I move my head up and down and my chin tickle from a tear hanging on the end until I wipe it.

No, he say. Do. You. Hear. Me?

And I know that Im supposed to answer the question with the right words. Not with my head. I say, Yes, sir. I am awake. I hear you.

KEITH DOESNT TALK to me for a whole day and then he leave our house. Daddy take him all the way back home to Victorville, and he dont come back for two whole years. When he come back, he changed. And he the same.

WE'RE GOING BACK home. That's what Daddy always calls it. I never feel right saying that because Tennessee isn't my home. California is my home. But I love, love, love riding in the car. And Mama and Daddy are always so happy to be back home. Daddy and Mama are in the front and I'm in the back. Keith and his mama are driving too. Owen is riding with them to help. Sometimes they are in front of our car and sometimes they are behind. Daddy only got one week for vacation, so he drives and don't hardly ever stop. If you have to go, you better hold it for as long as you can.

We will get from L.A. to Tennessee in two days sleeping in places where you rest with a bunch of trucks all around and Daddy and Owen taking NoDoz. Now Daddy is driving and Mama is sleeping and my favorite is right now, before we get South, when we are in the desert. In the daytime I can see all of everything pass by in colors like purple and green and gold and pink and yellow. But the sky at the beginning of night is purple, the desert in New Mexico is gold and pink and sometimes purple and it all passes by so fast. When we get in the South I won't like it at night so much. It will smell good, fresh, fresh like mountains of grass. But at night. Late at night it is black, but I will stare out the window trying very, very hard to see something. I hope I see Bigfoot and then I hope I don't see Bigfoot. It's just fake, I know, but if there is a monster out there, I think it is better to see it than not to see it. Or people out there in the trees. I don't like trees as much as I like desert, it's hard to see things in trees. I think that maybe I will see the shapes of people. Maybe I will see somebody walking around in the trees lost. I think, What if there is a secret world of people in the trees that only come out in the darkness and they blend with the dark, and only people who look for them really hard like I do can see them?

Daddy turns down the radio, but I like hearing that song Listen What the Man Said, because it sounds like a country song in a movie to me, and it fits the desert and the nighttime. The wind is blowing in my face hot and dry like I just opened the oven and I say, Turn it back up Daddy, but Mama says, Ain't nobody want to hear that country mess. But Daddy turns it back up. That's not country, he says to me, he says, You like Wings? I say, Yes! He turns his head to the side just a little bit to look at me, and then he looks back at the road. They all right, Daddy says. He turns his head just a little bit to look at me. What you looking at, Ave? Nothing out there but dark, he tells me, but I don't want to tell Daddy about the people I'm looking for because if I talk about the people, Daddy will tell me they are not out there walking around. I might sound touched but I'm being for real. I don't want to be told nobody's out there because I know they are. They are all in the dark, Daddy'll tell me, Ain't nobody out there Avery. Can't nobody get you. But seriously, I don't believe Daddy. I bet you ten dollars somebody is out there. How could they not be? That's a lot of space for people. Somebody has to be in that space somewhere.

II

WE SIT IN the middle of the living room, on the rug, like we used to do when we were kids in each other's rooms. There is a garbage truck on a nearby street somewhere in the neighborhood, making noises like a distant moan, the abrupt clunk of something heavy being put back into place. Brenna says, "At least call Massimo," and now I know how unsettled she is. She thinks something should be done.

She chews on her fingernails, what little of them she has left, works them on the tip of her tongue and spits them out. It pains me to look at Brenna's hands, yet I am always looking at them, the map of them reminding me of who she is. Wisps of scars like white worms between her thumb and index finger from an accident when she worked at Arby's in high school. Calluses from the jobs she's had. Housepainter, McDonald's, waitressing. She even worked as a truck driver, just as her father did. When we were children, she bit her nails so much that her fingertips rose over the thin line of the nail, like half-formed, flesh-colored bubbles, a hint of blood just visible on the nail's edges. They were the ugliest hands I'd ever seen, worse than my mother's hands, which were discolored, thick, and misshapen by so many years of endless factory jobs and cleaning houses without gloves. My mother's hands were always like that, and she was a grownup, anyway, I reasoned then. But Brenna was just a kid. I used to look at Brenna's hands with wonder, but I would never tell her to stop biting her nails, not until we were older. "Don't you know how terrible those look?" I would ask her, never asking her what she was so nervous about, why she bit her nails in the first place. She chews on another finger, frowns, her eyes fixed on the rug at her feet.

"There's no need for Massimo," I say, but I don't believe it. I'm lying. I know: When Massimo comes home to find that someone has come into his house and taken what has belonged to him, to us, and I have waited all day long to tell him, have not filed a police report, have not taken action, he will be in a bewildered rage, so mystified that he will be pulling at the curls on his head, asking, "Why, Avie? Please explain this to me." So many times I have disappointed and infuriated him because I could not answer that one question.

Brenna touches my shoulder. She says, "Massimo is a pain in my ass, but it will be worse if you don't call him. He'll get pissed and want to call the police and make it all worse." Make it all worse. And there it is. Both of us know who has come into the house. I had told her about the calls from Keith, and now I know that she knows. She says, "He can't just come into your house and take things," and pauses, as if waiting for me to disagree, knowing I won't. And it's true, I'm thinking, Maybe it's a good thing that he has come and taken what he wanted. To consider this relaxes me, like pain medication finally taking effect, slow increments of peace between the pain. After all, Brenna and I were sitting around a pool in the middle of the day, a workday. Lazing, listening to music and singing together, laughing. The two of us, not three. The air conditioning was humming quietly. We were laughing, and I had my mind on the showing tonight, seven hours away, trying, as always, to close the door on my cousin. A door. I think about this door, and it is never a solid, heavy door made of wood like the one he walked through today. But instead it is a sliding glass door with a screen as well, a door that slides open, Keith standing on the other side, me standing back from the screen pretending that what is on the other side of the screen is something else. A chair maybe. A bench. But not a person.

"Avie. Do you hear me talking to you? What are you looking at anyway?"

And now it is me staring off into space. Until this moment, I have not really been looking at anything. "Nothing," I say. "I'm not looking at anything." But this isn't true. On the white wall in front of me, where Keith and I used to be, there is nothing, yes. The portrait is gone. But the outline of it is there, the faint brown coloration containing what could be a smooth, white canvas. Clean.

12

BRENNA AND I sit outside by the pool, too uncomfortable to stay inside, though we have not said so to each other. Brenna sips her Red Bull and vodka, and I am still on my first and only glass of wine when Massimo's silver BMW eases up the driveway. As soon as his plane landed, after I called Massimo, I made Brenna promise. I said, "Please. I don't have the energy for what you two usually do." "Fine," she had said in a flat voice, and I could tell she was not thinking of Massimo at all, but of Keith.

The car door opens and closes with a muted, sucking sound, not the bang of a door connecting to its other parts of metal. Massimo loves this, the quietness of his car. Everything hums or quietly clicks as if padded. I don't know why, but both of us stand as he comes in through the gate. His round golden green eyes shift from me to Brenna and back to me. He comes to me, and I know that he wants to hug me, but something stops him.

"You are sure." He squeezes his car keys, and some of them stick out from between his fingers like weapons. "You are okay." He looks at Brenna but then his eyes come back to me. "Both of you."

"Yes," I say, and Brenna says, "Uh huh," and because she answered him I know she is trying and because Massimo asked if she is okay, too, I know he is trying. But some things about each of them will always make it hard for them to get along. For Brenna, the things she can't stand about Massimo aren't who he is as a man, a person with heart, blood, brain, bone, and muscle. But rather, it's the details of the things he owns. She hates that he drives a car that doesn't make noise, that his shoes are the kind of shoes that OJ wore, not because he killed his wife in them, but because they are so expensive. "Only a true idiot would pay that much for shoes," Brenna had said when Massimo asked if I knew where his Bruno Magli's were one day. She said, "At some point a shoe is just a fucking shoe to keep rain and dirt and shit off your feet."

For Massimo, this is the problem with Brenna: Life should be beautiful, and should be lived beautifully. Her Red Bull and vodka are laughable. Her "uh huh" is coarse and unpleasant, does not show impeccable manners like my "yes" does. Now, he takes his cigarette from his shirt pocket and lights it, squinting his right eye out of habit, not because of the sun. "Okay," he says, "let's see what this is."

Brenna and I lag behind, scared of something that is not there. The day has made us wary, but Massimo doesn't hesitate and he isn't bothered by what he sees. Maybe it's because I've told him what to expect, what's missing. If you know what to expect to be missing, when you see that it's gone, it's okay because you've been prepared for the loss. On the phone, I said that I wanted to wait until he got home to call the police, but now that I see that he doesn't seem to be upset, I will ask something more. His eyes travel around the room, falling on furnishings, taking inventory. He frowns, pulls a chair from underneath the table just off the entranceway, sits down and taps his cigarette into the ashtray, a misshaped, glazed bowl the deep orange of a tangerine. My failed attempt at pottery.

"Why didn't they steal this?" He holds it up and grins at me, and the dimple just underneath his right eye never fails to charm me. So many good times have come with that dimple, and it is only lately that I recall the bad times, how things didn't fit the way they should have fit. The way I used to make them fit, just to get along.

Brenna snorts. She and Massimo, two of the many things that don't fit, at least agree about the ugliness of my ceramics. When Brenna laughs, he looks at her as if he's forgotten she's in the room with us. She stares at him a little too long without a smile on her face, the two of them in a silent face-off. I say, "Do we have to call the police?" Massimo shakes his head, puts out his cigarette. "Of course we call the police. Why wouldn't we call the police?" His eyes shift from me to Brenna, and suddenly, he's looking at the blank space on the wall before him in the foyer.

"Your cousin did this," he says, finally saying the thing that Brenna and I did not. He folds his arms across each other, spreads his legs, and slouches down in his chair, settling in for a fight. "Avie. Come on. Really. I'm supposed to let some—" He stops, reaches into his pocket for another cigarette but doesn't light it. He holds it delicately between his fingers and tries again. "We can't just let him come in here and walk away with whatever he wants."

Brenna, who has been so good, just like she promised, comes to the table where Massimo and I are sitting and leans up against me, resting her arm on my shoulder. Lightly she places her other hand at the base of my neck. Her hands feel like the whisper of a scarf settling on my skin. Massimo refuses to look at Brenna, but instead looks at me, his eyes flashing with decisions. I reach across the table because I want to take his hand in mine. I turn his hand over and pry open his fingers so that I can place my fingers on top of his and grip them. But he pulls away, puts his unlit cigarette in the ashtray before him, and makes his hands into tight fists on his lap.

I wish these two people would know the things about each other that I know, the things that would change them from ideas to people. Massimo and I, when we first met and were getting to know each other, were just ideas to each other. But now we know better. Once you know someone's story, or even pieces of it, it's hard to dismiss them to pretend you know all there is to know about a person. I know this about Massimo: The hand that pulled away from mine is the softest hand I have ever felt, man or woman. Massimo's hands are the hands of a man who used to be a carpenter. Hands that should be calloused but are not. He built things as a young man in Abruzzo, before making his way to Rome and then, eventually, making the difficult journey to America, to who he is now. Before, though. Before, he built beautiful tables and chairs. Houses. He used to steal when he was a boy, running the streets with a "fuck you" ready for anyone who told him to stop. He couldn't be at home, because at home, his father beat him and beat him, for just the smallest of things. Nothing, they had nothing, just a simple life with simple things. His uncle Nuncio tamed Massimo by asking him to sand the legs of a table he was building. "You should have seen Uncle Nuncio," Massimo said, the first time he told me the story. "Hands so rough they felt like pieces of rock trying to find their way out of his palm. Beautiful things, his hands made, Avie. I was too stupid to see, until I made something not even half as beautiful. But my chest: Out. So proud." "But how are your hands so smooth?" I had asked, unbelieving. I took his hands and kissed the palms, took one hand and placed it on my breast. "Beeswax," he said. "I coated the handle of my hammer and tools in beeswax to keep my hands smooth so that now," he ran his hands over my hip, up my side, and over my breasts, "I can feel you and you feel me. Not hard things like rocks." He held up his palms like something had disappeared from them, like magic. Hands. Because his father's hands harmed him, Massimo has never struck anyone, no matter how angry he gets, no matter how much he rants and throws things, destroying objects rather than people. Anyone who looks closely, into his eyes, can see traces of pain, a man holding off heartache with the pursuit of grandness, by acquiring still more things. Brenna will not see this pain, thinks I am making excuses, that there are many people far worse off. But it's not that his pain is more valuable than Brenna's or that mine's more valuable than hers or that Keith's has us all. Just look at a person holding his heart in his hand, with parts of it torn up, as his way to explain something—that's all I am asking of anybody.

"He didn't always have money," I said to Brenna at the beginnings of her hating Massimo. "He wasn't always a lawyer. He used to be a carpenter."

"Yeah, but so?" Brenna had said. "Look at him now. He's a motherfucker."

And Massimo is always considering Brenna, what he sees as her rude intrusions on what would be an easier life with me if only she weren't around. Massimo understands little, though I have tried and tried to tell him. Look at her hands. She's like my sister. Even without Keith in common, she and I would still be family. Still, he has no interest in what Brenna and I have in common. What he and Brenna have in common. And if he ever does, she makes sure that his interest doesn't last long.

The light has shifted in the house. Massimo's watch says three o'clock, and I have so many things to think about. "Baby," I say. "Can we just take some time to think about this for a while?"

Just wait.

✳ ✳ ✳

I SWEAR TENNESSEE reminds me of Little House on the Prairie in places, because we have to go up a really small road to get to Granny's house, a road that has two lines in the road, with the grass coming up between the lines. Every summer I come, I think I'm lucky that I can always come back to this place. Brenna is so jealous because she is stuck in West Covina. She says it's bogus I'm going to be gone for most of the summer. I asked Mama and Daddy if she could come, and Daddy said No. No way in the world. The country is good, but there is something about it. I already told you. I like the way the woods look. Looking at them is okay. I just don't like to be *in* the woods. Daddy says I'm already a city person, that I like too much noise, that I can't even run barefoot on the rocks and dirt, that I'm scared of every little bug that comes my way. It's too late for you, Ave, Daddy says. L.A. done run the country out of you. Should have been born in the country like Owen. But Owen don't fit in Tennessee neither. He always acts like he is bigger than the place and everybody in it, and anyway, that's not it. Just because I'm the only one in the family not born in Tennessee. He doesn't know that there are a lot of ways to be in a place. How I like to walk by myself, or sit on the porch and play music, or just listen. Listen to the way people talk. I like the way people sound in the South. The way they tell a story. Make it seem like you're inside the story, like you're there, like you are them. Like I wasn't born in California, even. Like maybe I was born here. But the woods are different. I stay away from the woods.

IT'S JUST THAT the trees are like a scary movie. In scary movies, people always get caught in the trees. People are always chasing you between the trees. Like in Roots. That show scared me. Kunta Kinte runs and runs and runs through the woods for nothing because you know he is going to get caught. When it first came on, I wasn't sure I wanted to watch it, but I had to because if I wanted to watch TV that's all there was. Roots. Daddy said, Avie needs to know her history, and Mama said, We don't know all that much ourselves. But after that, I didn't want to know all that much about history. I didn't know. When was this slavery? How long ago? Mama said, A long, long time ago, Avery. And Daddy said, Not that long ago. I was wanting to believe Mama, but usually, Daddy is right about these kinds of things. He said, Ain't no need of you worrying about that now, Ave. It's over now. That made me feel a little better. But I still don't know. When did it begin? And why? When I asked Daddy, he said, Some people just don't like black folks, Ave. But to me, what kind of answer is that? And then I think, Maybe that's why at school Harry is always messing with me, not just because he's a dumbass.

So that's why I'm not all that excited to pee in the woods, but there is nowhere else to go. We are almost to Granny's house, and I have to pee really bad. Keith too. Both the cars pull off to the side of the road so we can go. It's getting dark and I don't want to go in the woods, but we have to go deep enough so that can't nobody see us pee. We stand far enough apart so we can't see each other, but I keep calling out, Keith, Keith are you there? I can hear him, but I hear so many other things, too. It's so loud here in the dark. Bugs that sound like a bunch of ten speed bicycles speeding at the same time. And birds that make so much noise, sound like they are screaming and saying, Who? Who? Hey, Keith calls out. I hear something. You hear that? I hear something coming at me, he says. Mama yells from the car, You all better stop playing and come on here. But something's breaking the branches and I hear running, so I holler and Keith holler and I'm running for the car calling out, Keith are you behind me? Are you out there? Hurry. Hurry. Run. And he says, I'm right behind you fool. You better run Avery. You better run, because I think I see ghosts.

WE DRIVE OUR cars up the road and you can see the holler, that's how they say it. Holler, not hollow, and it looks deep like a V. When we drive up the hill, getting close to Granny's house, I love the sound of the rocks underneath the tires. I never heard that sound in L.A. Never hear it in West Covina. Crunchy. It sounds crunchy like something being crushed, or even like something is boiling and boiling. It is so hot. Maybe something is boiling. I ask Owen, Do the tires sound like they crunching or boiling to you? He squints his eyes at me like, Stop asking stupid questions. For real, I say. Tell me. Crunch, stupid, he says, and then the sound stops because we're here.

It's like everybody is trying to get out of the car at the same time. I push the seat forward so I can climb out from the back, and Mama's not even all the way out of the car yet. Wait, Avery, she says. Let me get out this car first! Aunt Judy comes running out of the house first, with her hair cut short like Mama. And then Uncle Cesar with his big afro and pick in it, wearing one of those button-up shirts he always has on, and then Uncle Laughlin with his limp because of his accident when he jumped in the creek that didn't have enough water. Aunt Judy screams when she sees me and Owen, Oooh that boy getting as tall as his daddy! Avery looking like Darnelle's picture! Then she sees Aunt Janice and Keith and screams some more, Girl you done gained some weight! Keith you better come over here boy and give your auntie some sugar. And then she says, Hey Darnelle, and her smile isn't as big when she looks at Daddy. She still gives him a big hug and when she lets go she shakes her head, smiling. I say, Where Tina and Joe and them? and Aunt Judy waves her hand. They around here somewhere, probably doing everything but the right thing. And I want to go find my cousins but I don't know where to look, so I stay with Mama. Me, Mama, and her sisters sit on the porch and watch Daddy, Owen, and Uncle Cesar drive away. To run the streets, Mama says. But I know different because Daddy told me. He likes to come home to see his people, his friends, his cousins, and so that is where they're going. He never sleeps when we come because he tries to see everybody he's ever known, it seems like. It seems like he doesn't want to miss anybody.

I don't care about them. They are missing out because the porch is the best place to be. Tennessee is the only place I have seen porches in real life, and it's my favorite thing about Granny's house. No porches in L.A. No porches in West Covina. Only concrete or yards. You have to be careful, though. You have to watch the nails that stick up. And pieces of wood that's about to crack in half if you step on them too hard. And another one of my favorite things changed. You used to be able to lean out the window and practically be on the porch, but now the glass is broke out of it and they got cardboard in the window so you can't lean out. The porch leans to one side, too, and now they got bricks underneath holding that part up. But that's nothing. If you scream, Hello, the holler will answer you back from across the way, Hello, hello, hello. And you get to hear Mama and everybody talk about stuff they don't care that you're hearing about, even if they say you are only eleven years old and too young to hear about grown folks' business like Charlie, Nancy's girl across the way that come up pregnant because she is just as fast as she want to be and Johnny B up the road act like his wife don't know he running around with that light-skinned heifa up at his job and Owen think white women special since West Covina and Daddy don't never be home no more and Avery getting fat but at least she ain't fast.

Yet, Mama says. Yet.

Uncle Cesar got something wrong with him and Keith, if he ain't trying his hardest to turn into one of them bad niggas, and Granny just sits on the porch listening and quiet and sewing like she don't hear nothing, acting like that half Indian they say she got in her.

THE HILLS ARE alive with the sound of music, and I like it because I'm in the hills of Tennessee and somebody is always playing music. If it's not me playing this movie, then somebody else is playing what makes them happy. The hills are alive with the sound of music, I sing and Keith says, The hills are alive with the sounds of shit. Turn that dookie off, Avery, for real. But I walk around with my eight-track player and play all of it, over and over again. Me a name I call myself! Raindrops on roses! Whiskers on kittens! I hate to go and leave this lovely sight! Keith and my cousin ReRe play Al Jarreau singing We Got By. They love the line when he says, You bring the beans girl and I'll buy some wine. They sing that part loud and drag out wine like wiinne. ReRe got her fatigues on from the National Guard and she is smoking a joint, and they are sitting on the porch with Anne Marie that lives down the road with Uncle Jo Jo, who Mama said aint none of my uncle, but why we call him that then? I can't find my tape. I have been looking and looking, and I am very careful with it because I play it like it's going out of style, ReRe says. Keith has it, I know.

I ask him. Where is it?

Stop asking me about that bullshit tape, Keith says. ReRe laughs and the smoke puffs out her mouth. That's a crazy tape, Ave, she says, and then she takes another puff. Granny is sitting in the kitchen in the house like she always does, and so I know she can hear him. Why doesn't he care? He should care about Granny hearing him, at least.

For reals, Keith. Where is it?

For reals, he says.

Tell me, I say.

Keith says, Tell me.

But Anne Marie scratches her cornrows and then she tells me. Look under the porch.

I get on my hands and knees in the road and I look. I see my tape. Smashed. It's all smashed and the tape is pulled out, looking like a whole bunch of brown worms all curled up on each other crawling all over my tape. I scooch under to get my tape. I don't like being underneath the porch. This is where Granny's dog King went to die after he got the mange. It's dark and cold, and I know there are a bunch of bugs here crawling around. Roaches, fat earthworms, and ticks, a whole bunch of little red ticks that get on you all at the same time and crawl up your legs and look like somebody is coloring your legs red from the ankles up. Ticks that suck your blood. They get on you and you don't even know it until they are so big, something growing from up out of you and you can't believe you didn't know they were sucking on you all that time. And bones, I see bones. Whose bones are those? Are they King's bones? Are they chicken bones? No. They're too big to be chicken bones. I crawl backwards on my hands and knees and pull my tape out with me. Whose bones are those underneath the porch? I'm asking Keith and Anne Marie. She shrugs and swings her legs off the edge of the porch and hums to the song and sings Al Jarreau, Flying, trying, sighing, dying. Why do you care? she says. And she sounds just like Brenna to me when she says that. Even looks like Brenna. Anne Marie is golden red with freckles on her face too, but they look different on her because her skin is already on the way to being the color of those freckles. And people say she's got red hair but it's really orange. Exactly ten cornrows of orange hair.

Yeah, what you care for? Keith asks.

It's scary. Don't you think it's scary?

Keith starts to mess with me. He makes his eyes big. He starts singing in a spooky ghost voice. The bones of Kunta Kinte, the bones of his mama, the bones of his sister and his daddy and his brother. The bones of Kunta Kinte, the bones of his mama, the bones of his sister and his daddy and his brother.

ReRe says, Leave her alone, Keith.

Anne Marie starts singing the song with Keith. They sing it over and over. Keith jumps off the porch and does a African dance. He throws his arms and legs all over the place like something jumped in him and is making him do the dance, like he isn't doing it because he wants to. Idiot. I hate this song. I hate this song. I pick up the biggest rock I can find in the road and throw it as hard as I can at Keith's head. The sound is nasty, like a stick hitting another stick. ReRe says, Don't do that Avery, but she stays on the porch watching and keeps smoking her weed. He screams and holds his head and blood drops fall on his T-shirt and spread open like little flowers. He comes at me but I take off. I'ma get you and I'ma beat your ass, he hollers. You watch! But he doesn't catch me that day. Not on that day.

13

THE LIVING ROOM is heavy with all of us. Massimo with his clenched fists, hiding the softness inside, Brenna lit up from the windows, soft light falling on her red hair, making the split ends on the top of her head look like soft sparks crackling above her. I am thinking of them both. Of myself. Keith. If I can strike a balance between so many things, maybe this will all turn out all right.

Brenna is still leaning on me. She softly pinches the back of my neck, something she used to do to annoy me when we were kids. Usually with cold fingers, because of a Slurpee or a Big Gulp or ice that she'd been pulling out of cups and eating. "Cut it out," I'd say. "Why do you always *do* that?" "To shock you," she'd say. "Sometimes your uptight ass needs to be shocked." But now she does it absently, out of habit, and it soothes me.

"Brenn." I pat her rough fingers on the back of my neck. "You should leave. It's going to be all right."

Massimo raises an eyebrow and then lowers his head, nodding. When he looks up, his eyes glance over things in the room, finally landing on me. I can't read his face. I don't know if those sharp eyes and clenching jaw are pleased that I've asked Brenna to leave, or if he is angry that I took too long to ask her to leave. Brenna circles the table so that she is across from both of us. She tells us, "You're not going to call the police." I stand and walk toward her. When I reach her, I pull her to the door. "Massimo and I have to talk about this. It's better if you go."

Brenna knows that at least if the police are called, it won't have been because I called them. She knows that if the police are called, it will be because I lost some kind of fight. I may have tried so many years not to see Keith, but passivity, looking the other way, is not the same as putting someone in jail, I tell myself.

"Okay, then," Brenna says. She hugs me, perfunctory and light at first, but then sudden, like a spasm, she squeezes me, and without a word to Massimo she is out the door. She does not close it behind her, and Massimo and I are still as we listen to her start up her Honda, hear its fading chug as it backs out of our long driveway. When I cannot hear her car anymore, Massimo asks his same question.

"Why, Avie?" He lights another cigarette and takes a deep puff before he answers the question, himself. "For years I have heard this. She is my sister. We have known each other since we are kids. That you are all tied together." He gets up to pace and his voice gets louder. Higher. "But do you know how much shit I eat for that—" He inhales and pinches his lips tightly. "For *Brenna*, to be in my house treating me like I'm less than *nothing*. Even when she does not open her big mouth, this is what she is saying to me."

"But she didn't even say anything," I say. Thinking about how unpleasant she could have been. He walks away from the table, getting farther and farther away from me, getting angrier. "That's right," Massimo says. "She says nothing, as if I am not worth talking to."

In the kitchen, standing behind the counter, he pours some water from the tap and drinks. He tosses the glass in the sink, and something breaks. There is a high splintering sound that makes me cringe and cover my ears. "My-a God, Avie." His pronunciation makes me feel tenderness for him; all these years in the States and he still can't say "my God." His face has shaded into a deep red, and when he smokes his hand holding the cigarette shakes.

Fury. He is not good at containing it, as I used to be until recently, at keeping it moving underneath his skin slow and quiet like a stream. Instead, he fights with his fury, struggles and thrashes against it, like it's holding him down and trying to drown him.

"There is Brenna," he says. "And now your cousin. What do I do? What do you want me to do? Give him a key? Make gifts of everything I have worked so hard for? Whenever I want you to ask me for something, just to tell me what it is you want, you won't. You act as though I treat you like a whore, and anything I ask you is to spread your legs a little wider. But my-a God. When you do ask me for something." On the floor next to the kitchen counter there is a pile of books. He kicks the pile hard and pages flutter, opening and closing like wings. Suddenly he's sitting in the middle of the floor, breathing as though he's just run a long distance. I make him so tired. He gives and he gives and sometimes feels as if it is never enough, but that's only because we are not using the same currency. We can't decide what's being traded and how it's being paid for. He says he will give me anything, and he gives me a lot. I say that I don't want to be given anything, that I just want to be free. He says money is freedom, but I say only if everybody has it.

He is sitting halfway in the kitchen and I join him, setting myself on the cool tile of the floor. He lets me take his hand this time. "Massimo." I squeeze his hand. "I understand everything you are saying to me, but listen to what you are asking me to do. You are asking me to put family in jail. You are asking me to pick up the phone, to stand by while you pick up the phone, and send Keith to jail. You are telling me that I have to put my cousin in jail."

"He will have put himself in jail."

This is true and this is not true. This is what Massimo cannot be made to understand, unless I figure out a way to make all the stories I have told him come together so that he can understand.

14

MASSIMO IS IN the kitchen now, cleaning broken glass out of the sink so he can cook. Making things. Food, the occasional piece of furniture. These are the things that keep us in the world, he is always saying. "Contracts are not exciting, Avery. But making things is." He hums. Occasionally pots and pans clash as he rummages for the right one. Plates clatter in the cabinet, and I know that he is pulling a plate from the middle of the stack, only to put it on top and search for another, changing his mind as to which dish he wants to use and in what order. He steals glances at me, tosses his gray-streaked hair out of his face only to have it fall back in his eyes. I am curled up on the couch, drawing. I keep thinking of the two drops of blood on the bed, so that's what I'm drawing on my white pages. Dots of blood. But they don't look right. They just look like polka dots, and blood is much more than that.

Massimo and I never finish the argument. We have just decided to ignore the problem for now, even though we know that never works. The house is quiet, except for Massimo's work sounds in the kitchen. He calls out, "Avie. Dodgers game, no?" I look up surprised, and his wan smile fades as he turns back to his meal. Of all the things we have taught each other since being together throughout the years, this is the most surprising. Massimo has been a soccer fanatic all of his life. But I got him to see some value in baseball, to care when he pretends that he doesn't care at all. I turn on the radio and find the game. They are home, the Dodgers, and so Vin Scully is announcing the first few innings, urging Los Angeles to make sure they are well insured with State Farm and catching up the city on injuries, averages, and losses.

Vin Scully is telling everybody who is listening. It's 2–0, Padres. Full count. Bases loaded.

THIS SUMMER IS the best cause of baseball and *The Sound of Music*. But Keith messed up my day. He took my tape again even though I just got another one with money Mama and Daddy sent me. I got a whipping from Granny because I busted Keith's head open with a rock. He chased me, but I was too fast that day. Granny always hits hard with a green switch she keeps against the wall on her back door. Man it hurt. This is going to be the last time I'm going to get hurt for doing something. I ain't doing nothing no more. I hid in the woods even though it's scary, cause Granny is way scarier. I came out and sat on the porch because I'm thinking I'm in the free and clear. But she got me. She came up real quiet like a Indian. I'm sitting on the porch, humming Bless My Homeland Forever. She comes from the back of the house, from the kitchen, where she's always sitting staring out the open door into her garden of greens, tomatoes, and onions. She comes around the side, and I don't hear her because I'm humming. You think she is weak cause she's old, but she grabs hard and whips me. She says, Stop that crying. Stop it. You don't never treat kin like that, hear? You cousins and here he is bleeding all over the place. My legs are on fire. She stares at me with them gray eyes that all the kids on the hill are afraid of because they're gray, not brown like everyone else's, gray like that old well water bucket we use. They got light rings around the outside, not dark ones like they're supposed to have. She stares at me with them eyes and then she says, Keith right. That music shit, and then she takes her switch and limps to the back of the house.

I'm sorry when I see that rag wrapped around Keith's forehead later. I'm lying in one of the two beds in the house on top of that lumpy mattress. I love the smell of the bed, salty and sour and smoky like dirt. I'm only afraid of the roaches that crawl along the wall and in between the wallpaper that's peeling. They sometimes crawl in the bed with me and my other cousins. I'm lying on my back with my eyes closed and when I open them, there is Keith on the side of the bed with a box of cupcakes. Hostess. Hey, he says.

I say, Where'd you get them? Those? I say.

Stole 'em.

You going to get in trouble. Why? I say.

For you.

I can't eat all of those, I say. I'm fat. Everybody says so.

Naw, dummy, Keith says. Look on the bottom.

I turn the cupcakes over and I hear them bump up against the box and slide up against each other. There are three baseball cards on the back of the box. Rick Manning. Cleveland Indians. J.R. Richard. Houston Astros. And Ron Cey. Dodgers. Ron Cey. *Ron Cey*. He's my favorite. Stubby. Big forearms like Popeye. When he bats, he grinds his back leg in the dirt over and over again, digging in, and when he runs, he waddles. The Penguin.

Keith says, I know you like that fool. You weird, but. He shrugs and then scratches his head.

Yeah, I say. I'm staring at the box. Man.

Keith gets some old timey heavy scissors, and I cut out the Ron Cey card. I don't collect cards serious like other kids. I just keep Dodger cards whenever I find them or buy them at 7-Eleven or pull them 3-D cards out of Kellogg's. If I get a card that's not a Dodger though, I don't care. They go in the trash. I stare and stare at that Ron Cey card all summer long but keep it in my suitcase to be safe. I'm going to be the first woman pitcher in the majors. I'm going to come up with a special way to pitch. People are going to say, How did she get past us with that? And I'm going to be the peacemaker of the team. I'm going to be fair, treat people right. We're going to always win. Ron Cey is going to say, You pitched a good game, Arlington. A good game. He's going to think I'm perfect. Even better than Cindy Garvey. There's not going to be anything to change about me. We live in

a nice big house and have lots of money. Brenna never understands. Gross, she always says. He's such a fucking grandpa. But
she doesn't know about being together on the same team, how
bad that would be. Seriously dynamite.

WELL WATER IS super good. Super cold with a taste like nick-
els and dimes and quarters if you put them in your mouth. I
never taste water like this, except in Tennessee. Water in California smells like water in Joan's swimming pool sometimes. It
practically burns your nose, it smells way like chlorine. I like the
adventure of the South, but everybody always tells me to shut up
when I say it reminds me of *Little House on the Prairie.* I'm not
talking about Laura Ingalls. I'm talking about Granny's house.
Wooden, like a cabin, but with shingles on the roof. Granny's
bathroom doesn't work anymore because the pipes are all messed
up. So we take baths in a tub on the porch and we have to boil
some hot water to mix it in with the well water. And the toilet
doesn't work, so we use the outhouse Mama says she used when
she was coming up. We brush our teeth in the kitchen and spit
the toothpaste out of the back door. Granny cooks on a stove, but
the flames are inside of the stove, not on top. They make the flat
top hot from the inside. In the middle of the living room, there
is another stove that goes all the way to the ceiling, through the
roof. There is a couch, and some chairs, and a television. That
is the only thing that is not like Laura Ingalls. The television.
Sometimes, if it is too hot, Africa hot, then we can sleep on the
floor in the living room with the door open, just the screen. I
love this. It feels like sleeping outside. In L.A. I could never, ever
do this. Not even in West Covina would they let me sleep in
my own yard. Too much wrong with the world, Mama says. You
don't need to be outside at night. Something liable to happen,

she says. But Tennessee is different. We even have slept on the porch on pallets, Granny calls them.

I tell Daddy this. How much I love that I get to feel a little like Laura Ingalls. He looks at Mama and they both laugh. Big laughs and for real. They never, ever laugh like that. Nothing is ever that funny to them. Daddy gets a serious look, though. He says, Avery, I need to tell you something. It's 1978. You know that much, don't you?

He always does this. Why is Daddy talking to me like I'm a baby? Yes, sir, I say.

And when Laura Ingalls live?

Pioneer days.

Daddy says, And are we in pioneer days?

And I'm getting mad because I feel like Daddy doesn't know how smart I am. He's asking me questions, and that means he's trying to argue with me about something. That's his thing. I am not stupid. Of course not. Of course this is not the pioneer days. I say, No. We are not in the pioneer days.

Why Miss Lucille got pioneer stuff then? Why she got an outhouse? Do we have an outhouse in West Covina? Did we have one in L.A.?

No we didn't. We don't, but so what? We live in the *city*. We live in the *suburbs*. So what? He and Mama wanted progress and moved to West Covina, but Granny is country. Maybe she likes things that way. That's where she lives. In the country. She will sit for hours and hours, I swear, watching her garden. She doesn't even watch TV. She says she ain't stuttin' no TV. Rather look out her back door. I even asked her once. Come to California, just once. Daddy's mama, Mama May, does. She likes it. Comes to Dodger games and everything. But Grandmama Lucille says ain't nothing in L.A. for her. I tell Daddy all of this. He stares at me and shakes his head. He looks at Mama and she just shrugs. I win the argument. I answered all the questions. He usually wins, but I win this time.

But Daddy is still talking. Listen to me, he says. Miss Lucille is poor. Now I know you know what poor is.

Poor is when you don't have anything to eat and no place to live. To me, Granny's house isn't being poor, it's just different, and I don't mind what this is. It's fun. It's lovely, like Joan would say. The porch, the sound of the cicadas. Well water. Even Brenna says it's cool to come here. It's a nice place to visit. I just want to stop talking about it because he's not going to understand what I'm talking about, so I just agree.

I know what poor is, Daddy.

Because you need to understand, Daddy says.

Yeah, I know, I say. I think of what Brenna would say if she were talking to her daddy. She'd say, Yeah, geez, all right, Dad. God.

Daddy says, What did you say?

Yes, I say. Yes. I understand. Sir.

YOUR WHOLE GENERATION including you. That's what we say to Uncle Cesar if we think he's too far away to catch us. If he tells us something, we curse him like that. To us it means something like Brenna would say. Fuck you. But maybe not as mean as that. Maybe it's more like shut up and go away. Yes. Shut up and go away. He doesn't ever run, but he will stay perfectly still so you think he's too bored to be bothered with you, and then he'll grab you and give you a Indian burn. He will take your arm with both hands and twist the skin in opposite directions and burn your skin. He's a weirdo. He's never lived anywhere on his own. He's never had any job. He's never had any girlfriend that anybody has ever seen. Not even holding anybody's hand. He didn't go to school no more after junior high, even. All he does is stay in the house or go to the library. He walks down the hill and into town and he comes back with so many books. Books on science, about planets and universes. Books on math. Books on history. Books about art. I saw one of those books. *Art, Music, and Ideas.* I look at the pictures of art mostly, don't really understand the part about ideas or music. We're in the back bedroom and it's dark even though it's sunny outside. There are two pictures I like in this book that Uncle Cesar is showing me. One is a picture of a statue. A woman holding a man that looks like he's dying. She's sitting on a chair and she's wearing a robe, a robe or a cape, maybe, that has folds and folds that look so soft like clothes. Not hard like rock at all. You can count the man's ribs, he's so skinny, and you can tell that she loves the man. She is trying to take care of him. Or maybe just make him better. The other picture I like is different. It's just lines and colors. Black and white and blue, yellow, red. I like it because it seems clean, maybe? Or easy? And that there is so much more that you can do with plain old colors like that. Plus it looks like the Partridge Family's bus. I tell Uncle Cesar this. We're on the bed in the back bedroom. He has brown eyes like the rest of us, but he has a face like Granny's. His bones make his face seem like a cartoon, a face made with lines like a box. Light skin like Granny's. But his brown eyes are the only way he is like the rest of the people in Tennessee. His voice doesn't sound like the rest of the people. Cesar sounds like a lawyer on TV.

He says, Avery. This is Mondrian. He's Dutch. *The Partridge Family* is a silly television program that borrowed these images for their bus. That is the only thing the two have to do with each other. He looks at me like he's worried about me, like Mama sometimes looks at me when she thinks I'm sick.

He touches the page on the book and his fingers go over the lines in the picture soft, like he's petting a little cat. They say everything in his life is reasoned or calculated. If a table has not been laid with perfect symmetry, it upsets him, Uncle Cesar says. But what is he talking about? What's a perfect cemetery? What's calculated? Uncle Cesar rolls over on his stomach and lifts his head up like he's going to look out the window, but he can't because of the cardboard there. What's perfect cemetery? I ask him. He rolls over on his back and then brushes a roach off of his arm. Symmetry, he says. Lie back, he says, and I lie down next to him. We look up at the ceiling and I'm looking at another roach crawling over us that I hope doesn't fall on my face.

Uncle Cesar turns his head to kiss me. He has done this before. I like it. He pats my face soft, like soft little slaps, and then he kisses me on the mouth. He talks to me. His lips are almost touching mine and his breath smells sour and smoky like cigarettes. He says, Michelangelo. The sculpture you like is a Michelangelo. Remember that now Avery. And then I hear Keith's voice. He's in the doorway and he says, Avery getting down with Uncle Cesar. You nasty! When he says that, I feel nasty, but I didn't feel nasty before. Uncle Cesar grabs my arm when I try to get out of bed and get to Keith. Shut up. Shut up, I tell him. Uncle Cesar pulls me down on the bed. He says, Shhh. It's all right. But it's not all right. Something is not right. I say, Let me go, nasty, and I yank my hand hard and I'm finally off the bed.

Uncle Cesar sits up in bed and looks at me. Calm. Just blinks at me. You're being silly, he says. Come here.

No, I say. You're an idiot.

Uncle Cesar smiles and blinks at me like he's playing a game. You're an idiot, he says.

Dumbass, I say.

You, he says. You are. You're a stupid little girl. He is smiling. Your whole generation, including you.

Uncle Cesar laughs. Do you even know what a generation is?

Yes, I say. But I don't, even though we say it all the time. It's the final word when you say that. Nobody can come back from that. I don't know what a generation is, how long that lasts. Is it a short time or is it forever? Uncle Cesar knows this and he laughs and laughs. I can still hear him laughing when I run out of the house.

MAMA AND DADDY call from California. They're back home now because Daddy only had one week vacation. Mama too. All the grown folks had to go back, but me and Keith and Owen stayed. They always leave us behind for the rest of the summer and then we take the bus back home. This is good for us, Daddy says. Sometimes California ain't, Daddy says. I asked him why when he and Mama were getting ready to leave. Why did he and Mama move all the way to California if it's not the best? Daddy was checking out the car. He was looking under the hood. He closed the hood and tied it with rope because the hood doesn't work right anymore. It pops up sometimes for no reason, right when you're riding in it. Daddy wiped his hands on his pants. He said, Both places have some bad, and both places have some good. What are those good and bad things? I asked him. But he just said, A lot of different things, Ave. All kinds of things. Hot, he said. It's hot. Blistering. I *mean*, he said. It gets hot in California, but that kind of hot I can take.

I like it. I like Tennessee, even hot like this, Daddy.

That's right, he said. You and the pioneers. You gone rough it? I guess we may as well send all your stuff down from California so you can go head on and stay out here then, you like outhouses so much.

But he didn't understand me. That's not what I said. I wasn't thinking one or the other. I'll always want to go home, to California. Daddy was trying to show me, but I would show him. I would try to make him make a choice.

Okay then, I said. If I stay here then you have to stay yonder in California and never come back.

Unh, Daddy said. Yonder? He laughed. We both gone want to come back and forth and all around so we gone have to figure out something different. But better drop that yonder. That ain't gone work nowhere but here, talking like that. And you ain't staying here.

And then he yelled to Mama, Come on now, Vicky Sue. It's time to go.

But now he's on the phone sounding worried and tired.

I tell them about the sugar toast. Sugar toast is very good, but now I am sick of it. It's all we hardly ever eat anymore. For three weeks, at least.

Now he tells me to put Aunt Judy on the phone.

Judy! I call out, and Daddy says, You don't just yell for somebody that's grown. Yes sir, I say. I put the phone down and walk to the kitchen. She's down in the garden with Granny. Daddy want to talk to you, I say.

What he want?

I don't know, I say.

She comes into the living room and leans on the stove while she talks to Daddy.

She says, Spent it. I know you did. I ran out, is what happened. Bills. Phone liked to got cut off. Lectricity too. I don't know Darnelle.

She doesn't say anything for a long time. She's nodding with the phone against her ear.

Uh huh. I know Darnelle, she says. But wasn't nothing to help it. She's nodding again. About three hundred be good. All right, then, she says. Bye.

She hangs up the phone and looks like she wants to hit me. Why you tell your daddy we wasn't feeding you?

But I did not say that. I only said I was sick of sugar toast. I didn't say that, I say.

Sugar toast ain't good enough for you? Rice ain't good enough for you? It's food and you eating, ain't you?

I don't know how to answer these questions. It's true what she's saying, but we've been eating that Sunbeam bread and white rice forever. When we first got here, at least we were eating more greens. Had some possum and rabbit too. Sometimes fried to-matoes and fried potatoes. But I wish we could have hamburgers sometimes. Pizza. Chinese food. Spaghetti like Mama makes. I tell this to Aunt Judy.

She chews on her bottom lip for a while. She says, You bet not call your mama and daddy again talking about we don't feed you. She slaps me. Nobody but Mama has ever slapped my face before. I'm so surprised it doesn't even hurt. It's just that her hand came out of nowhere. Like a magic trick, it shocks me and surprises me so much that I don't even know where I am. I'm standing somewhere else, it feels like. Like I don't even know where I am with my face tingling, seeing stars in front of me and far away into Granny's garden outside the door, and the hills even farther away, like I'm traveling to Mars and Jupiter or home to California.

15

MASSIMO IS HUMMING and smoking and cooking in the kitchen. Humming is what he does to calm himself. Cooking, too. It's true that one of the reasons I fell in love with Massimo is because he cooks. Only, to say that he *cooks* does not describe what it is he does for us. For me. The house is filled with smells I love. Fresh smells. Garlic, which my mother never cooked with, and which I, myself, only ever used in powder form until I met Massimo, who was horrified when I first cooked spaghetti for him. Mushy, sticky spaghetti with butter, canned Heinz tomato paste and water, in which I mixed ground hamburger meat seasoned with Lawry's Seasoned Salt and garlic powder. I never tire of the memory of the moment nearly twenty years ago when I served Massimo, sitting cross-legged in the middle of my studio apartment. I knew that I didn't cook well. Or cook, at all, by Massimo's definition. I opened things out of cans, heated them, and ate them. My favorite salad was iceberg lettuce dressed with bacon grease—hot, salty grease poured on top of crisp, crunchy lettuce was one of my favorite meals that my mother made for me as a child. Delicious. But there was no convincing Massimo of this. And his face when I served him his spaghetti.

"What are you laughing at now," Massimo says from the kitchen. His brow is knitted in concern, as though my laugh is evidence of some sort of crack-up. "Nothing," I say, but his face then. I'd served us on plastic plates, Barbie plates that I'd purchased ironically, my twenty-one-year-old humor. I'd mixed the sauce and the spaghetti together, adding a dash of mustard, something my mother always put in her spaghetti sauce. Massimo took a bite. His eyebrows, eyes, and mouth all struggled for a pleased expression, but he couldn't help it. I had to put my plate down so that I could roll on the floor with laughter without spilling my spaghetti.

"Awful," he said, finally laughing with me. "Truly awful." But I liked it. It was food, wasn't it? Good food. I wasn't laughing at me and my spaghetti. I was laughing at him. I learned when I was a kid, just a chubby little girl, to eat what was put in front of me. Pigs' feet, hog maws, boiled turnips, chitlins, hog headcheese, turkey necks, chicken gizzards, frozen pizza, Chef Boyardee. Sandwiches on white bread and mayonnaise. Saltine crackers with ketchup squeezed on top.

Massimo thinks that Americans don't know how to eat. I tell him, It's class. People with money eat differently, and anyway, my family knew exactly how to eat. No one ever gives you credit for making the most of what you have, for mixing and matching, for the creativity of it all. The artistry of it. Instead, they tell you that your food is disgusting. Your clothes are tacky. You're trying to be white. Or you are acting ghetto. When truly, you are only trying everything that is you. Massimo said at the time, "Bullshit. I had nothing when I was a child. Nothing. And everything we ate was fresh. The vegetables, the bread. Not, that, that, *plastic* bread you eat out of a *plastic* bag with polka dots."

Then and now, I often have to tell him. "That is in Abruzzo, Italy. And now this is West Los Angeles, in the hills. Once again, you are confusing other places with West Covina and Los Angeles, and other places elsewhere, in California."

I lie flat on my back on the couch. I smell sausage cooking in the kitchen. It's organic, I know. Sweet Italian sausage, which tastes good, but not as good as Farmer John's. Vin Scully is confirming this right now. I close my eyes. I hear the pop of a cork above the sounds of frying and the murmur of the radio, and then I feel Massimo standing over me, even though I can't see him. When I open my eyes he stands in front of me, holding out a glass. I sit up and give him a lopsided grin, gently taking the glass out of his hand. I am comforted by the warmth of the first sip and let the feeling roll down my throat, spread throughout my chest, and settle in my stomach. Wine. Something else that came to me through Massimo. These small things, a meal being cooked for me with care and consideration. Fresh things, things just handed to me by a man as I sit, not me cooking and giving things to a man as he sits. During that first meal at my house, laughing and grabbing me around the waist, Massimo took two more bites to prove his love for me. My mother had handed things to me. My father. But because these things were common and handed to me in haste, without ceremony, because these things were thrown-away parts of something else that didn't match, I took them for granted when I was old enough to know better.

Massimo is asking. What kind of salad do I prefer? Arugula or a mixed green salad? "I have leftover cherry tomatoes," he says. "Best to use them before they go bad." "Yes," I say. I agree. It's best to make use of whatever you have left over, before it's too late.

Putting my show together for this evening, I thought about leftovers. I am always wondering what to do with them, the left-overs of my childhood. How to represent them in art? But leftover is just another word for legacy. What remains. Keith is family, and family is what we have until we die, whether or not we acknowl-edge them. That is the legacy. And art. Art is what we have until we die and after, if we are lucky, to keep talking about what's left over. That's what I want the people to see tonight.

❋ ❋ ❋

GREASE. IT'S PLAYING down at the Mi De Gay, and three times I've seen it. Daddy and Mama sent extra money so we could go to the movies, but it's the only one I want to see. Saw the giant ants already. We have only one more week here in Tennessee, so I'm going to see it one more time. Keith saw it already and thinks it's only good for one time, even if Olivia Newton-John is fine. And she is. She is so beautiful. I like her even before she changes to the nasty girl that John Travolta is going to like. In her saddle shoes and ponytail. How it bounces whenever she turns her head or jumps up and down. The way her sweater is around her shoulders, stuck by a gold chain holding it there, not with her arms through the sleeves. The skirt with a dog on it. It looks so fun when she dances and it swishes out all around her and then twists around her body again, heavy and fluffy at the same time. She's so clean and pretty and perfect. But wait until she changes for John Travolta. The first time she shows up in them black pants I die. She is cute before, but this is different. I don't even know what I'm feeling, a feeling like John Travolta looking at her. Like he can't wait to get down with her and I think this too. I want her too. I want her and want to be her. I want John Travolta to want me like he wants Olivia Newton-John.

I'm going to change like that someday. I don't know how, but I'm going to.

It's going to be like people don't see me at all, don't know my name or even think about who I am. Or maybe they will see me and think about who I am. That's even better. I'm going to change and then they're going to see me. You watch. I'm going to be choice.

After the movie is over I walk back up the hill to Granny's, singing we'll always be together, thinking about that halter top that ReRe has, and some red platform shoes she has. When I get in the house I put that halter top on and stuff it with toilet tissue and put some of Aunt Judy's lipstick on. I even put it on my eyes to make eye shadow. I wait until I'm out of the house and off the porch to put on the shoes. It's hard to walk in the road with these shoes and the rocks, but I don't care. I keep thinking of Olivia Newton-John and John Travolta and his blue eyes. We'll always be together. We'll always be together, and I'm trying not to fall. If John could see me now with my long legs and lips and titties. We'll always be together. A car is coming. It's behind me, getting close. I get over to the side of the road but I can only go so far because there is a ditch and if I'm not careful, I will fall into it. But the car is getting closer to my side of the road. I want to get out of the way, but where do I go? There is no space for me to go anywhere.

Hey Gal! Somebody yells out of the truck. Hey big legs! Where you get them juicy legs? And when I turn my head to see who it is, I twist my leg in them platforms and fall in the ditch. I did not want to end up in this ditch, but here I am, anyway. I get little rocks and dirt all in my elbows and knees. One of my paper titties is in the ditch, like a regular piece of tissue somebody blew their nose on and threw down.

I am stuck in this ditch and it is hard to get out of. I should have never put on these shoes that don't fit me, but if I take them off and try to get back home barefoot, it's going to hurt. Before I climb out of the ditch, I put my paper tittie back in. And I put the shoes on because at least I'ma get up the road, even if it don't feel right. Even if it hurt.

16

I LIVE IN this house, but I do not own it. I love this house. A house with immaculate floors, bamboo, even though I am not the one, necessarily, who has cleaned them. Furniture that does not have ugly patterns and rough textures, Prairie Era furniture, I was delighted to be told by Massimo. I had never heard of the Prairie School, but my favorite furniture in the house is a barrel chair with a deep red cushion and a table made of Parkton cherry that we use as a seat, table, and footstool. In this house, it's elegant, but it reminds me of another place and time, my dreams and memories of the country. Such furniture doesn't have to be in this house. This furniture can fit anywhere. And something else I did not know I dreamed about until I had them: sheets that are soft but sturdy and heavy on my legs, belly, and breasts. Sheets with an impressive number of threads. I did not know that there was more than one kind of sheet. I didn't know about sheets, but now I can't go back to not knowing about them. Massimo, almost done preparing our early meal, agrees. But after this agreement we part ways because he isn't grateful. Why should he be grateful? He has worked very hard. He had nothing. Now he has something. "Avie," he says, "you had nothing. Now you have something. So?"

"So?" I had asked him, thinking about all my people who had nothing. Who still have nothing.

"Avie," he says now. "Come and eat. And them. The radio. Enough. They will lose anyway."

I push the button on the radio. Off. "No loyalty. None at all," I say from across the room. I see the last of the day's light shine on his strands of gray. "Don't you know how far loyalty goes? If you wish really hard and think really hard, what you want to happen will happen. The Dodgers will win." And I still believe this, time after time. "But *your* fair-weather bullshit?" I point at Massimo. "You undercut the magic."

He turns down the corner of his mouth, his cigarette still holding on by the thin paper of his filter. "There is no magic. No luck. If you play hard, you win. *Sometimes.* The Yankees will win this year. That's it."

"Listen to you." I am amused in spite of everything and grin at poor Massimo who thinks he knows something about baseball.

"They always win because they always buy up the best players," he says.

My eyes follow Massimo around the kitchen. I have nothing to say. He strikes me as being right, and I feel foolish for not thinking about baseball in this way, when now, this is one of the truths of the game. But it doesn't have to be the only truth. Just ask the Oakland A's. They once had nothing, but they figured it out and won. "As if you know what you're talking about. Baseball," I say. "We're talking about baseball. Not soccer." I pull a chair from the beat-up round table in the dining room. Beat-up on purpose, but still I like it. "Let me handle the American sports, and you can share your soccer wisdom with someone who cares." I say this with anger, though I don't mean to. Misplaced as it is, I am angry but don't know at whom, exactly. I say, "You don't always win because you have money. If that were the case, what would be the point of playing the game?"

"Okay, okay," he says. "What the fuck do I care? Eat," he says, sitting down. He points to my plate with its yellow cloth napkin sitting beside it. "Eat." And when he says this, I always know that it's not because he simply wants me to eat, but that he intends to show me: On my plate, there is more than meat, some vegetables. Bread. Look how much I care for you. You don't think I do because I rant or am often gone. I am feeding you something that I made. So I care for you.

We eat in silence, and I watch Massimo as he bends over his plate, elbows up around the plate as though he's waiting for someone to grab one of his sausages. Such an elegant man, a man concerned with how things should and shouldn't be done. And yet, here we sit. My back is a trick. Perfectly straight, as always. I imagine a string connected to the top of my spine, the last bone that attaches itself to my skull, someone pulling me up straight. A puppeteer. I never, until recently, thought it strange that I did not think of it as pulling myself up. My posture, keeping the posture, was a very difficult thing at first, but I've gotten used to it. I'd much rather slump over my plate, keep my face hovered over my meal, enjoying it as Massimo does. My space, my table, my plate, my food. This is what Massimo looks like now. This is mine. I am enjoying it very much. You will not take this from me. And no, I am not grateful, because this is how it is all the time, for everybody.

"What?" He holds his knife in one hand, fork in the other, spread apart in question.

"I will not call the police, and I don't want you to either."

Massimo breathes through his nose and shakes his head. His utensils fall on his plate with loud clinks. "I'm not going to. I want to, but I'm not going to. I suppose I knew this from the very beginning."

I nod. I suppose I knew this from the very beginning, too. The fear never was about what Massimo was going to do, but what about me? What choices was I supposed to make? What was I supposed to do?

Massimo rubs his face violently, pulling down on his cheeks so that the insides of his lower lids are exposed. He reminds me of a trick that Keith used to do when we were kids. He'd flip both his bottom and top lids up and under so that the bloody-looking flesh was exposed. He'd chase me around because he knew it disgusted me. "I am a zombie!" he'd cry out with his arms outstretched, stepping toward me with stiff legs. "A zombie! I will get you. I will get you!" and I'd scream and scream, even though he'd walk slowly like the zombies in the movies, so far away but always catching up to the living somehow. "I want to help," Massimo says. "Tell me what to do, Avie, and I will try."

He picks up his knife and fork again, cuts his meat slowly, as though he's afraid something is wrong with it. Then he stops, pushes his plate away from him, and folds his arms, waiting.

"I just don't know," I say, and I allow myself to get lost in the last traces of sunlight fading from the tablecloth.

"It's not my place, Avie. You have to tell me. Do you want to call somebody else? Your brother? Your parents? Keith's mother?"

Yes, I think, *Yes.* But I'm too old to call on parents and older brothers. He came to me.

"Do you want to wait? Get your show over with and deal with this after tonight? It's impossible to do anything tonight, yes?" Massimo leans forward, hands out, as if I need convincing.

I take my plate, reach for his, and rise from the table. Yes. It's impossible for now.

❀ ❀ ❀

SOMETIMES YOU CAN'T get any dumber than Brenna. My mom agrees with me. She says all the time: That child act like she touched.

And she is so dang bossy. She's like, Why are you wearing that old-timey shit, or, How could you let that fucker Harry talk to you like that, or, Why can't you just climb out of your window after your mom and dad go to sleep? She knows all this. My parents don't have extra money and her parents don't have extra money, but I'm not going to steal clothes like she does. So I wear whatever clothes I get and make them look as normal as I can. That gross Harry makes fun of me, and Cheri with her Jordache and her Chemin De Fers. She looks at me and says, What did the little bird say when he saw the Kmart sign? Cheap, cheap, cheap. She's perfect. I can't stand her. But at least I put stuff together in a way that's totally decent. Like my favorite. These light blue pants with the crease stitched on in the fronts and a green V-neck sweater with one of my dad's old shirts underneath. Brown with little orange sunsets all over. I think they're bitchen duds, but Brenna says I still look like Kmart. Kmart from thirty years ago! Wha-wha! she says loud in my ear. I tell her, Ha ha. So funny I forgot to laugh. But I wish I had new. I don't. So I figure out something different. Something nobody else is wearing and could never put together in a million years because they don't have the pieces that I have. So what? I can't stand Brenna sometimes.

She won't even go in Kmart. She says everything about it is vomitus, and anyway just go to fuckin' Miller's Outpost and steal the shit that you want. So. She looks like she has some money and I never look like I have some money, which I didn't even really think about until this year. Eighth grade sucks and I can't wait until high school when I can get around some normal people who won't even care about this kind of stuff like that greasy fat Harry or perfect Cheri. Brenna says she doesn't care what other people think, especially dumbass Cheri, she says. She only cares about what she thinks and what she likes, and OP and Sasson is what she likes so why shouldn't she just wear the threads she wants?

But I care. I don't want to hear stuff from my mom. I don't want to get in trouble with my dad and I don't want Owen saying nothing to me and I don't want to be fat Kizzie like Harry calls me.

Brenna has a plan for me. She's gonna make me look normal, she says. It's after school and it's hot, and she has on pink Dolphin shorts that she stole and she stole a pair for me, too. Green ones. Dolphins are great. They are thin and light and have high splits on the sides and they are so short that your booty cheeks hang out the bottom. Brenna looks good in hers but she didn't get a big enough size for me. She got a medium and I need a large, maybe even an extra large. But still. I like these shorts. They make me feel like somebody, like a foxy guy will have to look at me in these shorts. He'd see my booty and then it figures that he'd see me. Brenna gives me one of Tate's old OP shirts too. Hers wouldn't fit me because she's flat. It's almost like my dad's shirt. Brown with a sunset and a bird flying against the sun. But it's better. I don't know why, but it just is.

We're in my bedroom with the door closed and Brenna is checking me out. I pull up my red tube socks. The elastic never lasts long on these things but at least my fake Vans look okay. I drew all over them with stuff I like in different color pens. Led Zep. Hang ten. Disco sucks. Peace. And this one thing I saw on a purse at Zody's: A Good Man Is Hard to Find. So now they don't look like imitation, they just look like all the stuff I like. I'm tired of being called Imitation. That's what they always call me. Imitation. Because everything I wear is like something else but not the actual thing it's supposed to be. My Izod shirt really isn't Izod Lacoste. It's got a horse on it instead of a crocodile. My boat shoes aren't the real Top-Siders that cost too much money. Plus the stitching split open at the toe after the first week I had them. Every year at the beginning of school my dad buys me two new pairs of pants and two new skirts and two new shirts and underwear and shoes. It's Zody's and Kmart, and I don't say anything but Thank you Dad because the last time I said I wanted something different, something better, he stopped right in the middle of putting his key in the car. He froze like we do when we play freeze tag. He said, These clothes are new. *New*. And you lucky to get old ones. Get in the car. It was stupid, what I said. I know. But sometimes I don't think about what I'm saying before I say it, and every time I do that, I get into trouble. I'm thinking about that more and more now, thinking about thinking more and then saying something after I've worked it all out. I still wish that I had better stuff, though. All I can do is mix and match and improvise to get to something kind of cool. I can't steal like Brenna because Mom and Dad would kill me and bury me twice. Mom always says that.

Brenna looks better in her clothes. Why didn't you steal one big enough for me? I ask her. Brenna puts the needle on "My Sharona" again. What a faker, goody-goody. Stealing's bad unless I steal for you? She sings Oh my little pretty one, pretty one, when you gonna give me some time Avie! She blows watermelon Hubba Bubba and squints at me. You look rad anyway. Just do something with that hair. You look like you got electrocuted.

I stick my hair under my Dodgers cap because that's all I can do with it. It's half nappy and half straight because it hasn't been pressed in a week.

Brenna blows more bubbles and checks me out. Imitation my ass, she says. You look all right.

I pull the shorts out of my butt. I don't know. She's probably not even serious. I have to just believe what Brenna says when she looks at me. Let's book, she says, and sings, Runnin' down the length of my thigh, Sharona!

We bump into Owen coming out of the room. He smells like Dad's Old Spice. Groovy, he says, and smacks me upside the head. It's so old. He says it like every time he sees me and Brenna together. Jan and Marcia! he always says in a stupid voice. His white voice. But I don't mind being called Marcia, actually. Brenna is Jan, because she looks the most like Jan, so that makes me Marcia. Brenna always rolls her eyes, but she likes Owen all of a sudden. She thinks he's some kind of big deal all of sudden. She turns her back on Owen and sticks out her ass and slaps it. That's what I think of you, man, she says. How you like these apples?

I think your little ass bet not talk to me like that again is what I think, Owen tells her. But he's laughing at her until he sees me. Ave, where your clothes at?

Don't worry about it. I pull my shorts out of my butt again and I know I'll be doing that all day now, pulling and tugging because they don't hardly fit.

Ave, for real. Owen stands in front of me, between me and Brenna. You ain't going nowhere in them short draws.

None your business, doofus. Brenna pushes Owen shoulder but when he turns around and looks at her like, You must be crazy, she puts her eyes on her feet and picks at her nails. I know I have to do what Owen says, but I hate it. I hate this feeling, like everything I want to do has an answer for it and that answer is always no.

He waits until I go in my room and change into my cutoff jeans, long down to the knee. My shirt is still tight, but as long as my butt ain't hanging out of my jeans, Owen says. I'm going to work, he says, but I got eyes in the neighborhood so you better watch out. He thumps Brenna on the head hard and it sounds like it would hurt but Brenna just flips her hair at him and says, Let's go Ave.

We walk down the hill, in the middle of the street until the sidewalk starts up at the bottom of the hill. That's when Brenna takes her comb out of her sock and starts bending over and flipping her comb through her hair. She's forever flipping her hair and keeps stopping to do it. I keep pushing all my hair under my Dodgers cap and I keep trying to think, At least the sun's not in my eyes like it is in Brenna's. That's a good thing. She pulls cherry lip gloss out of her other sock and puts practically the whole tube on her lips. I don't wear it since Harry called me bongo lips and said it made my lips look even fatter than they are. That they just looked big and greasy. Stop eating so much fried chicken, he told me.

I kick a stone in front of me and it goes too far for me to keep kicking it. It's in the street now. That last time I tried to look better than I look, I ended up in a ditch. Stop trying to look all slutty, I say. I pull my Dodgers cap down on my face. She rubs her hands all over her chest and sticks her tongue out like Gene Simmons. I'm not trying to look like a slut. I *am* a slut, she says and bumps me with her hip. I can feel the bone. Gross, Brenn. Nobody wants to be a slut. I'm saying this, but I don't believe it, not really. This is what I think for real: What would be wrong with it, exactly? To have all the guys drooling over you and to have anyone you want, whenever? Like in *Grease*. Olivia Newton-John turns into a slut for John Travolta. She calls him stud and shakes her butt in his face and that's it. It's over for him. She tells him no. Not the other way around. And everybody thinks she's so much better in the tight black pants and those Candies. You can tell. I like that. Everybody thinking you're what they want and you giving them what they want and all of it feeling good. I say, Two weeks and junior high is over.

Yeah, Brenna says. I can't even wait. And then we don't say stuff. We just keep walking.

I'm bored in school. I get As in everything except math—and PE, but that's only because they make us do stuff like a thousand push-ups and jump over walls and run like eighty miles like we're in the Army. It's the California Presidential Exam or something. My Dad was all, How you get a C in PE? Didn't say anything about the As, but the C in PE was like I did something terrible like stab somebody in the eye. He's in school part-time now on the side of work because he said he doesn't want to work in a factory putting together cars that other people get to drive his whole life. He wants to be a real estate agent. You make money in that Dad? I asked him, but he was still stuck on that C in PE. You can do better than a C in PE, now Avery, he said. I wanted to tell him how hard it was, all the work they make us do and I can't do it. It's too hard for me. For other people it seems really easy, but not for me. But I didn't say anything to him. That's talking back and you don't do that to Dad. Or Mom.

I pull on my Dodgers cap again and sing my favorite commercial, this old one that never gets out of my head. Baseball, hot dogs, apple pie, and Chevrolet. Baseball, hot dogs, apple pie, and Chevrolet.

You know you sound retarded, right? Brenna says. That's what she does all the time. Mess up my good feeling about something. So I sing it in my head.

Finally, we're at 7-Eleven. And it's Carlos from school eating donuts, leaning up against a low-rider, all green and sparkly. Carlos. Way foxy. Black hair slicked back. He wears Dickies all the time, walks all slow and hunched over with his feet pointed out. Black eyes that are practically closed all the time. When he talks, he sticks his chin up and looks at you and squints even more. I don't even know how he can see you when he's talking to you. He calls everybody Homes, except for me. Sup, Avery Day, he says when he sees me. Don't even ask me why he calls me that. He doesn't talk to Brenna and Brenna never talks to him. When he was new, last year, Brenna tried to get in his face after she cut in line at lunch. He told her, I'm in line, Homes, and Brenna says, So? Now I'm in line too.

He pushed her. She pushed him back. He told her, I'll fuck you up. Fuck you, fucking cholo, Brenna said. White girl, Carlos said, you don't even *know*. His put his hand up like he was going to smack her but he psyched her out. Brenna jerked her head back anyway, so he won. And now she acts like he's nothing. He's not there, but when he's around, I can tell that's all she thinks about.

Hey Carlos, I say. Come on, Ave, Brenna says, and she's trying to pull me into 7-Eleven when the door opens. I feel cold air hit my legs and face and then I see a girl that I know must be Carlos's sister or cousin or something. Get off my car, foo, she tells Carlos. Serious makeup on. White eye shadow. Eyebrows look like they're shaved off and drawn back on all skinny. Black lipstick, black Dickies. Black hair. Feathered perfect. Like raven wings. And white Nikes. She looks scary. I've seen girls that look like her before, but it's like she's not just wearing stuff to make her like that. She *is* the stuff.

She stares at me and Brenna and then pulls her car door open. She gives us her chin like Carlos does. Sup? she says. Nothing, I say. Let's go, Brenna says. She's still trying to pull my arm out of my socket or something. But I'm staring at this girl. My sister eh, Carlos tells me. Chrissy.

Hey. I raise my palm to her and then I think. Dumbass. It looks like you're telling her to stop.

Leaning on my fucking Impala, she tells Carlos. You tripping? Let's go eh.

Later days, Carlos says. He throws his donut wrapper on the ground and gets in the car. When they turn on the car I hear that old song about the girl who has two lovers but ain't ashamed because she loves them both the same. I swear they look like a movie driving away. The way the sun hits the car all sparkly green like Fourth of July. I think about it flying up in the air like the car in *Grease*. I keep hearing, Eh? Let's go, eh? In my head, I'm adding it at the end of any sentence and it sounds bad. I'm cool just by saying eh at the end of stuff. What if I was a chola? Looked like Chrissy? Nobody would tell me nothing because they'd all be scared of me.

The hell, Ave, you deaf doofus? Come on. Let's get something to drink, Brenna says. We're looking. A bottle of Sunkist? Or a blueberry Slurpee? A Big Gulp? I grab a Coke and go look at the magazines. Flip through them all. *Mad* magazine. Something in it always makes me laugh, even though it makes like no sense to me a lot of the times. But when I do finally get stuff, I feel like I know something that nobody else is paying attention to. And the fold-up on the last page is the best. The situation is one thing before you fold it up and then it's totally something else. I pick up *Seventeen,* but then I get tired just flipping through it. Nothing in it ever applies to me. The hair stuff that's supposed to de-frizz or the blue eye shadow I'm supposed to buy or the clothes I don't have the money to buy. Plus all this stuff you're supposed to do to get dudes to like you. What. Like not be me? Brenna is next to me, smelling like watermelon gum. *Mad* magazine, she says. Whoever does that thing must be high all the time. Makes no sense.

She picks up a magazine and pulls on the straw of her Slurpee so that it makes a squeaky noise when it goes up and down. God, this issue of *Dynamite* is so bogue. Mork in that dumb *Popeye.* Who cares? She turns the pages hard. They sound like she's tearing them. Now we're talking, she says. Erik Estrada is coming to you! she reads to me. And that makes me think of Carlos because they've both got Spanish names. Be right back, I tell Brenna. I need to check the baseball cards. She rolls her eyes and puts *Dynamite* down and picks up something else.

At the register, it's some guy I never saw before. Old. White hair and everything and gold John-Boy Walton glasses. His tag says Ed. I put two packets of cards on the table. And this Coke,

I tell him. And that'll do you young man? he asks me. He barely even looks up. And then he does. Looks me up and down and tells me he's sorry. It looks like you don't have any hair, he tells me. Thought you were a boy, young lady. I don't say anything, so he says, Buying cards for your brother? No, I say. They're for me. He smiles. Tomboy, are you?

No. I just like baseball.

Well that's good, he says. I hold out my hand and he gives me my change. Who's your team?

What does he think? Who else is there? Uh, Dodgers? I say, and shake my head, like, What do you think?

I open the cards right at the register, looking for Carlos's favorite. Pedro Guerrero. A black man speaking Spanish like Carlos does, and Carlos likes him. I finally asked Carlos one day at school was Guerrero some kind of Mexican, even though I'd never seen a Mexican that dark before. Naw foo. Dominican, he said. He was squeezing the white stuff out of his Twinkie and licking it with his tongue. I stared and stared at him doing that.

Two packs of cards and no Guerrero. No Dodgers, even. A waste of almost a whole dollar.

Brenna socks me hard on the arm. Hello? Hello? Earth to Avie. Let's jam. Her mouth is already red from her Slurpee. You look like Bozo, I say. I grab her Slurpee and drink some. Your Mama looks like Bozo, she says and snatches it back. And the door goes ding-dong when we leave the store. Ed says, Bye-bye young ladies, and Brenna does her nose like something stinks. Probably Chester the molester, she says.

It's like all we ever do is walk around in the hot sun. Damn, Brenna says. Hot for reals and it's not even summer. She finishes her Slurpee and throws the cup on the ground. We pass a house with the door open. You Can Ring My Bell is playing and I love how the lady's voice goes, Ring it, ring it, ring it ring it ahhh! all high. When

I sing it, Brenna asks me, Who sings this song? And I forget and fall for it. I tell her who sings it. Let's keep it that way, she says. I tell her, That's so funny I forgot to laugh, and then I get an idea.

Will you steal me some Dickies?

What are you, are you a cholo now vato? All into that disco ring my bell shit too.

Just get me a pair.

Why?

They're cool.

They're beaner clothes.

You steal all the time. Why do you even care?

She doesn't answer me at first. I won.

But she takes her comb out of her sock and starts flipping and combing. Steal your own damn Dickies goody-goody chola.

But I'm never going to steal anything, so Brenna wins.

Hey, she says. Did you see that thing in *Seventeen* where you could get a lip reduction surgery if you wanted to?

I stop walking. What? They have a surgery for that?

Yeah, I saw it. This one article on stuff you could do to make yourself look better. One was this lip surgery thing. They cut some off the inside or something to make them thinner.

I don't say anything else. I keep walking. I'm excited. My lips. This is something I can change. Finally they put something in that magazine that'll help me.

How much money, though? I ask Brenna.

Fucking get the magazine and read it. I don't even remember.

Why didn't you tell me about it in the store? I could have got it.

You were too busy buying your goofy baseball cards. I forgot. I can just see you with your new lips all black with chola lipstick. What a dreamboat.

I'm thinking that Brenna makes me sick, but I don't say anything. I wish I had something to bag on her about, but there's nothing. Her hair is fine. Her face. Her body. There's nothing to pick on because she looks like everybody else.

We always stop on the corner when we get to our street. I go up the hill and she goes down. Later days, dude, she says. When I get home, Mom and Dad are there and I feel that feeling that I feel whenever they are at home together. Sick. Better if one or the other is home, but not both at the same time because they always are fighting about something. Last time Mom started a fight because Dad wanted to watch TV. He turned it on. She turned it off. He turned it on again and it was like she tried to make him hit her, but he wouldn't. He just got up and left. That's what he does now. They don't hit each other anymore. It's like they're both too tired.

Avery, Daddy says. Come here and sit down for a minute. And I'm scared. I'm thinking, Uh oh. My ass is grass. What am I in trouble for now? Sit down, Dad says again. And Mom says, What are you doing with your hair. A baseball cap? You need to do something to it. I don't have anything to say because I really am just sick of my hair. But that's the least of my problems. Stupid Owen said something, I know he did. He acts like my father half the time. I took the Dolphins off, wore the cutoffs. What else do they want me to do? God.

Listen, Dad says. Something's going to happen and you need to know about it. Your Aunt Janice has really been having problems with Keith running around and stealing and staying out and not coming home. She asked us if he could come stay here for a while. He looks at me and scratches his beard.

I don't know what to say, but I don't think I want Keith to live with us. I know what he's been doing. Everything but the right thing, Mom says. Him and John smoke weed. Keith takes money from Aunt Janice. I don't even see him whenever we go to the desert. Every time, I'm like, Where's Keith? In the streets somewhere, his mother always says, and then I end up just sitting in the house watching TV until Mom and Dad are ready to leave. You too old to be running around with boys anyway, Mom said the last time we were there. Don't need to be running the streets with them.

And now he's coming here to live.

Where is he going to sleep? I really want to know. Owen still lives here even though he's not in school anymore. He works. He's saving up. And I know he's not going to share a bed with Keith. He's only got a twin bed, like me.

On the couch, Mom says.

For how long?

Long as he know how to act, Dad says. We ain't gone put up with all Janice put up with, tell you that right now.

And I'm thinking, How are we going to pay for him? They're always talking about how we don't have enough money. The house note is always late. Mom is always calling the phone company to get extensions on the bill. And I can tell: Whenever we have real meat for dinner, we have some extra money, but if we don't then it's neck bones and Hamburger Helper. And I swear it's like we have Hamburger Helper all the time now. Don't ask me why, since it's not like anybody's spending money on anything actually good, like better clothes or new furniture or whatever. It is what it is, Mom always says.

That's what we're going to do, Dad says. Okay?

And I say, Okay, because it doesn't matter what I say. What they say, goes.

ALL HE HAS when he comes is one bag of clothes and a skateboard. Him and Dad come through the front door and Keith's face looks totally bummed, like he had to drive the whole hour and a half from Victorville listening to a lecture, which he did,

I'm sure. Keith's standing there looking like he'd kill to have something to do. Dad takes off his cap and goes into the living room to watch TV, so that's out. What else are we supposed to do? I don't even know what to do with him.

I point at the skateboard. Since when?

He pulls it away from his body to look at it. John gave me this. He just got a new one.

Oh.

I look at him and he looks at me.

Where you going to put that thing?

He shrugs. You can put it in my room, I say. There's nothing in there anyway. We go to my room and stand around after we put the skateboard against the wall. Now what?

There are two games on my floor. Connect Four that Brenna brought over and Monopoly. I hate Monopoly because I have to count money and think about money, and I can never count up fast enough and I just hate dealing with it. I swear, everybody I've ever played with gets all crazy too. Mean and stingy and have to own like every single property. And Keith. Oh my God. He used to be the worst.

I sit on the floor and pull the game over to me. Then I put a cassette tape in. Keith watches me. What's that? he says. Please don't let it be no *Sound of Music*.

Shut up. It's The Who. Keith likes them, I can tell by the way he nods his head. His mouth is moving to the words.

I take the lid off the Connect Four box. It's been taped around the corners a hundred times. Want to play Connect Four?

I guess, Keith says. He's still standing.

Sit down doofus. Why are you still standing around like you're going to go to jail or something? He's acting so weird.

You start, I say. He puts a black checker in. I put a red. He puts another one. I do mine. He puts his in and wins.

Anh! Lucky break dude, I tell him, let's do it again. Let me go first this time.

I don't care, Keith tells me. He looks around my room. What's up with them Raggedy Ann curtains?

Quit bagging on my curtains, I say. They're like four years old.

Damn, he says. He shakes his head.

Shut up. Let me concentrate. My legs are stuck out in front of me in a V, so I kick him. I think about where to start. If you start right, you can win. I start with red this time. Keith goes. I go again. You lose, he tells me, and drops his last checker in.

One more game, I say.

Okay, but this is really boring Ave.

Shut up, I say. Start.

He starts and then he wins. We play four more games and I can't beat him. I'm not even mad about it. I just want to figure out how he does it.

Tell me, man, I say. Seriously.

I don't know. Keith stretches his arms out to me and pushes up his shirt sleeves like to show me there's nothing in them. I can just see it, he tells me. I can see how I can beat you every time.

But you got a F in math. My mom told me. Maybe you're just lucky.

I don't know, he says. It's just four checkers. That ain't math.

Maybe you're lucky.

I don't care, Ave. I'm bored than a motherfucker, is what I am.

We end up getting out of the house. I tell Dad we're going skating and he says all right. I get my skates that look like sneakers and Keith gets his skateboard and we skate down the street. It's a big hill, and then there's another big hill. It's so rad for skating. Keith is always ahead of me, going real fast, and I get scared sometimes that he's going to get hit by a car. I won't go as fast as he does. Are you kidding? Slow down dude! I call out after him. You're going to get hit. When I catch up to him at the bottom of the last hill, he's laughing and smiling. Whew! he says. Damn that was fun. We don't have big hills you can go down where I live.

Seriously, Keith. Be *careful*. I look up and down the street but it's kinda empty. It's always empty, but sometimes there's cars and people. You just don't know when.

Negro, please, he says. He wipes sweat off his face with his shirt. He tilts his head to the side like he's listening for something. Do you see anybody? See any cars? Ain't nothing in my way.

17

I CLEAN THE kitchen. Putting away leftovers that I will eat, that Massimo will not. He says they don't taste as good. One of the Fiestaware bowls is chipped. The big yellow one he always uses to serve things that are red. He is arguing with someone on the phone over somebody's contract. "No," he says. "This is not what we agreed we would do. No. No. Absolutely not." Massimo pauses. "I'm more than happy to meet you halfway, but we must be reasonable about such things. Surely you must understand," he says, pacing. He picks up an ashtray and his glass of wine and steps outside to the garden. Working, he is always working, and so it has always been a surprising conflict between us that he thinks it unnecessary that I work. My only job should be making art, otherwise I'm not really trying. This is something that he, in my estimation, has always been unreasonable about until he finally threw up his hands and said, "Fine. Do whatever you want. If you want to work yourself to death for ten dollars an hour, you are welcome to it. Good luck to you." He brushed his hands together and waved them through the air as if the argument were something trifling and dusty. He has a very particular American dream, which somehow includes a woman who doesn't have to work because that's one of the ways in which he measures his achievements. When I wanted to work, though, he thought I was somehow giving up on my American dream, the dream of being an artist. But for me, this was not a small thing, work. When we first met, I didn't have a job. I had lasted about a month as an administrative assistant at an educational testing company, my first job after graduation. I had trouble finding a job because most of my interviewers couldn't figure out how someone with a degree in business was not doing anything with it. But I just didn't want to, which made me a fuck-up and a failure with a degree. I was in the middle. Too qualified and too inexperienced for the waitressing jobs I wanted, which I thought much more interesting than working in an office. I considered being a cleaning woman for a short time, to set my own hours, have some flexibility—until I could find a real job. It was a way to be invisible but make some money. Nobody would be asking me about why I had not lived up to my potential in those circumstances. My mother had done it, so why couldn't I? Massimo, lying beside me in bed, threw up his hands in frustration. "What will people think, Avie?" he said. "I can take care of you."

"I want to take care of myself," I said.

"Have some respect for yourself. Don't clean people's toilets. You are educated at a university. You are smarter than all the idiots I know. It's stupid, this idea. Look." He punched a pillow and turned over on his side, his back to me. "I won't let you do it." That time, I let him not let me do it. But that was the last time.

And so I work. I worked. I fell into jobs that required little of me. I taught art to children with learning disabilities and physical disabilities for a few years—a job I was recommended for through April, an old college friend with whom I am no longer in touch. The years passed and all I know is that she is somewhere out there. The last job I had, Massimo helped me, too. He knew someone who knew the person advertising for the position. But I felt that Massimo being involved with my whole venture compromised my goal. I didn't want to be a hypocrite, working merely for show.

"Avery," he had said, stroking my face, genuinely amused. "How do you think people get jobs? Do you think everybody is lucky? Do you think that magic happens simply because you work hard?"

"Yes," I said. "Yes. Exactly."

He laughed his big, booming laugh that I love so much. The laugh of someone who marvels at and enjoys the misconceptions of a child. "Avie baby," he said, wiping the moisture under his eyes. "Half the people working at my firm are the daughter or the son or the cousin of some idiot."

I suppose I have always known that, but I have never been the one to think it's okay to take advantage of such arrangements. Why should anyone have much more, do much more, get much more, when they have not worked for it, but their mother or father or spouse has? And why should someone have so little when they work and work? But my scruples crumbled. I took the job. "And now I'm the girlfriend of some idiot," I said, which made him laugh again.

The job I had was not hard. I taught basic drawing, which I'd learned autodidactically, as a child and in college. Things that anybody could learn and teach. Exercise in techniques like still life, figure drawing, landscapes. There were eight students in the class, and even though I had taught before, I didn't know how to be. What would be me? I thought of all the different possibilities. I could be the professional, measured and single-minded. The compassionate instructor, all soft touches of encouragement, smiles after gentle entreaties to take the charcoal off the page. *No need to press too hard or think about the task at hand.* Or I could be the teacher who was jokesy and folksy, the coolest thing in the room. I settled on all of them.

When I first walked into the studio, there were only three students there. A painful-looking young girl, her body trying to disappear, hunched over and apologetic before she had even met anyone. She smiled at me, a quick, nervous flash before she looked away. Abigail. Her name was Abigail. An older woman, maybe six-ty or so, sat across from Abigail. "Hello! My name is Sally," she had announced loudly. "Sal!" She pushed up the sleeves of her sweater and pulled on the neck of her black Bob Dylan T-shirt. Her big hands were a jumble of turquoise and amethyst. Sal was the first to speak, but John was the first one I noticed. He was tilting back in his chair, his arms clasped behind his head. How was he managing, I wondered, leaning back dangerously in his chair, with no hands anchoring him to the table? Effortless. But no, the tip of his Con-verse was hooked under the table. He had black hair that stood up in chunks. A silver hoop earring. He said nothing. He just stared at me with gray eyes, without a smile on his face, and I thought, He is trying to make me nervous. He is trying to intimidate me. I used the trick of staring back to show that I was not nervous or intimidated. But I was. "Hey everybody. I'm Avery," I said with the most casual cheer. "Glad you're here. Let's wait a few moments until the others get here, before we get started." When the others did ar-rive, I could only think about John. I only knew his name was John because I had finally asked him at the end of class.

"Hey, I didn't get your name," I had said. He was walking out, his back to me.

"Oh," he said. "It's John." He didn't turn around fully to face me. He had said it over his shoulder. And his tone was such that I remember it exactly. In my ear. In my head. Right now. It was as though I had asked him a question to which there was only one answer. Later that evening, when I told Massimo about my first day in the studio teaching, I told him about it all, except for John. He said, "Nobody you wanted to fuck?" He asked this, laughing, to joke, but I knew he wanted an answer. I threw a pillow at his head. "Shut up," I said. "Shut up."

"Shut up," I say. I'm startled to hear Massimo's voice, now, asking me. "What?" He puts his hands on my shoulders.

"Nothing. I was just talking to myself." He looks at his watch. He comes to me. He holds my face in his hands. "Come here," he says. He kisses the back of my neck. He takes my hand. "Lay down with me." I have to start getting ready soon. It's late afternoon. But I let him pull me. I would like to go to sleep.

❋ ❋ ❋

OWEN'S BEEN WORKING practically since we moved here. Gives Mom and Dad money to stay at home. He says he can't stand to be without money and he hates to ask Dad for anything. He's always saying, Don't mess around and try to ask Dad for more than two dollars at one time. Might as well be asking for a million the way the old man be acting. And that was *before* Keith came to live with us.

Everybody has to work because of the pizza me and Keith ate, and the leftover meatloaf, which Dad totally went spastic over, because of what Mom had to cook in place of the pizza. But we didn't know. We were hungry, so we ate it all. Mom came home from work and was going to heat up the pizza and the meatloaf and make some greens to go with it. But it was gone.

I'm in my room when Mom gets home, goofing around with my baseball cards, putting them together in groups of color that kind of match, even if they don't match exactly.

Avery! she yells, and I know I'm in trouble about something. Where the meatloaf at? She opens the oven door and closes it. Where them pizzas that was in the freezer?

Me and Keith ate them, I tell her. She shakes her head. Don't nobody get paid until tomorrow. Ain't nothing in this house.

She looks in the cabinets. She says everything we have. There's a can of mackerel, some Jell-O, half a box of grits, and some pinto beans. Only got half a bag of them, she says. I'm waiting for her to just let us have it. Keith is standing next to me, and when I look at his face, he crosses his eyes while Mom's back is still looking in cabinets. If I laugh, forget it. She will go off on us. Just because she hasn't yet doesn't mean she's not going to. I look away from Keith but when I look at him again, he's not making goofy faces. He's just looking down at his shoes. Fake Nikes. Instead of the swoosh thing, they have these weird squiggles on them. I told him when he first got them that I could draw stuff on them to make them better, make up some totally different kind of shoe that's even badder than Nikes, and he just goes, I don't care. They're shoes. But you don't like them, I told him. They could look way better if you tried. He just shrugged. What about these high-waters? This gay-ass little kid shirt with a bear on it? I guess he was right. He couldn't even steal anything. Mom and Dad would totally be able to tell if he did.

While she's going on about the food, I'm surprised that Mom isn't even more mad. Sometimes she's real pissed but most of the time lately she just acts like she's tired. She lets us slide this time. She makes something crazy with everything that's left in the cabinets. It's crazy, but it's good, too, I swear. She boils the beans. Then she fries them up with the mackerel. She boils the grits. Lets them get kind of hard and then she fries that up with little pieces of bacon we have. Two pieces left. We have the greens with all that. I think it was good, but nobody else does.

When Dad comes home, he looks in all the skillets and pots. What in the hell is this? He takes off his cap and scratches his head. We ate earlier. At all kinds of different times because no one eats together in my house. Never do.

What *is* it? Mom says. It is what it *is*, she says, smoking her cigarette.

Well, if that what it *is*, Dad says, we gone have to do better than that.

Better make some more money, then, Mom says. Or quit your school, she says. But Dad isn't for that. He thinks school is everything. All of a sudden, he decided that he was going to night school for a real estate license, and so that's what he's doing, so there's less money.

And that's why everybody has to have a job.

Keith picks up money mowing lawns and helping people clean up junk out of their garages. He even helps Joan sometimes.

I'm a babysitter. That's what I do this summer. Joan got me

the job. It's her daughter's kid I babysit. He's a nice little kid, Jonas. A brat only some of the time. Joan trusts me better since I'm a little older. She never held what happened at her house against me. She's a real nice lady. I can't figure her out. She's just so *nice* all the time. I don't care, though. I get two bucks an hour and sit for three hours with the kid, usually a couple of times a week, and then on the weekends I can even make ten bucks. Joan told me. She said, I knew you'd be good at it. You're so watchful and observant. Like it's hard to watch a kid. He's six. There's not that much to do.

It's July and I'm watching *Family* and I'm babysitting Jonas because his parents are on a date. They're seeing Whitesnake play, which is so cool. I told Jonas's mom Lee, and she just stares at me. *You* like Whitesnake? she says. She pulls up on her bangs to make them stand up more. Big blonde bangs just like the lead singer in Whitesnake. Huh, she says. Okay. She smiles at me. Don't let Jonas stay up after eight, she says. C'mon! Let's go, Jonas's dad yells. He's not that hot. He doesn't have a chin or something. And his red hair doesn't look as cute on him as it does on Jonas. And he's not that nice. They had to get married right out of high school. Eighteen years old. Owen told me. Married bliss, Brenna says.

Somebody's knocking on the door and I get scared because it's dark and who would be knocking on the door? I get up and go to the door. I turn down the TV. Stay here, I tell Jonas. He gets up and comes with me to the door. He never listens to me. Who is it? I yell at the door.

It's yo Mama! Brenna says, and I can hear Keith laughing through the door. I open it. You guys better get out of here, I say. But they push through the door.

Yeah, get out of here, Jonas says. He puts his little hand in mine.

Nice, Brenna says, looking around and picking up stuff. She picks up this bowl of jewelry that's on the kitchen counter, where

Lee keeps all her jewelry. This place is nice. Brand-new and just built, but they don't hardly have any furniture or anything.

I swear to God if you steal something, I will tell them you did it, Brenn.

And for once Keith can tell I'm freaking out a little because I really, really want to keep this job. C'mon, he tells Brenna. Avery's parents don't play. They will whip both our asses. He sits down on the couch though, and puts his feet up on the coffee table.

Off, I say. Feet off.

Why, he says. This ain't your crib. Ain't nobody here to see me.

Yeah, Brenna says. Pull it out. She always says that. She means pull whatever I have stuck up my ass out of it. She sits down next to Keith and I notice something right then that makes me scared. I don't know why I am scared but that's the feeling. She puts her hand in his hand, like nothing. Like it's their house, that's how they're sitting together on the couch. Jonas walks over to Brenna. He holds out this red fire truck he loves. Look at this, he tells her. You want me to go put out a fire for you? I can do it, he says.

Nah, Brenna says. Keith just stares at him. She tells Jonas, Don't put the fire out. I like fires.

SO WHAT IS going on when I come home from babysitting? Mom is bent over our kitchen table shaking and wiping her eyes. She tries to puff on her cigarette but can't. She has to put it down or drop ashes all over the floor and table. Keith is doing some kind of spastic dance that has a lot of crazy steps that don't make sense together. Funky chicken and then the robot and then he kicks up his heels like Dick Van Dyke in *Mary Poppins* when he does that really cool dance number "Step In Time." Then the swim. That's his favorite dance to do when he's acting stupid.

Look you guys! he says. Look Auntie Vicky.

He swims through the air and hops on his toes then holds his nose with one hand while the other hand moves down making Ss in the air like a snake. I'm drowning, he says. You guys, help me, I'm drowning! He's yelling in a high girly voice. Mom is almost on the floor. She's telling him, You need to quit playing, you need to stop. You a mess. You so silly.

Ave, do the swim with me, he says and pulls me next to him. I don't even know what to do at first but I don't want Mom to stop laughing. She looks at me and her right eyebrow is up like a upside down V. I can't have fun like Keith, though. I'm thinking about too much. How do I look? Does it look good? But it's not supposed to look good, the swim. It's supposed to be a joke that I'm playing but I keep taking it all way too serious. Come on, Keith says, and tries to do the bump with me like when we were real little kids. We made up dances to songs. We did the bump to the Jackson Five singing A, B, C, it's easy as one, two, three. And that one song I used to really like. One bad apple don't spoil the whole bunch girl. We didn't even have to practice. We could say, okay. Four bumps, three "Kung Fu Fighting" kicks to the left and then to the right. Then robot for a little bit and then march in place. But Keith isn't telling me what we're supposed to be doing. I'm not sure what he's going to do next. I just stick to swimming in place for a minute and then I drown until I'm on my knees and can't go down any more. It's not funny anymore to Mom. She smokes her cigarette and stares at me. I try one more time. I just do free moves, that's what Brenna calls them, like the hippies. I twirl around and sing, When the moon is in the seventh hour and Jupiter aligns with Mars then peace will guide the planet and love will steer the stars. I twirl and twirl, thinking Treat Williams is such babe. I love that movie.

Mom's mouth is open now. Keith stops dancing. Mom says, What you call yourself doing? She's smiling, though. That's something.

She's having some kind of fit, Keith says. Somebody done hexed her.

Something, Mom says. She mashes out her cigarette. You doing your own thing though, that's something. Don't know what it *is*, but go head on with it.

I stop dancing and take a bow. Free Moves. I'm the queen of Free Moves, I say.

Okay, Free Moves, Keith says. I'ma call you that now.

All right, Mom says. Messing around with y'all. Got to get my work clothes ready for tomorrow. Go and sit down somewhere. She gets up and empties her ashtray in the trash. Got to iron something for me to wear, she says. So me and Keith stop dancing.

Let's sit down goofy ass, Keith says. We both sit down at the table and swivel in our chairs. Keith makes a song with his fingertips on the table. Guess this song, he says. I listen real hard but it's easy to figure out anyway. I move my head to the music. I sing, Fame! Is it any wonder you are too cool to fool?

Too easy, Keith says. Why you home already? They must have not stayed at that concert long.

No. They didn't. I slide the placemat around the table. I got driven home by Jonas's dad Caleb and he didn't say five words to me. He goes, Hey. You ready? Night. Thanks. His hand stayed on the steering wheel and I was daydreaming that it would be kind of cool if he would just take his hand off the steering wheel for a second. Put it on my leg. Say, Avery, you're cute, you know that? But no. All I get is, Night. And he doesn't even wait until I'm in the house. He totally burns rubber on me. What if there was like, some weirdo who jumped out of the ivy and tried to strangle me or chop me up in a million pieces, like in *Halloween*? He doesn't even care.

Whitesnake is shitty anyway, Keith says. They look like girls. Girls with white snakes.

What are you talking about?

Girls with dicks, dummy.

What?

That's what whitesnake means, dummy. Keith gets up and starts talking in a high voice like a girl. Look at my long white snake. He puts his hand in the front of his jeans like he's holding a big hose that's all out of control and spurting water everywhere. Then he does a curtsey and skips around the table.

That's funny to me, Keith skipping around the table. I am a dummy. How come Brenna never told me what Whitesnake meant? She's always knowing what something nasty means. Keith slaps his hand down on the table. Wake your ass up! I'm talking to you negro!

Shut up, and don't come over to my job anymore. I smack him across the back of his head when I get up to go watch TV. Nobody else is watching it now so I can watch whatever I want. *Don Kirshner's Rock Concert* if it's on.

I sit on the floor close to the TV and Keith sits next to me. It's on. Cool! I say. We watch Bachman-Turner Overdrive and Keith rolls his eyes.

I say, What's up with you and Brenna anyway? I've been wanting to know this all night but couldn't ask in front of Mom because she would be all over it, telling Keith that he has no business going around with Brenna.

Look how you look at them dudes. You want to get down with all of them, I can tell, Keith says.

I watch them throw their hair all around and thrust their crotches at me and point their guitars at me. At me. Yeah.

But I say, Gross. I don't want to get down with anybody. You. You're the one, Keith. Are you making out with her or something?

He scoots closer to the TV and turns up the sound.

You hate them. Why are you turning up the sound?

He doesn't answer me.

So what, it's none your business. She kiss good, too. She's my hoochie coochie girl.

Stop saying that! God! I say, and I don't know what I'm feeling. This feels like something about me. This is what I start thinking: I'm fat. I look like a boy. I got nappy hair and I don't even know what to do with it. And nothing I wear is ever cool and nothing Brenna steals for me looks good on me. She lies when she says I look rad. She's a liar. Didn't even tell me about Keith.

I turn the TV up even more. A Mustang commercial is on. I say, Mom and Dad bet not find out.

How they going to find out? I pull down my shirt because it always rides up over my stomach. I say, I don't know. They just can, that's all.

You bet not say anything or I will beat your monkey ass, Keith says. I will too. I don't care.

Like I care, I say.

He looks at me for a long time and then stands up. I can't stand this shit you watching, he says. And Aunt Vicky won't let you hang out with Brenna if you go run and tell like a big old baby. He shove the back of my head real hard but I jerk it back straight like, So? You pushed my head but it's right back where it was. Fast. Like a ball you're trying to push underwater. It's always going to pop right back up, so there.

THE NEXT DAY, I walk to Brenna's house and her dad comes to the door in his boxers. I woke him up or something. I stare at his chest hair like a moron. I ask his chest, Is Brenna home? He yawns and runs his hands through his hair and it just stays up. He points to Brenna's room and leaves me standing there. Close the door, he tells me over his shoulder. I stand there staring at Brenna's door. I can hear Rod Stewart singing If you want my body and you think I'm sexy. It's too loud so I have to knock hard.

What's the password? Brenna yells.

It's Avery, I try to yell and whisper at the same time. I wait there, waiting for her to tell me to come in, even though she always just walks into my room like it's hers.

Come in dumbass, she yells.

She's sitting on the floor, drinking an Orange Crush with albums and 45s all around her. I get on my knees and look through all the records until I can't stand the loud music. Turn it down! So loud! You deaf?

She turns it down and whispers. My mom and dad were going at it and I had to turn it up to keep from barfing up my ramen. Who wants to hear that crap? I think of Brenna's dad all sweaty and making out with me and my hands are running through all that red hair on his chest. Yeah, I say. That's pretty gross.

I want to give Brenna a chance to tell me about Keith. If she's my best friend, why isn't she telling me everything that's happening? Nobody ever tells me what's going on. I say, I talked to Keith about something.

So? Want a biscuit? You live together, you must talk to him about *something* like a thousand times a day.

Why can't you have a normal conversation without being a smartass all the time? I bite my lips and I swear I want to punch her all of a sudden. She makes me so sick sometimes. She says whatever she wants and does whatever she wants and nobody ever tells her anything. The first thing I do, everybody's got something to say about it.

What was that all about when I was babysitting yesterday?

What? Brenna scratches Rod Stewart when she takes him off the record player.

So you're not even going to tell me.

What? she says like she's talking to some little kid. Spit it the fuck out already.

You made out with Keith and you weren't even going to tell me about any of it.

What's there to tell? I did it cause I wanted to and I didn't want to tell you because I knew you'd go all crybaby on me.

It? Just kissing, right?

Ave. Brenna bends her neck and tightens her halter top string. Keith's right. She says. You're half retarded, if not 90 percent retarded, I swear to God.

So it's even worse. They totally got down. I wonder. When did they do it? How did they do it? How many times? And where was I? Sitting with a baby.

I ask Brenna. When did you do it?

Where are my normal records, Brenna says. She shuffles all the records like giant cards. Van fucking Halen, she says. Aww yeah. She pulls out the record and looks at the sleeve like she's reading the words to the song but she knows the words. She always knows the words before me. She doesn't even like music as much as I do, because she can take it or leave it. She gets bored easy with it. But not me. Every time I hear something, even if it's a dumb song to everybody else, I keep it and it's like I pull it out of my pocket like it's a little medicine telling me it's cool, Avery. Like, Ray, a drop of golden sun, me a name I call myself, far a long long way to run. Don't you worry about a thing mama cause I'll be standing on the side when you check it out.

I ask Brenna. Have you and Keith been doing this all the time? I'm pissed. I'm so pissed just thinking about them knowing something that I don't know. Liars.

She sings, What a sweet talking honey with a little bit of money can turn your head around.

I ask Brenna, How does it even feel?

God. Brenna frowns at me. I don't even know, Ave. What kind of question is that, even?

I want to hit her so bad. Just sock her hard in the face. I make myself calm down by talking very, very slowly. I say, It's a normal question, Brenna. A fucking. Normal. Question. How. Does. It. Feel. To. Have. A. Dick. Inside. You.

Brenna pays attention to me finally. She has a weird smile on her face. You should be like this all the time, Avie baby. Brenna still has that crazy smile on her face.

Why? Is that what whores are like?

That hurts, Brenna says. I'm crying. Can't you see these huge-ass tears running down my face? She lies down on her back with her hands behind her head and then she crosses her leg over her knee. She jiggles her foot like we're lying somewhere else, on a beach in Tahiti or our personal island, staring up at the sky instead of lying on her dirty green carpet. I like it, she says. I like Keith. So what? What did I even do to you? She sits up all of a sudden and puts her face in her hands. We stare at each other and out of nowhere I think, That's a nice picture, her face in her hands like that, like her hands are frames. White frames with brown dots all over them like cinnamon sprinkled over some milk with a little bit of Strawberry Quik mixed in. That's the kind of white Brenna's skin is, the kind of white that is not the same as any other white. She squints at me and all I can see are slits of green. Her red hair is all the way to her waist. But it's not red, either. It's brown and orange and blonde all mixed in so we're all calling it red but that's not right. It's not even specific enough.

Hey. Brenna kicks me. I asked you a question stoner. What did I even do to you?

It feels like she and Keith did something to me. It does. But I don't know what. There's nothing I can say and I guess I'm not that mad anymore.

You could have told me about it, I say. That's all. You always tell me everything.

Okay, then, she says. All right. I hear you. Sorry. Next time you will get all the blow-by-blow details, *if* you know what I mean.

Gross. Not what I mean, Brenn.

Okay. So we're solid then.

Yeah, I say. I stand up. Brenna reaches her hand out to me and wiggles her fingers. Pull me, she says. Pull me up. I do and she throws her arms around me. I love you, I love, I love you, she says and makes wet kissing sounds.

I push her away. Stop it. That's not funny. She laughs and then looks at me dead serious. I'm not kidding, Ave. It's not supposed to be funny. You always think I'm fucking around, man. Even when I'm not.

18

I CAN'T SLEEP. I get up. Massimo is lying in bed and I think, *Call Brenna*. Don't worry about Keith. She thinks of him all the time, I know, though she pretends not to think of anything that would trouble her. She thinks of a family even I, myself, have not imagined. Tones and hues and surprising colors popping up in hair and eyes. From people and places no one has remembered or imagined. When I try, I see this family in abstract, geometric shapes and patches of brilliant colors that allow us to see each aspect of these children, without the specifics of what they are made of obscured or melted into a pot. Each fragment of the collage is conspicuous and astonishing, as valuable as the other, pulsating on the canvas with its own little song.

I stand in the bathroom, having forgotten for the moment what it is I meant to do once I entered the room. I look at myself in the mirror, a mirror I love. It's large, wooden, and white, with the paint chipping off of it, revealing the brown wood underneath. It's half gone, and Massimo is frustrated with it. "Either we start with a new one," he says, "or paint over this one," but it's antique, remnants of someone else's life, and I think we should let the paint run its course. And anyway, it's lovely, this weathered combination of brown and white.

Always, since I've traveled the long distance, the half hour from Los Angeles to West Covina, Brenna and I have been together, or, I should say, friends, except for a brief time in high school when I didn't know what to do with all that had happened. I had decided that, whatever had happened to her did not happen to me. Therefore, it was my right to ignore it. Me and my rights, my freedom, as if such liberties have anything to do with how one should treat another person. And besides, I had reasoned at the time, my parents told me to stay away from her.

Brenna has two jobs. She works at her mother's day care center during the day, and at night, she waitresses at Chili's. She has been working like this for years. Jobs in pairs that don't go together. Truck driver/mechanic, short-order cook/saleswoman, barista of impossibly finicky orders with varying degrees of foam, milk fat, and temperatures by day, mixer of cheap vodka at the local dive bar at night. Sometimes she keeps these jobs for a very long time, and sometimes, almost right away, she ends up inviting someone to go fuck themselves. I begged her to apply to college—junior college—but she said the notion of school bored the turds out of her. No one could ever tell her anything, especially me. Now, whenever I tell her it's not too late, she says, "Thanks, cheerleader Muffy. Besides," she says, "you went to college and studied something totally useless to you and ended up broke. Until Massimo."

I have argued this point with her, that education is simply synonymous with opportunity. Brenna, though, calls bullshit. She says that sometimes opportunity is synonymous with, "So what? I'm too fucked up to take advantage of any of your precious opportunity." This may be true of some people, but Brenna— Brenna is just some bewildering combination of stubborn and disdainful. "It's America, man," she always used to say whenever I would try to tell her something. "It's a free country and I'm free, so shut the fuck up."

Back when I was painting more instead of doing found art and collages, one of the last things I painted was a portrait of

s on my left. Her image is reminiscent ngstocking, who I adored when I was a Brenna hates. If you didn't know Bren- e of thinking that was who she was, just ome funny little girl. Big eyes, freckles, a nt red ponytails jutting crookedly from portending weathervanes. In the paint- ssed and her middle finger is extended. heeks of a child, circles of pink on my cheeks like a circus clown. My two braids are stiff and pointed down and away from my face, but my eyes—I was more careful with my eyes. They don't commit to anything. They look toward Brenna's middle finger with a hint of worry. My hand is wrapped around her wrist as if I mean to pull her hand down. But why is the corner of my lip turned up in a grin?

Now I stare at myself in the mirror. I try to duplicate the grin of the portrait. I think, after all these years, finally, that the woman in the mirror looks okay. There is nothing to fix about the face. The lips are good. Big and fat and in style now that white women are buying them. The hair is at long last inconsequential. Not of value to me, not of interest. It is simply short. It is simply there. Breasts that are large and heavy. Belly and thighs that feel good to me. To Massimo. This realization is both sudden and expected. But satisfying. Like a middle finger. Though I'm not sure when, exactly, I first began to extend that finger.

From the bathroom doorway, I can see Massimo lying on his side. His long eyelashes flutter slightly as if he's dreaming, but his eyes are open when I thought they were closed. "What are you grinning at?" He reaches out to me and I go to him, take his soft hand, and he pulls me closer.

"Nothing. I don't know. I was just thinking that some people are brave, or stupid and brave. Some people just lie down and die."

"Which are you, my love?"

"Not so brave, for sure. A little stupid. But I don't want to lie down and die."

Massimo frowns. Traces my lips with his fingers. "What's this? Why are you talking in riddles?"

I sit on the bed and run my fingers through Massimo's curls. Stroke his gray temples. "My grays," he says. "I should dye it, no?" He takes my hand and kisses my palm. "I am getting too old for you, I know. I will be old and alone." He sighs, squeezes my hand and grins at me, but it is a sad grin. He thinks that what he's saying might be true one day, even if he will never ever be alone, because he has money. He can always get a girl, because rich men can. A girl who loves him or a girl who is hungry or a girl who is both. But now I know, in spite of everything, all he truly only ever wanted was me. I tell him something that is a truth I have never said out loud. I lie down next to Massimo. I make my body fit into his and pull his arm across my belly. I tell him what I am thinking at this moment. I say, "I'm afraid of Keith."

I first became afraid of Keith many years ago, when he had called me from his mother's house. Before that, I had not heard from him in a very long time. It had been ten years. I had graduated from the University of Southern California, and he had called from prison to congratulate me. "You a fancy motherfucker now, ain't you?" he said. "Good for you, Ave. Good for you." I had been happy to hear from him because it had been such a long, long time. It was early in the morning, hours before I would leave for the gallery where I taught. It was the kind of day I love, the kind of day you can't find anywhere else. Bright, windy, the Santa Ana winds blowing through and making the air crisp and full of static. Clean. The sky was a sharp blue with no clouds. And I was thinking that there was no place more beautiful than here. California.

I keep talking to Massimo fast, like a confession I'm trying to be free of. "I should have visited him. I should have called him, but I don't want him in my life. I don't want to take care of him. He's going to pull me down into his shit, and there is Brenna not saying but thinking that I need to do better by him since my life is good in a big house on a hill with a swimming pool, and I just don't want to deal with any of it. I want to think only of myself. That is what I want. To think only of myself."

"Yes," Massimo says, his breath warm on my neck. "I understand this."

"I mean, we were supposed to let him come in here and lay around doing drugs and God knows what else? I could just see it. Brenna and Keith and his buddies sitting on our couch, eating our food, being loud, telling me, 'Chill out, Ave. Relax.' This is a nice home. I mean, how are we supposed to control them?" I sound terrible to myself, but I mean it as I say it. There is us, and there is them.

"Avie," Massimo says calmly. "Already you have moved everybody in. That will not happen. We know this, so you just have to make it all right in your head. That it is not because of me that you didn't want family in this house. It is because of you." He keeps talking to the back of my head. "In any case, there is only so much you can do, and you better start thinking about how dangerous this person can be. Family or not."

But that's the thing. So much I can do. But what have I done, exactly?

"How is it in there," I had asked Keith, already wanting to get off the phone that day. "Aw, you know," he said. "Bullshit. They be sweating a nigga for real." After a long silence, he said, "Member the time we put hot sauce on Joe and Tina's sugar toast? Shit was hilarious." I recalled this, something I hadn't thought of in years.

"The hot sauce was your idea," I said. "But we both got the belt." Our cousins were happy when we sweetly offered them sugar toast—two pieces of bread like a sandwich—but when they took their bites, their tongues caught fire. "We were mean," I said. "What little assholes."

"Sugar toast!" Keith laughed. "They ate that shit up. But that's your problem if you just gone eat any shit a motherfucker gone hand you." And then, he was saying that he had to go, that he would see me when he saw me.

Back then, Keith was new to prison, but he had done his time and now he was out, after a second stint for armed robbery. He was out, and he was here.

SUMMER *WAY* SUCKS if you're working. But at least I have some money saved. I haven't spent that much of it. I only saw *The Blue Lagoon, Fame,* and *My Bodyguard,* and then I bought a pair of black Dickies and some red jellies. Still, though, if you're not working and after you've bought a bunch of stuff and saw some movies, it gets to be boring. You end up just staring out the window sometimes. Dad's mowing the lawn. Come here, Ave, he says. You want to go to a game tomorrow? Double-header on Sunday? He says, You and Keith been working hard. Me too. Everybody needs a break. He's got five tickets. One for him, and then tickets for me, Brenna, and Keith. Mom won't go. She never goes. And she's not talking to Dad anyhow. There's some other woman calling the house and hanging up now. So there's one more left. Carlos. I want to bring Carlos.

Dad stops pushing the mower and leans on it. Who is Carlos?

I can tell by the way he's asking me that he thinks Carlos is somebody who wants to make out with me or something. I wish. Yeah Dad. Carlos has ulterior motives. I drive him mad with desire. I go, He's just a friend at school. He's nice.

He Mexican?

Yeah, I say. He's Mexican.

Dad stares down at the grass. There's this one patch that's a perfect triangle. It's the only piece left. He looks at me with one of his eyebrows raised. What kind of people are his family?

I bite my nails for a second. I don't even know what kind of question that is. I think. *Kind of people.* I know what Dad is asking me, but I guess I'm just wondering how should I know? I only met his sister once and she was mega awesome. So.

Dad says, He not one of them cholos, is he?

Dad, I say. I don't know. Why would he be a cholo?

The thing is, he is kind of a cholo, but I think cholos are cool and I don't want to get into a whole thing about it because Dad always thinks he's right about everything, so I don't even try.

I'm not saying he is, Dad says. I'm just asking if he is. Because you don't need to be running around with people driving around in cars and doing whatever it is they're doing.

I wish. I wish I could ride around in Carlos's sister's glitter-green car listening to oldies. But I just say, Dad. He's really nice. You can see for yourself. If he comes to the game.

All right then, Dad says. He can come if he want to.

I go to Carlos's house that day and ask him. I know where he lives because I followed him home one day. He's watering the lawn, when I get to his house, standing in tan cutoff Dickies and a white T-shirt. I go, I got a ticket to the Dodgers tomorrow. Want to come? He goes, For real, Avery Day? Don't play girl. And I know he's coming. He doesn't say yes or no, that's all he says. And I'm so nervous about the game today. I figure out an outfit to wear. Tan Dickies that are going to be pressed straight down the middle. Cuffs sharp like blades. My blue Sasson polo shirt and my green jellies. I can't go full-on cholo because dad will have a cow. But it's close. It's my version.

Nice threads, Brenna says when she sees me. I'm so confused, she says. That outfit is confused.

But *I* put it together with the parts that *I* wanted. I'm not confused. Carlos is riding up front with Dad and all I can think of is I hate our car. It's crap. It used to be green, but now it's brown and yellow and green. And it's trashed inside. Dad's a maniac about a clean house, everything has to be spotless all the time. But his car. Man. Newspapers everywhere, books, Kentucky Fried Chicken wrappers. Jack in the Box. And the lining on the roof of the car is torn so it's hanging down in the middle of the back seat. Also, Dad never fixed that piece of metal that sticks out of the passenger side door and sliced my ankle open last summer. Keith and Brenna don't care anything about how the car looks, but I'm sorry. It's embarrassing. After I know Carlos has noticed the three different colors on our car, and the trash in it everywhere, when Carlos is getting into the car, I have to tell him, Carlos. Watch your leg. That metal thing can cut you. And then I want to kill myself.

It's cool, Avery Day, he says. My dad drives a bucket too. Yeah, I think, maybe. But at least your sister doesn't.

Dad turns up the radio so he doesn't have to talk to Carlos. This is what he always does when somebody's in the front seat with him and he doesn't feel like talking. Vin Scully and Jerry Doggett are announcing. Bobby Castillo is pitching today. I'm sitting in the back behind Carlos. Keith and Brenna are sitting together, of course. I lean forward and look at the shiny tip of Carlos's ear. If I kissed it, Dad would never even know, and Carlos would maybe think it was on accident, since I had to lean in to talk to him. But I'm chicken. He'd probably turn around and say, Avery Day what up with you? I stare and stare at his ear, all shiny and brown with just a little red underneath. I say, I miss Sutton. Last time I saw him pitch he was on fire!

That's right, Dad says. He likes Sutton. Sutton's his man. But now he's always talking about a player named Valenzuela. Dad says that dude is bad and we're going to see a lot more of him, watch and see.

But Carlos is stuck on Sutton. So why you like Sutton better, Mr. Arlington? Carlos asks. He totally scores points for just adding Mr. Arlington at the end of that sentence.

Well, Dad says slow.

No! I know that when he says *Well* all slow we're going to get a long-ass story. He turns down Scully and Doggett. Oh no. Here we go.

He says, Sutton comes from *nothing*. And I mean nothing. A tarpaper shack. You all know what a tarpaper shack is? Oh no! We're getting ready to get a definition, *too*. Somebody just say

they know what it is so we can move on. But Dad's got the definition ready. He goes, Tarpaper is just paper that's got tar in it. It's
tough. But you think it's tough enough to keep the wind and cold
away from you? You think it works as good as a real wall?

Nobody says anything.

Sutton is a hardworking dude, Dad says. Hasn't missed an
opening yet, not cause he's sick, not cause he's hurt, not cause of
nothing.

Okay Dad, I'm thinking.

And let me tell you something else. He was telling the truth
when he let everybody know that Reggie Smith is the money on
that team, not that pretty boy Steve Garvey. Smith work hard like
Sutton. Born on the same day, Sutton and Smith. Bet y'all didn't
know that.

Brenna looks at me and rolls her eyes. Like this even has anything to do with baseball, she says low, so Dad won't hear her. But
I totally get it. Dad hates lazy asses and people who get other people's credit just for looking like they ought to. Everybody thinks
Garvey and Cyndy are all perfect and pretty. But they actually are
to me, though. I don't tell Dad that.

All American, Dad says. Folks don't know what American is
if it's just gone be some dude with a pretty face.

Nobody can say anything until Dad is done with this whole
Sutton thing. And I'm sorry, but Steve Garvey happens to be a fox
and a good first baseman, so why blame him for anything? Like
it's his fault people like him.

Dad turns up the radio, so he's done with all that anyway.

Traffic is slowing down and we're almost to the stadium. It
only takes about forty-five minutes from home and then you're
eating a Dodger Dog and peanuts. You can always tell when you're
almost there, because of the old wooden houses with their paint
peeling off on the right side of the freeway. White houses with blue

paint underneath, right in the middle of apartments too. Bars on all the windows. I like those old houses because they don't seem to fit where they are, right next to the freeway, looking like they're from a million years ago or someplace else that's not L.A., like Cape Cod. I don't even know what Cape Cod is, exactly, but that's what those houses seem like they are.

Then I hear something that sounds like it fell off the car.

What's that noise? Keith says.

Yeah, Brenna says. She sits up straight. Turns around to look out the back window like she's looking for something behind us in the road. The car is coughing and then there's a rattle. Our eyes are all big and Dad eases off to the side of the freeway. Then, the car just stops. Dad turns the key but the car just screams without moving.

Dad says, Shit. He gets out of the car and opens the hood and we all sit in the car watching other people get to the stadium.

Rad, Brenna says. Really. This is awesome. Great ball game.

Keith slides down in his seat. I don't care if we get to the game or not, he says. I'd rather play than watch these other fools play. But Carlos is bumming like me. He turns around in the front seat so he can shake his head at me. Avery Day, he says. *Man.*

Dad leans into our side of the car. Y'all might as well get out the car. It's hotter in there than it is out here. He takes his Dodger cap off so he can wipe his head and then he puts it back on. Bring the radio so you can listen to the game while you're out here. Let me try to figure out what's wrong with this car.

We all get out of the car and sit on the freeway ramp. Carlos has the radio and turns it up as loud as it will go. It's still hard to hear, though, because of all the cars, and the game is going to start in like five minutes. We're going to miss the beginning of the game, I say. I kick a smashed Burger King cup that's by my feet.

Einstein, Brenna says. Does it even look like we're going to make it to the game? Call your chauffeur, why don't you. Tell him to pick us up.

Yeah, Keith says. He puts his hand on top of Brenna's. Tell him to have some refreshments waiting for our asses, too.

Shut up, eh, Carlos says. He's got the radio up to his ear. I can barely hear the game, he says.

BFD, Brenna says and Keith gives her a kiss on the cheek but only because Dad's head is under the hood and he can't see us. They better watch it. They totally better watch it.

Now there's a truck pulling up behind Dad. A rusted-out truck that looks even crappier than our car. It's a Fix Or Repair Daily. A Ford. A man gets out. We all stare at the guy. Even Carlos stops listening to the game. The man's kind of crazy looking. A long ZZ Top beard. A T-shirt that's got stains all over the chest like he just wipes his hands on it all day long. He says something to a little girl sitting in the front and then gets out of the car. His belly's sticking out from underneath the shirt and he keeps pulling up his jeans. He's got a long blonde ponytail sticking out the back of his Dodgers cap. He ignores us and goes straight to Dad. It's Avery's husband, Keith says. Moron.

Hey man, the fat dude says to Dad. What's wrong with your car?

Don't know, Dad says. Can't figure it out. They both take off their caps and stand with their hands on their hips. They stare at the car. Let me check it out, the man says. He's not under it long. Can't tell what's going on, he says. Well, Dad says.

You going to the game? the man says.

We was, Dad says.

I'll give you a lift in my truck, the guy says.

Dad looks at him, thinking about him, I can tell. Dad looks at all of us sitting on the side of the freeway. Brenna leans into me and whispers, Total serial killer.

Yeah, Dad says. I'd appreciate that ride.

Yes! We are going to make the game. That's all I care about. We all get in the truck and the man puts the kid in back with us so Dad can sit in the front. She's scared of us since she's so little. She stares at us with her mouth open and holds on to this baseball like we're going to grab it from her. Keith pretends he's going to steal it. No! she screams, and we all laugh. It's pretty funny. A Dodger's going to sign it, she says.

What's your name, kid, Brenna says.

Monica. Her blonde hair is swirling all around her face from the wind. She holds her ball up. Like her name's on it or something.

Which Dodger's going to sign? I ask her.

She stands up and almost falls back down because the truck's moving. She turns around so we can see her shirt. Scioscia. Nice.

Hey, Brenna says. Sit down, kid, before you bust your ass.

She listens to Brenna and sits down, holding on to that ball real tight.

Carlos isn't paying attention to the kid. He's listening to the radio. His head is bent close to the radio and his black shiny hair looks like it's got blue in it, it's so black. I love you Carlos, I want to make out with you so bad. Hopelessly devoted to you. I'm going to totally transform myself, for reals. Not halfway like today. And then you're going to be way into me.

I pull the radio from Carlos. They start? I put my ear to it. What's this? I frown but I don't mean to. All I hear is in Spanish.

Yeah, foo. Jaime Jarrin, mofo. Carlos winks at me. You like Scully, he says. I like Jaime.

I pass the radio back to him. Well, tell me what's happening, at least.

He holds his finger up. Lopes at bat, he says. He hits real good off of Steve Rogers. He keeps his finger up to tell me to be quiet.

Yes! he says and smiles real big. What I tell you Avery Day? Base hit. He's on first now.

Keith and Brenna don't even ask about the game. They don't even try to act like they're not into each other. They sit there holding hands and talking to each other. They better not let Dad see them, I swear to God.

We are at the stadium now. Finally. The man parks his truck and we all jump out. Brenna helps the kid out and holds her hand until the man takes her. Dad shakes the dude's hand. I really do appreciate the ride, Dad says. The guy goes, Nah. Glad to do it. He's holding the little girl's hand and he picks her up, puts her on his shoulders. Double-header with this one, he says. He pulls on her foot and she laughs. I thought I wanted a boy, the man says, but old Monica's all right. For now. He smiles real big when he says that, and he's got the whitest most perfect teeth. How did he get those teeth? He looks at all of us. Enjoy the game, he says, and then he walks off with the kid on his shoulders. Hurry up, Dad says. Come on, y'all.

But what are we going to do about the car, Dad?

Don't worry about it, he says. We'll get towed home. Cost a damn fortune but it was gone cost a fortune whether or not we see the game. May as well get our money's worth. We done drove all this way. Keith and them walk in front of us, like they even know where they're going. They don't know the stadium.

I ask Dad. Who was that guy?

I don't know. Nice fella, though.

I mean, you didn't even get his name?

I didn't ask, Dad says. Don't matter no how. Looked a little rough, but he was just as nice as he could be. Dad looks at my hands. Who's got the radio?

Carlos, I say.

Good, Dad says. He squints at Carlos's back like he's trying to see him even though he's right in front of us.

Something just happened because the whole stadium is cheering. I love hearing that sound, a whole bunch of people sounding like they all agree that whatever's happening is the best possible thing for everybody here.

But walking with Dad, I see them again. Brenna puts her hand on the back of Keith's neck, real quick. I think nobody sees but me. I have this feeling in my stomach, like when Dad comes home too late on a Saturday night and Mom doesn't say a word. It's like Dad is invisible. You know something is going to happen, something so scary, maybe a loud something with screaming and shouting or something so small you don't hear anything at all, but when you wake up in the morning, the house feels like everybody's a little bit sadder, and that feeling's forever.

I AM LOOKING at something I will always remember, like it's a photograph. I have that kind of feeling. Keith is standing in the kitchen holding a baloney sandwich. Want half? He holds up the sandwich. Ain't no more bread so we have to split it. He wipes his hands on his white T-shirt and pulls up his dirty blue jeans. He's leaning against the refrigerator, green like the inside of an avocado. He takes a bite and chews, and the light from the sliding glass door is coming into my eyes, but I keep looking because I think, I will remember this, before Keith knows what he and Brenna did.

No. Thanks. I sit on a barstool next to the stove. Stare at him.

What? Take a picture, he says. Damn. Keith is standing still. My picture of Keith is changing into something else. His eyes are moving to things all over the room. The wall behind me, the clock on the wall behind me. Mom's plastic yellow roses in the middle of the dining room table. At me. Just past me. I don't know for sure what he's looking at, though. I can only guess. I can only look where I think he's looking and still not see.

I don't like how you staring at me, Ave. Go find something else to do instead of staring at a motherfucker. But he looks nervous. His face is doing a lot of different things. His eyes are squinting. His mouth is open like there is something strange he can't figure out. Then he closes his eyes like he's standing there sleeping. When he opens them they look dead, like doll eyes. You know those doll eyes that flip open? You can look at doll eyes forever but they will never look back at you like they can see you. They're always crying but then they look at you like they don't even know who you are. He sneezes. He gets a pitcher from the fridge and pours a cup of Kool-Aid. Then he goes to the sliding glass door with the sandwich in one hand and the cup in the other.

He tries to balance everything, but then tilts his head at me. I can't get this, he says. I'ma spill my drink or drop my sandwich. Open the door for me, Ave. Don't just sit there. Help a nigga out.

EVERYBODY COMES TO our house. Brenna's mom and dad. Aunt Janice. They all sit down and I stay in my room and listen through the door.

Well, this is a fucking mess. Brenna's dad. I won't lie, kid. I want to bash your fucking face in.

I wish I can see Dad's face when I hear this.

Joe. You can kick his ass but our kid's still going to be knocked up. Can I smoke in here? Brenna's mom.

Then Dad says, We are responsible. He's living with us.

You don't teach him he can't just do whatever he wants? That's what he does? Just run around screwing little girls?

Brenna's dad is way off base. He's talking about Keith like he's some old dangerous molester guy.

Then Mom tells him like it is. Mom says, They the same age.

Look like you let her do whatever she feel like doing. Brenna didn't know how to keep her legs closed?

Vicky, Dad says.

Brenna's father says, You ain't got nothing to add to this bullshit disaster?

Naw, Aunt Janice says, real quiet. I almost don't hear her.

Then I hear mumbling and mumbling and then Brenna screaming. No! I am not killing it! I'm not going to fucking do that! I will run away, I swear to God. Try and stop me. Better fucking tie me down.

After that, all I hear is more mumbling and then people walking and then the front door closes.

I open my bedroom door. Brenna and them are gone. I sit at the kitchen counter just looking at everybody. I'm so scared. It's so scary to not know what is going to happen.

Aunt Janice has those doll's eyes like Keith had. Then all of sudden, she smacks him across the face, and not even one sound comes out of his mouth.

Don't, Janice. Dad says. It's too late for all that now. What's that gone do now?

Adoption, Mom says. That little heifa bet not turn around talking about she want to keep it.

Fourteen goddamn years old, Dad says.

The ashtray I'm playing with makes a clink on the counter and everybody looks at me. Like they want to hit me too.

Aunt Janice scratches her scalp. Her hair is pulled back tight with a blue rubber band. She crosses her arms. Shakes her head. Well, she says. Pack up your stuff, Keith.

Ain't got much to pack up, Mom says.

He leaves his schoolbooks behind because school has just started and he'll have to start up again in Victorville. He has a box of clothes and that's it. When he's leaving, I remember his skateboard and it makes me sad. I want to cry thinking of that stupid skateboard. Don't even ask me why.

Hey, I say. You're leaving your skateboard.

He looks at me and I know what he's thinking because his eyes aren't doll eyes this time. He doesn't say it, but his eyes look like, Man, Ave. Fuck a skateboard. But because Mom and Dad and Aunt Janice are standing around him, he just says, You can have it. I don't need it.

Everybody stands around like they are going to say something, but nobody does. Until Dad. He says, You don't have to keep traveling down this road, and Aunt Janice nods. Aunt Janice is hugging herself, but nobody's hugging Keith. Dad says, You need to just straighten up and hit the books. That's what you need to do.

Keith is looking down at the white floor with black scuffs all over it. Either Mom or me, we're always taking scuffs off the floor. Keith crosses his arms and puts his hands underneath his armpits.

This don't have to be the end of the world, Dad says. Keith takes a deep breath and I'm thinking, You need to answer my dad.

You hear Darnelle talking to you, don't you? Aunt Janice says.

Yeah, Keith says. I hear. I know. I will. It's not.

Come on here, Aunt Janice says. She pulls on Keith's shoulder. Get that box and let's go.

The box has Del Monte Pears stamped on the sides. I think the red behind Del Monte looks good outlined in yellow and the words Del Monte in white. Mom says, Give me a hug before you go, and I'm still thinking about Del Monte when I see Keith's face while he's hugging Mom. His eyes are closed, but will he open them to tell me something with his face? He doesn't. He keeps his eyes closed the whole time and then he picks up the box.

Bye Keith, I say. Aunt Janice has the door open and the bright light is coming in from outside. It's Saturday and usually on

Saturday we walk around. Keith and Brenna and I go to 7-Eleven or catch the bus to the mall if there is nothing better to do. Or we just hang in Brenna's room and play records. It's the kind of sun on a Saturday that's just awesome. Gold and orange and bright and a beam behind Keith. But it's blinding me so I can't see his face. It's gone, all of a sudden, his face. I wish I could do something, but what can I?

Bye Keith, I say again, because I feel like this: If I keep saying bye, at least he knows that I care he was here, that I'm going to miss him. I hate it when people don't say hello or goodbye to me, like at school or anywhere, like I'm invisible.

All right then, Ave, Keith says. He looks down and then looks up again, right in my eyes.

He walks out the door with Aunt Janice and Mom. Mom is standing at the top of the driveway waving. I know it. I don't even have to be out there to see it. It's like the last thing she wants to see is someone go. So long as she's standing there and waving she can see you. You're not gone. But I don't go outside to say goodbye, because I already did. And I'll see him again. He'll be back. It's not like he's going to some other planet or something. It's like Mom says. Every goodbye ain't gone.

Dad sits down at the kitchen table. He lights a cigarette and looks at me, puffing. I'm in some kind of trouble. I can tell by the way he's looking at me and not talking. Somehow, Brenna and Keith have something to do with me.

Avery, Dad says. Sit down.

I do what Dad says and that's when Mom comes in. You talking to her now?

Yeah, Dad says. Right now.

Good, Mom says. She says, You right there with them all the time and you ain't seen nothing that was happening?

Vicky, Dad says. Sit down.

No, Mom says. I don't believe I really want to sit down.

Dad smashes his cigarette. You know why we talking to you, don't you Ave?

I'm thinking what to say. I didn't do anything. I never do anything. Not really. I go, I didn't do anything.

That's right, Dad says. But you knew what was going on and you did nothing. Didn't say nothing. That's worse. When you know something ain't right with what's going on and you still don't say or do nothing. You just gone sit on the sidelines.

I don't answer him. Dad says, You know Keith and Brenna was doing something they shouldn't have been doing.

Like I'm supposed to be everywhere they are, watching out for them like I'm God.

But I just look down at the table. I say, I didn't know everything.

Mom comes and stands close by my side. If I were a little kid that would have freaked me out because she would have smacked me for sure. They don't have to hit me anymore since I listen without it. I don't get smacked because I'm already trained.

Mom says, That's it for her.

Look at me, Mom says. That's it. You don't do nothing with Brenna. You don't go to her house. She don't come here. You don't do nothing with her after school. If it don't have nothing to do with school or work, you ain't doing it.

That's impossible. But Mom, I say, Brenna is my friend.

Well you don't need them kind of friends.

Okay. She's crazy. I'm supposed to just blow her off whenever I see her? How am I supposed to do that? How is that even going to work?

Avery, Dad says, and he says it quiet, real quiet. So I know I better not say anything. Just listen and take it, like every other day of my life. Dad says, Brenna is obviously doing some things that she don't have no business doing, and you really don't want to go down that road. She already off to a rough start. Ain't no telling what all else she's doing. Drugs. Drinking. Everything but the right thing.

Mom nods. This is her favorite thing to say and since Dad already said it, all she has to do is agree.

Oh my God. Brenna doesn't even do drugs. She thinks stoners are dumbasses. And she doesn't even drink. Smoke, yeah, but so what? I don't say any of this, though. I still have to just sit there and take it.

Dad wants to know. Who all else she run with?

I shrug. I don't know, I say. Just me, really. We don't really hang out with anybody else.

Well, you gone have to start, Mom says. All I'm gone tell you is this. Keep your legs closed. If you come up pregnant, might as well hang it up. I feel sorry for you cause can't nobody help you then. You on your own.

I want to tell them, Nobody wants me. Nobody cares, seriously. Nobody has even *tried* to touch me, not since John did that time and called me Aunt Esther. If just anybody would. And if they did, I'm not stupid. Only stupid girls spread 'em so easy, like they don't have any sense, and then get knocked up and that's why I'm mad at Brenna. She's not stupid. She's not. And now look.

Are you listening? Dad says.

Yes sir.

This is what you're going to do. You're going to go to school. He looks at me and waits for me to agree.

Yes, I say.

You're going to do real good and you're going to keep your job. Yes.

And you are not going to end up like Brenna. You hear me talking to you?

Yes, I say. I'm not going to end up like Brenna.

I TRY TO talk to other people all the time. But nobody talks to Brenna. People stare at her, though. That's the girl, I hear them say. Some black man did that to her, they say. But Keith isn't a man.

There are these two girls. Perfect. I sit by them at lunch and ask them if they know what time it is or do they have a pencil. Abby Batista and Letty Cruz. They look right out of *Seventeen*. Abby's always in something Ralph Lauren. She'll wear a jean skirt with argyle socks and a pink sweater with a turtleneck. Top-siders or loafers. Her hair is always pulled back in a ponytail. Not one. Strand. Loose. Not one. Letty is always wearing super tight Calvin Kleins and plaid Laura Ashley blouses. She puts Sun-In in her hair so it's kind of brown and blonde at the same time.

I always wait until they get their lunch before I get in the county line for mine. They pay for their lunch with money, but I get a silver chip from homeroom every day. It kind of looks like a quarter, except it's not. When I was a kid, and in junior high, your name was always on some list so it wasn't a big deal. But now that I'm in high school, they call your name and you have to go up to Mr. Celaya and take the chip from him. You have to feel people watching you. And then, at lunch you have to get in the county line for free lunch. That's what everybody calls it, like we're on county welfare. It's a totally different line from the kids who pay with money. I can't even tell you how much I hate standing in line with a chip in my hand when other people have actual money. It reminds me of when I was a kid and saving up Blue Chip Stamps with Mom, trying to buy something. I was always asking, Why don't we just pay with money? But I was still happy to get those stamps.

So I wait until Abby and Letty sit down with their lunches and then I get mine and take it to their table. Sometimes they say hi. Sometimes they don't.

Excuse me, I say, Do you have any extra ketchup packets?

Abby says, Here, and tosses one to me. She doesn't even look at me. Knock yourself out, she says.

Oh my God, she says to Letty. Did I even tell you? Marcus is totally trying to scam on me, like he's even close to being my type. It's like, are you serious? Gag me. Not for a million dollars, burnout. In your *Pinto*. I'm sure! I need a Clydesdale, sweetums, not a jackass. She shivers all crazy like she's having a fit, and Letty laughs and then puts down her sandwich. She only took a bite. I watched her. Gross, she says. I can't eat any more of this or else I'll be a cow.

Look, Letty says. How sad. There's that girl. And I already know who they're talking about. I watch them look at Brenna eating at a table all by herself. She looks back at us and they keep talking about her and looking at her. They don't even care that she can see them looking. Her life is over, Letty says.

I heard she's not keeping it, though, Abby says. She picks up her sandwich and tears it into a lot of small pieces and pours some milk over it. There, she says, and then she pushes her food away.

It's going to be a black baby, Letty says.

Abby rolls her eyes. How can it be a black baby? Look at her. She's all pink and like, *red*. You can't get a black baby out of that.

Yes you can! Letty says. It depends.

I'm still thinking about this when they stop talking and I know they're looking at me. I can tell. I don't even have to see them doing it.

Can't you get a black baby out of that? Letty points her chin in Brenna's direction.

Yeah, you should know, Abby says.

Not mean, though. She just thinks I should know.

But I don't know what the baby will look like. And they said *that*. They pointed at Brenna and said *that*. I go, All mixes are different. I guess you could get almost anything if you mixed all kinds of colors or people or things together. Anything is possible.

19

MASSIMO STAYS IN bed, still resting, satisfied with all the work he has done, having helped his brother's son purchase a new house in Rome. He stayed curled up in the sheets when I left him there, moaning that he was happy to be home.

I have four hours until I have to be at the gallery. I'm expecting not to sell my art but hoping to sell ideas. It is truly a rare thing, a privilege, to have an audience, even if, ultimately, they don't care and still won't know what I'm trying to say.

I play a CD I made for myself, one of many I play when I'm working or at gatherings. This one starts out with Bay City Rollers chanting exuberantly that it's Saturday night and ends with Talib Kweli singing "every poor person is a nigger now." They always unsettle Massimo, not only silly relics from the past like the Bay City Rollers, but all songs with the word "nigger" in them being blared through speakers during a dinner party or while you're quietly reading the Sunday paper. Somebody is bound to be disturbed. But to my mind, it all belongs together, so why segregate the music for each listener's comfort, playing safe, inoffensive music sure to go down easy for everyone? Still, I make sure that the music is down low and only coming out of the outside speaker so I don't disturb Massimo.

There is a breeze now and the day is ending, so the mountains are shaded at their edges in purple and burgundy. I can step outside myself and see the picture. The clean simplicity of a person and a landscape, elegant like a Hockney painting. But can it be true that Hockney is too simple? Facile? True that nothing is captured in his images? Sure. In my picture of a woman sitting by a pool, for example, there is simply this: A person. A place. And yet. Underneath all of that, there are layers, invisible as they may be.

I have my phone sitting next to me on the table because I'm sure that I will get calls from people with last-minute questions and regrets about tonight. In my family, people don't go to computers for info, so they won't be looking up all the information that I've sent via e-mail. Dad doesn't have a computer. Neither does Mom. And Owen, there is one in his house, but he just doesn't care. Smart phones are too much of a bother for him, even. "Does it still call people?" he asked me when I complained about his obsolete phone. "That's all I need it to do."

The phone rings. I think it's Owen on the other end of the line, but it's Mom.

"You home?" she says. "It sounds quiet. Thought you'd be running the streets."

This is something that she always accused Owen and me of, running the streets rather than staying still, not knowing how to stay home and just sit down somewhere.

We catch up quickly about everybody. I ask, "How's Aunt Janice? Anybody hear from ReRe lately?"

"Oh," she says, "you know how everybody is, fair to middling. ReRe call herself starting her own cleaning business, but we'll see." This is what she says about everybody all the time, even herself. Nobody is ever great. No one is ever terrible, even if something terrible has happened. There is always somebody in limbo, and I always saw this in colors when I was a child. Middling was orange, but on the bad side there was only black and blue and on the other side, the good side, the color was brilliantly golden yellow.

Everybody is in limbo, and she is sorry that she won't be coming tonight. Tired. Don't feel like being around a bunch of folks she don't know. "The next thing, though," she says. Now, so many years later, now that she and my father are no longer swimming against the tide of their individual burdens and resentments, she doesn't seem as tired and tough as she used to be. Home used to be where trouble was, but now my mother simply wants to be home. Because I have her on the phone, I tell her about Keith. In these situations, a long time ago, there was never a middling. The finality and clarity with which she and my father declared what was the right and wrong thing to do was oppressive when I was younger, but now it strikes me simply as a solution to the problem.

"Keith showed up over here, Mom."

"You see him?"

"No. Brenna and I were at the store."

"What Massimo say?"

"He was mad, but he says it isn't his place to do anything about it." I wait but hear nothing. "Hello? You there?"

"Yeah," Mom says. "But there ain't nothing to do. He in his own way, been in his own way for years."

"Yeah, but he wasn't born getting in his own way."

"Well," Mom says, which means she agrees, but. So much more could be said, but what, exactly? "We did the best with what we had," Mom says. "And you all came up every which way, did whatever you wanted to do. You didn't come up the way we did."

This strikes me as outrageous, this business about me doing whatever I wanted to do.

"Seriously? You and Dad ran a tight ship. I mean *tight*. You don't remember?"

"I remember everything," Mom says. "Everything. And all I know is your brother married a Korean? And you living with a Italian? Over there making stuff with Popsicle sticks talking about it's art?"

When she says all of this it sounds like a madcap adventure, the premise of a wacky television program with bizarre characters. It makes me laugh and makes her laugh, too.

"And Keith," she says, identifying the one dark element of the adventure. I can imagine her shaking her head. "If you all had come up in Tennessee, wouldn't be none of that."

"Well we didn't, though," I say. "And I'm glad. And you're glad too or else you would have gone back."

"I guess you right. Ain't no need of talking about what didn't happen. I like my little house. Hold on." She pauses. "I smell something," she says. "Let me get off this phone. My cornbread about to burn up."

"You all right with money, before I let you go?"

"Could use a little change," she says, and I let her know it's on its way.

When my mother hangs up, I think about her liking her little house, the house I grew up in. I wonder what could have been different, to keep us all together in the new house that promised stellar living. But there is not one or even two things that we could all agree on. It was, and is, still floating among us, waiting for us to grasp it someday. And I think of the Popsicle sticks Mom brought up. Once, when she was here, I was working on a house, using canvas and Popsicle sticks and paint. I had painted the side of a house, thinking of the house next door to us. White with blue trim. And then, I adhered Popsicle sticks to the canvas, creating the fence dividing the property. Below the fence I tried to replicate the gummy bright blue of dried Popsicle juice, to allude to a swimming pool, or maybe the sky, turned upside down. Just a house, a fence, water, and sky. Sticks and glue. Nothing and everything.

When we were kids, Brenna would complain about the tight ship I grew up on, the *S.S. Arlington*, I now imagine, barely staying afloat on treacherous waters, the threat of us drowning as we headed to an unknown land. Brenna thought my mother, in particular, was a strict co-captain, the Bitch, she would always say. Mean. And me, I was always wondering why my mother was so angry when I was younger, so exhausted in later years, and content now, without the trappings I've stumbled on. No care in the world about the difference between a Hockney and a ham hock. I used to wish we could have conversations about the difference. But now. I see: I was looking at the picture of who we were—and are—all wrong. I knew nothing of aesthetics. My mother was looking at that picture with fierce clarity. In fact, she was the creator of the picture. An artist. Her family, her children, were an expression of her skill and imagination, the composition of which she, as the artist, wanted utmost control. Of course, I know now. Of course. An artist insists on her vision alone.

✳ ✳ ✳

WE HAVE TO do these drop drills in case of an earthquake, but earthquakes never happen at school. All my life every earthquake I've felt has been at home, in the middle of the night, so the drills are kind of dumb. Mom says I even slept through two when I was a little kid, that's how big a deal they were to me, I guess. Avery can sleep through anything, Mom says. That girl, she says. Shakes her head like it's a tragedy. I mean, she can sleep like she dead, I'm here to tell you.

Once a month they surprise us with these drills. You hear the siren and then you have to get under your desk and cover your head. Because that's totally going to help you if the ceiling falls on your head.

Mrs. Lardner is trying to keep these other two kids from talking to each other all the time so she makes the one sitting next to me switch to the back. Young people, she says. I'm trying to educate you about history. The Mayflower is very important. She rubs her hands together and her eyes are all watery and worried like she's going to cry on us. She better not cry, because if she does, it's over for her. Everybody'll make fun of her forever. So she makes Mike sit up front next to me.

Then we hear the siren and we're under our desks and everybody's laughing and talking. Class? Mrs. Lardner says. This is serious! Mike looks at me with his hands over his head and smiles at me with braces all over his teeth, all shiny and wire-y like a million highways and knots and bundles. I wish I had some. I keep telling Mom and Dad that I need them because I have a gap between my two front teeth. I want to close it. Get a retainer, at least. You know how much I hear them things are supposed to cost? Mom says. It's like I asked her for something crazy, like golden underwear.

Mike puts his finger on his mouth. Shhh, he says. Avery! Be quiet, man. Quit fooling around. But I'm perfectly quiet. I'm the only one that's quiet and I love that he's talking to me. No boys talk to me. We wait for the second bell so we can get up. Man, Mike says. That was really and truly lifesaving. And I'm into Mike now. Nobody thinks he's cute. He's got super tight curly blonde hair and a big head. A really big head that's way too big for his body. His eyes aren't straight. The right one is a little crossed in. And his cheeks are always red, no matter what. People call him fathead, but not to his face because he has money. His mom picks him up in a Mercedes and his dad drives him around in a BMW. Both new. I saw them at the store one time, him and his dad. His dad was good looking though. Kind of like Mike, but less all mixed up. Mike's funny looking, yeah. But not to me. Not anymore. I can't even believe it, but he talks to me all the time.

Today we sit between the portables, waiting for his mom to come. The portables are fake classrooms that are just plain old trailers because they ran out of space for everybody. So we get trailers. You never see schools on TV made out of trailers.

Hey, I say. Look. You can see the snow on the mountains. Look how pretty that looks, like milk spilling down rocks and the sun could be honey.

What? Mike blocks the sun with his hands and squints his eyes. He looks at the mountains. They don't really look like that, he says. What are you talking about?

To me, I say. To me it does. And we don't even need sweaters today. It's so sunny. Isn't it weird that the same place can have two different weathers? Down here, it's warm and sunny. But up there. I nod at the mountains. Look up there up at the very top.

I KEEP CRYING for no reason. Mike doesn't joke around with me anymore. I can't find him at lunch for like three days in a row. I'm crazy. I feel crazy. It's windy. Santa Ana winds that I usually love. All warm and super strong and the wind does make you feel a little crazy. Like you don't care because the sky is super blue and the air is clear and this is just like any other day but also a day that you'll never have again. So do whatever. Say whatever. It's almost the end of lunch when I find him. He's walking back onto school grounds. Weird. I run up to him. Where are you coming from? Where have you been for like, ever? I've been looking all over for you. Home, he says. I been eating at home this week. My mom picks me up and drops me off. I met his mom the other day when she picked him up after school. She looked like Bo Derek. I never saw a mom that looked like her before. Not even Brenna's mom. Blonde hair pulled back in a tight ponytail. Super tan. Black eyeliner and blue, blue eyes. Super skinny. She was playing Diana Ross on the radio really loud. Upside down you're turning me. She smiled at me. She was nice. Hello Avery, she said, and then she said, Mikey, get in the car.

Why? I say. Why are you eating at home all the time now? God, he says. Stop bugging me. And he won't look at me. He won't look me in the eye. He hates me now. Okay, I say. Okay. I talk to myself. Don't cry, Avery. Don't you cry you idiot. You stupid fucking idiot. But it's too late, I'm crying. I pull up one of my argyle socks. New. I bought them brand-new from JCPenney. I want him to see these new socks. There is nothing wrong with them. They are just socks like everybody else wears. He stares at my socks and higher. He's looking up my jean skirt. At my legs. His eyes are all over my body and he makes a weird sound almost like a whine, like a dog. Then he grabs my hand. It's the first time he's even touched me. He puts his hand on top of mine. I wish you were white, he says. I wish you were white so you could be my girlfriend.

I say, Me too. I wish I was white so I could be your girlfriend. But I can't be and he won't look at me anymore so I walk away, crying, feeling shitty. I don't look up while I'm walking. I keep looking at my feet on my way to fourth period, keep looking at the one loafer that's ripped. I stitched it together with red thread.

That's how cheap they are. I stitched them with my own needle and used red thread because I thought it might look cool.

Hey, Brenna says. She scares me because I wasn't thinking of her. Here she is. I stare at her belly and wipe my eyes. It looks like a joke, like she'll pull a ball out of her belly like a Harlem Globetrotter or something and say, Here. Catch.

She looks me in the eye and her face is frozen and I know that face. It's the fuck you face she gives everybody else. She keeps walking like she's going to pass me by, like she doesn't see me, even though she said hi. But she stops before she gets too far past me. Hey, she says. What's wrong with you?

I talk to her like I always have, like it hasn't been forever since we've talked and like her life isn't ruined. But I don't tell her everything. I just say I'm sad. She stands with one leg stuck out and her books on her hip. Tell me, she says.

I don't know how to tell her. I don't know what's wrong with me. I just feel awful. I say, Mike Abrile can't hang out with me. His parents told him so.

Her lip curls up like she's smelling her own lip and doesn't like what she smells. Mike Abrile? She rubs her big stomach. *That* doofus? She taps her head with her finger like, *Think* Ave. God, Ave, she says. For reals. He looks like Mrs. Potato Head fucked Howdy Doody and had a baby.

Nuh uh, I say. No he doesn't. Plus his mom's a ten.

Worse, even, she says. He looks worse than that.

He's nice Brenn, I say.

She keeps switching her books from one hip to the other so I take them and hold them. Thanks, she says. She puts both hands on her belly and keeps rubbing.

Are you okay?

Yeah, she says. He may be nice but he's a fucking tool, too. Duh. Just hang out with you at school. He's got to get Mommy and

Daddy's permission? Everybody loves his big head only because he's loaded. So what? Let him be all miserable in his big stupid house with his lame parents. They're lucky you were crushing on him. You *would*, she says, and squints at me. She shakes her head but smiles. Besides, I thought you were all in love with Carlos? What happened to that? Los Dodgers and all that crap.

I can't believe I'm smiling now when I was just crying my eyes out like a dummy.

Fuck yeah, Brenna says. Carlos over baby Howdy Potato. Ain't no bout a doubt it.

I feel better, but Brenna is kind of right and kind of wrong, but everything's all mixed up anyway. If I think about Mike's looks, my socks, Brenna talking to me, me being sad and Mike being sad, him putting his hand on top of mine, and Carlos, I feel better. It's better that everything is mixed up and true and not true. I take a deep breath. Okay, I say. I'm better.

Brenna says, Next time, tell that fool that you wish *he* was black! And this is the funniest thing ever. I can see Mike black and I'm tripping. I'm seriously tripping. But it's not a true black, like me. Just paint over his face. Same eyes and same hair. Same everything. Just black. Blonde hair with glitter in it. Blackface. I'm totally drawing that as soon as I can.

What are you laughing at, spaz?

You're crazy, I say. You're out of your mind.

Brenna's eyes get big and she holds on to a doorknob next to her. She has a big smile on her face. Did you feel that?

Yes, I say. Yes! Rad! I love earthquakes. I never get to feel them enough. We can hear people all around us asking, Oh my God. Did you feel that?

Wait a minute, Brenna says. She's standing still but rubbing her belly. Let's see if there's another one. A bigger one. An aftershock.

We stand still. Waiting.

20

I KNOW MY brother won't be able to make it tonight either, but I'm still waiting for him to call me, to tell me so. He drives a UPS truck and takes all the overtime he can get, and he really can't afford the time these days. I stand and stretch after what seems like hours. Waiting for my show and thinking about Keith has brought on a lethargy and stiffness that has manifested itself in a limp when I walk back inside. My legs tingle, trying to remember what they're supposed to do. The air has gotten moist, and it's nearly dark. Lights shine from neighbors' windows like invitations, making me wish, for a moment, that I could just wander into someone else's house and sit down with a cup of tea, rather than attend my own show. But when Owen calls maybe he will have some advice. I pause just inside the door and a photo of my nephew, Dae-Jung, catches my eye. In him, I see mostly Owen, who moved out of the house soon after Brenna got pregnant. He married Mika, diminutive and stunning, and they had one child, Dae-Jung, who was conceived almost ten years after they met. I'm thinking like any family member who inevitably believes their family is uncommon and extraordinary, thinking like a proud aunt, but this child, not a child anymore, is a work of art, a work in progress, so much like a collage I would make of someone who comes from parents such as his, a place such as he does. Greater Los Angeles. I remember meeting Mika vividly. Mika and Owen pull the sliding glass door open and walk into the back yard where Dad is deep-frying catfish. Mom doesn't say a word. Her eyes say everything. Nice to meet you, my father says. He stops poking the fish floating around in the grease to stare at her and shake her hand.

"Hello," Mika says, and nods her head. Her voice is soft, accented. And then, Owen goes inside to get sodas and leaves the door open, screen and all, and my mother doesn't tell him to close it. She just stares at it being left wide open.

"Lord have mercy," my mother whispers. "What *is* she?"

She's Korean and beautiful, and Owen is so happy.

I try to look at Mika without being seen. But she sees me. She smiles at me. She tells me something no one has ever told me in my entire life. Not yet. She says, "You're a cute girl. You should do something with your hair. Put some lipstick on. Earrings. You'd be a fox."

Owen looks at me like I'm a stranger, as if I've wandered in from outdoors and surprised him.

"Foxes are sneaky," Mika says. "That's better than being cute. You think they're doing nothing, you don't even know they are around, and all of a sudden, there they are. Don't forget it," she says. "Foxy Brown," she says, and nods at me like, *You hear me?* She smiles and winks.

Mika's hair is like black water down her back, and her eyes are light brown ovals. She has a huge mouth, and lips that seem to take up most of her face. They shouldn't go with her other features, but they do. When I was younger, I just wanted to sit her down in front of a mirror and color in those lips with all kinds of different colors. When I found out they were pregnant, I imagined that their baby would look like so many different things. Owen has light brown eyes and so does Mika. But that didn't mean the baby's eyes would be the same. Her hair is super straight. Owen's is kinky. What kind of hair would that baby have? What kind of skin, since Mika is barely brown and Owen is dark? Now, looking at Dae-Jung, pausing on his uniquely golden eyes that see the world in his way, I see that Dae-Jung doesn't really look like many different things, even though he is. In one picture at Owen's house, Dae-Jung looks like a character from television, a basketball player in *The White Shadow* maybe, who crashed some Korean people's party.

I keep thinking about those superpowers that Mika bestowed on me so many years ago. But now I'm still limping, hardly the gait of someone who can do something surprising and extraordinary.

"Avie," Massimo calls out, sounding groggy. "What are you doing?"

"I'm here," I say, noticing something on the floor, underneath the table along the wall, where Dae-Jung's picture sits. "I'm coming." I bend down to pick it up and realize it's a baseball card. Signed. Kirk Gibson in a Detroit Tigers uniform. I turn it over and over in my hands wondering where it came from, thinking at first that Massimo meant to give it to me and forgot with all the confusion of the day. But no, he would be sure to give me Dodger memorabilia. He would get the player and the team right even though he doesn't care. He has the resources and is meticulous. Keith, on the other hand, has always improvised, all these years, wrestling with whatever, however he can. He can't make his own opportunities, but he takes them. He is catch as catch can, and somewhere, someone is missing their signed Kirk Gibson card.

❊ ❊ ❊

I'M SUPPOSED TO be drawing apples and oranges in art class but I'm not really into that. I'm just goofing around when I start drawing, thinking of when Brenna and I saw Morrey earlier today. He was wearing dress pants with sneakers and a blazer. And a tie. He looked like a lawyer. And his hair looked better when it was bigger. If you ask me, he should let it grow out a little. Now it's back to being short and he looks like he's got a little peanut head. He's running for treasurer or something. He's so serious all the time, like it's real government. It's not real. It's just school. He gave this speech that we all had to pretend to care about during assembly but he said one thing that was cool. About making the lunch lines the same no matter how you pay. I'll vote for that.

Brenna just stared at him when we saw him.

I waited for Brenna to shred him but she just kept staring.

I think he's kind of cute, Brenna said.

Put your eyes back in your head.

But what about the *clothes*, Brenn? Who wears that?

She pointed at my saddle shoes and argyle socks. Brenna hates these shoes but they're part of my creation for today. Look at you, Happy Days, Brenna said. Who wears *that*? And anyway, he's trying to do something, at least. Look at you, she said to me. What are you trying to do?

I'm copying the front of the *Leave It to Beaver* house perfectly. I used to love that house. I draw it on regular sketch paper with a white pencil. Then I use a flesh-colored crayon to outline Brenna's body. I make her belly really big, like it actually is anyway, and then I draw Morrey in his suit and tie and holding Brenna's hand. He's outlined and colored in brown and he's got a briefcase on the ground next to him, like he's going to work. Then there's a half cat, half dog at Brenna's feet. I take all period to draw it, even though we're only supposed to be drawing some apples and oranges. I get the apples and oranges. Fine. One's orange and one's red. Ms. Joseph comes around checking everybody's work. There aren't that many people in the class because most people want to take home ec or shop so they can make stuff they can actually eat, wear, or use some other kind of way. I almost took home ec so I could make some clothes, but I didn't only want to make clothes. I want to make a whole lot of stuff. And besides, I can always improvise and work with what I've got.

Ms. Joseph stops at my desk. She goes, Avery, apples and oranges. She pushes up her glasses, these Buddy Holly glasses that I loved after I saw the movie. Of course you'd like that dork, Brenna said. She rolled her eyes and said Buddy fucking Holly. Ms. Joseph reminds me of that time. She always dresses like back then, some other place. Forties dresses, fifties dresses, always a dress. But she talks like the kids, even though she has to be up there already. Maybe even twenty-five or thirty. She goes, What happened to the apples and oranges? What is this, even?

I push the paper at her so she can look at it better.

It's Brenna Kiersted, she says. Ms. Joseph pushes up her glasses again and plays with her black bangs that are perfect across her forehead like a comb. The rest is in a bun. I tried to make my hair do that, but it wouldn't. Of course it wouldn't. I don't even know why I tried. All it does is look nappy or straight with nothing else to do but stick out from my head.

Hunh, Ms. Joseph says. She points to Morrey. And who's that?

Morrey.

Hunh, Ms. Joseph says again. That house. It's perfect. So *Leave It to Beaver.*

Totally, I say. That's so cool you see it.

Please, she says. I grew up on that show.

She pushes the paper around on my desk. It's interesting, she says. Subversive.

I've never heard this word before. I stare at my picture. What's subversive?

21

THE PHONE IS ringing again. This will be Dad, double-checking on the time and place. But when I answer, there is nothing but distorted music playing in the background. Some laughing. Somebody says, "Tell that bitch I want a hundred dollars!" and then there is more laughter. Silence. Then Keith's voice. "What's up, Ave."

This simple question confuses me, as if it's a trick question. I don't know what he's asking me, and so I ask the only thing that seems important in the moment. "Where are you?"

"Around."

"But where? Where are you?"

"Why? You scared?" The phone is muffled. Keith says to someone, "Hand me another beer, man."

"What is it that you want?"

Noises and other people's voices come from the phone. High voices and low voices. "I like that painting you had on your wall."

"I know. You took it."

I should be telling Keith that we're not going to stand for him coming into our home as if it is his own. Taking things as if he simply forgot them and is coming back to get them out of our way. I am supposed to be saying, "Stay. Away. Don't come back here. I mean it." I am supposed to be protecting everything that is ours because it is ours. We have worked for it. Massimo has worked for it.

"You took it," I say again.

"I liked it. It's worth some money?"

I have to think about this. I stare at my toenails, thinking. "No. I mean. It's worth something to me, but if you tried to sell it, I just don't know who would pay anything for it. Maybe, I don't know, something like ten dollars."

"*Ten* dollars? Dang." Keith drinks something after that. "Sheeit," he says. "That's *it*?"

"If people knew who we are. If I was a well-known artist, then maybe it would be worth something. That's how it works with art. It only has value if the right people say it has value."

"Yeah, well. Don't nobody know who we are, that's for damn sure."

We both say nothing for a long while. We just trade breath on the phone. I get up and kneel at the edge of the pool just to run my hands in the cool water and am momentarily soothed by the sound of the soft trickle that my fingers make moving back and forth in the blue.

"You can't come back here, taking things. Massimo isn't going to stand for that."

"Man," Keith says. His tone is both slow and impatient. "Fuck Massimo."

"Well then, for me. Just because you're my cousin and this— what do you want me to *do*?" I stand and wipe my wet hand on my leg.

"I want you to give me some money. You got money."

"No, I don't."

"You got money," Keith says again.

"No I don't."

"You got money."

"But it's not *mine*. I make some money, but not a lot. If you walk in here, it looks like I have money, but I don't."

"That's some bullshit, Ave. Niggas always talking about they ain't got money and then look how they living. *Nice* house. I mean shit is nice. What Massimo driving now? That BMW? You got that old-ass looking furniture and I *know* that shit cost something. White folks love that old shit. Expensive for real. Who else we know got that? Name me somebody in the family."

Of course, there is nobody. So I say nothing and I think about how Massimo doesn't quite fit into the group of white folks that Keith is thinking about, even though he is white. But just because somebody looks like something, it doesn't mean they are something. You might be on the same team, Dad always says. Or you might not. "Yeah," Keith says when I'm silent. "Yeah."

"Listen," I say. I look around the room, my eyes landing on things that might not be missed and knowing that's not the way to go, either. "Just let me think. Maybe I can do something. What are you going to do with it anyway?"

"What. The money?"

"No. The painting. I know what you're going to do with the money."

"Yeah. You always know everything, don't you?"

"No, I don't," I say. "I don't." But he has already hung up on me, and I still don't know where he is.

I meant to ask him something about the painting he took. What did he think of it? He thought it was valuable. But did he think it was valuable because I had it? Valuable because I did it? Valuable because it was us? Or valuable because it was a portrait of him, a person hanging up on a wall, someone you have to look at because there he is, right in front of you, staring you in the eyes.

✳ ✳ ✳

DAD SAYS I can't major in art. I have to major in business. He tells me, again: I'm the first woman in our family, ever, to go to college, etc., and blah, blah. And I'm not going to waste it on crayons and whatever else I'm supposed to be doing, he says. An education is invaluable, he says. How are you supposed to get ahead, he asks me. Do it on the side, he says, but not for real. So that's how I do art. On the side. I sketch and draw and think about what I would say if I could say it through art, write some ideas down. And then I just put it all away.

But at least I get to go to the school I want. I win that fight. They wanted me to stay home and go to the junior college up the street. But I never ever wanted to do that. I don't want to stay in the same place all the time.

I don't know why you stuck on leaving the house, Mom says. USC ain't but thirty minutes from here. May as well stay.

They are only thinking about the money. Me too. I did it all by myself. A gazillion pages of application. Filled out papers for financial aid. I have student loans and a couple of grants and I'm going to get a job on campus. I don't know what kind of job. Anything. I don't care. I'm going.

Mom watches me fold the box flaps over each other. I walked down to Stater Brothers and took them from the back where they throw them away after they're done. My stuff's in a Pampers box, a Gerber baby food box, and a Chef Boyardee box. I only have three boxes because it's not like I have a ton of stuff. Three pair of shoes. Some clothes. Some sheets and a blanket and a pillow.

You got everything? Mom says. She stands over my boxes and looks down at them. She's not looking at me. Dad is here. He doesn't live with us anymore. He's got this small apartment with no furniture, in another neighborhood. Never finished school. He had to quit a year after he started because of the money. He honks the horn one time, real short, so he doesn't make a lot of noise. I can hear the car, though. So loud. Chug, chug, chug. Loud. Like the Beverly Hillbillies' car. Embarrassing.

Go on then, Mom says. She pats me on the shoulder. Hard. She puts her hand down, but then pats me again. She says, You got everything?

I look around the house and I feel like memorizing everything. I didn't know that I would want to do this. I look at our round glass kitchen table with the white place mats with orange flowers. I look at our green fridge and I see Keith standing next to it, leaning on it. I look at the stove and remember how Mom used to keep a hot comb on it, to straighten my hair. She wanted my hair so straight for school. I remember that. She wanted my hair to be perfect. She dressed me in that yellow baby doll dress. The sliding glass door is open and some warm air is coming through. I can feel it. I'm thinking, Does that warm air feel as good to you Mom like it does to me? I'm thinking, I hope that air feels good to Mom too.

She says, You crying?

I shake my head.

Ain't no need of you crying, Mom says. You going now.

I'm not crying, I say. I pick up the Pampers box. I'm not crying. I'll be back in a couple of weeks. It's just a half hour away in the car and an hour on the bus. I'll see you then.

Mom stacks the two boxes I have left. She bends down and picks them up. I don't know how she can pick up all that weight. Those boxes are heavy. Mom, I say, put those down. Those are heavy. I'll come back for them. It's my stuff anyway. I'll carry it. But she doesn't listen to me. She says, Open the door. I got it. It ain't all that heavy.

COLLEGE IS GOING to be awesome. If it would just start. Dad is worried about me, I can tell. He's gearing up for a lecture. He's worried because I'm seventeen and a freshman, worried about my corrupted youth, but I'm going to turn eighteen in a month anyway. We're in front of the dorm, sitting in the car. But I want to get out of the car. I don't want people to see me sitting in this car, even though they don't know who I am. And there are so many people out there with all of their stuff. All these new people and I can't wait to just get out of the car and start. Nobody knows anything about me so I can start over. I'm going to be a brand-new person.

Dad turns off the car. I put my hand on the handle and open the door.

Wait a minute, Dad says. I want to talk to you for a minute.

Oh. No.

Listen, he says. I want you to understand something.

God! I understand! He always thinks I don't understand! What am I supposed to understand, exactly? I'm going to college. That's all I know. I want to get out of the car.

Dad pulls on his cap and then he rubs his hands together. Listen, he says. There's going to be a lot of stuff for you to get into if you're not careful. You need to be careful.

I stare ahead and want to snap my fingers like Samantha on *Bewitched* so I can get out of here.

A lot of drugs. Boys. Stuff you don't have no business doing.

He turns his head but not his body and looks at me. Then he turns back to stare in front of him. You need to keep your head in them books and you need to get a job.

I know, I say. I already know about the job.

In a week, he says. You need to be working in a week.

A *week*?

Yeah, Dad says. In a week.

I already have to think about work. I can't believe it.

This is really something, Dad says. Do you know that? Do you know where you are? And then he starts talking, again, about how I have this chance and how I should do it right because not everybody gets this kind of chance to go to school. A good school. Do you know that 80th Street just a ways up the road? Just a few minutes away? But this is a different world, Dad says.

But why should I have to be thinking about all of this now?

I tell Dad. I shouldn't have to think about all of this now.

Dad takes his cap off his head. Scratches his scalp and then puts it back on. He says, You ain't got to think about it. You right. Until you have to think about it. Mess up and end up like folks we know. Then you gone be thinking about it all of a sudden.

I should go, I say.

Who you living with anyway, he says.

Anika something. That's all I know.

She white?

No. She's black. They put us together to ease the transition, the letter said. I roll my eyes. But Dad says, No. That's good. Nothing but white kids here, seem like. Good to be living with a black girl. Y'all got more in common.

Yeah, I say. That's true, I guess.

All right then, Dad says.

I push open the door. Dad gets out and we stack all my boxes on the street. I pick up one and wait for Dad to pick up the other two. I wait and he leans against the car. Watching me.

Aren't you going to get those, Dad?

He crosses his arms over his chest. No, he says. You can handle it. I'll wait by the car. I'm not parked right and I don't need no ticket. It'll just take you two trips, that's all.

It's like ninety degrees and these boxes are heavy all by myself. I totally need help but he just watches me. I stack two boxes so I can get it done faster, but when I try to lift them, one falls and my pillow drops on the ground.

Shoot. I say. These are heavy, Dad.

You good, he says. You got it.

There are two beds in the room and I don't know what one to choose. I don't think it's fair to just grab something before somebody else gets a chance at it. So I wait.

Anika bursts into the room. She explodes into it. Her mom's behind her and they're like twins. Long black hair and expensive-looking clothes. Anika is wearing Calvins and her mom is wearing heels. *Heels.* These black pumps with black slacks and a white shirt with pearls *and* a gold chain, and I don't even know what to think about the pearls and the gold chain being together. I'm sitting on one of the beds when they come in and my boxes are in the middle of the room because I don't know where to put them.

Hey! Anika says. She sticks her hand out hard like she's going to punch me in the stomach. And then her mom is shaking my hand and asking me where I'm from and what my parents do, but her face is falling the more I keep talking. She says, Is that all you have? She points at my boxes. Yes ma'am I say. Ma'am? she says. How polite. Like I've said something that's surprising. She says, That's where you want to be? I shrug. I just sat here. I didn't pick.

Well, she says. Okay.

I want that one, Anika says. She points at the bed I'm sitting on. I really don't care which one she takes. She and her mom pull her luggage over. Real luggage. Leather with gold letters that have Vs with Ls going through them. I like Anika's shirt. It's striped, like a sailor's shirt. And then, just when I'm getting used to them, her father comes in carrying a TV. A *television.*

Wow, I say. That's great. I didn't think I was going to have a television at school. Man, I'm so happy about the television I can't wait to plug it in. Can we plug it in? We can plug it in here. I slap my hand down on the desk. It runs across the room, from Anika's end to mine. We could put it exactly in the middle.

In a minute, Anika says. We haven't brought up all my stuff yet.

Oh, I say. Okay.

I could be watching TV while they keep bringing up stuff. I don't see why I have to wait. They take like five trips and the room is full of all her stuff. Her brand-new word processor. All of her clothes. All of her shoes. A bookshelf. A plastic bin full of face and hair stuff. A guitar. A bike. They get it all in the room. The last trip up it's just her and her dad and he's got car keys in his hand and an envelope.

KiKi, he says. He looks at her, smiling. Guess what? You should have been paying better attention. You got a ticket. He makes a tsk, tsk sound and shakes his head. He puts the keys in her hand. It's locked now but you're going to have to move it. He leans against the wall with his arms folded and his loafers crossed over each other. Weird. He's not wearing any socks. Do people with money not wear socks with their shoes?

Shit, she says. How much?

Shit, in front of her Dad. Like Brenna would do.

Twenty-five bucks, her dad says. He waves it in front of her and puts it in his pocket. You should have gotten the pass from parking, he says. Your mother and I did.

Pass? What pass? Me and Dad didn't know about the pass. He was waiting outside for nothing.

They hug her goodbye and tell her to call if she needs anything. Anything at all.

Bye, Avery, her mother says, smiling. Her father nods at me with a smile on his face, and then they're gone.

Anika starts unpacking her stuff. She plugs in and turns on the radio. She starts singing "Raspberry Beret" really loud. I'm thinking, If I had her voice I wouldn't sing that loud. I'm thinking, If she plugs in the radio, maybe she'll plug in the TV, but she doesn't and I'm not going to ask again. You watch. I'm not going to.

She's weird anyway. She doesn't hardly even talk to me. She's all into her stuff. She acts like she doesn't want to talk to me. She's not mean. She's just ignoring me.

I try to talk to her. I say, Where are you from? I have to practically scream it over Whitney Houston singing that crappy song about saving all her love for some dude. It's the worst. And the videos. She's like a black Barbie. How does she keep that up?

Baldwin Hills! Anika says. She's got a comforter in her hands and she lifts it high so that it spreads out and lands on her bed big and puffy like a cloud. It looks so soft, I want to just flop onto her bed and roll around in it. I'm sitting on my blue blanket and it's okay, but I know it doesn't feel like that comforter looks.

Where's that? I say. Baldwin Hills.

You know, she says, looking at me like I'm trying to be stupid. L.A. It's in L.A.

And I guess I've heard of it. Or if I've heard of it I haven't thought about it. Where it is and who lives there. But now I know who lives there, who's been living there while I've been living at all these other places. 80th and Vermont, West Covina.

Later that night I call everybody. I call Brenna first and tell her everything. About all Anika's stuff. About the car.

What a bitch, Brenna says.

No, I say. No. She's just weird.

Yeah, Brenna says. Okay. Right.

Baldwin Hills, Dad says. They got some money over there. That's the kind of black folks go to USC.

And me, I say, and he laughs on the other end of the phone.

That's right, Ave, Dad says. And you. She might be ahead of the game, but you right behind her. You about to catch up.

22

I HAVE ALREADY been to the space that will hold my art this evening. I went this morning. Installed four pieces. I am just one of four artists in the show, Here Is Elsewhere. Massimo is in the kitchen, on his second espresso, listening to Lou Rawls live, singing about Tobacco Road. It's his favorite Lou Rawls. Listen to how he's talking to us at the beginning, Massimo always says. He loves the part where Lou Rawls says he left Chicago and then went out West, where it's the best. Me too. I always listen for the applause and cheers when he says that, wishing I could be in the middle of it all. "Avery," Massimo calls out now. "Do you want another espresso? It will wake you up."

I am already dressed for this evening. I want to be myself, so nothing fancy. I ditched my plans. No desperate statements of my worth and importance through bold jewelry and arch, sharp clothing. No black dress. Instead, jeans. A white T-shirt. A pair of blue Vans that are the same blue of the imitation Vans I wore in junior high school. In the kitchen, I reach for my espresso, and Massimo looks me up and down. "That is all? You look like a typical American boy. A very lovely boy."

The phone rings and when Massimo answers, I know he's talking to my brother. "Hey man," Massimo says. "What's happening? For real? Aw, Bro. Avery is going to be disappointed." He sounds ridiculous, but this is how they have always spoken to each other. Massimo thought that this was how he should speak to

Owen, and because Owen found it amusing that an Italian spoke this way, Massimo kept doing it. "Stop it," I'd say, when it seemed to become less a joke and more their lingua franca. But it somehow made them both more comfortable, that Massimo changed his voice. Massimo did not feel so much the foreigner—to either one of them—when he spoke to my brother in his language.

"Later, man," Massimo says now, and hands the phone to me. "You can't come?"

"Can't make that drive, Sis. If I come, I'ma have to just turn around and come right back, and I only have one day off before I have to go to work on Monday."

"All right," I say. "I'm disappointed but I understand. Next time."

"Dae-Jung coming, though."

"What? He doesn't even have a car. How's he getting here?"

"How you think? How every other person without a car gets around. The bus. And his skateboard. What's up with these kids and they skateboards now? When I was his age, I already had a car. *That I bought*. It was a jacked-up Pinto, but I had my own shit."

Dae-Jung is not the child my brother imagined he would have. Weird, in Owen's eyes. Father and son look a great deal alike in the way they walk, their hair texture, and their skin color, younger and older versions of the same man. "That boy is Owen's picture," my mother loves to say. But that's how pictures can be deceiving, as well as can be the flesh-and-blood person standing in front of you, if you don't have the imagination to really see what you're looking at. I love Dae-Jung for being impossible to pin down. He's a construction of so many things, which has nothing to do with what he looks like, but what he lives. "Leave him alone. Everybody doesn't have to get stuff all the time."

"Yeah, all right. You and Massimo can give up all your shit then."

I almost say, "You can have it," but Owen would know that I don't mean it, that I only mean it in this moment but will likely change my mind in the next moment. And anyway, if I were to say, "Take it. Take it all," Owen would say, "I don't need you to give me nothing. I got my own." Mainly, he's worried about his boy. He wants him to grow up to be respectable, line his pockets with money. Like Dad, he believes it has to happen in that order. Somebody in this family needs to make some money, Owen's always saying, with accusation, I think. It was supposed to be me. "Dae-Jung." I say. "How's he getting back to West Covina? Back home from L.A.?"

"I don't know," Owen says. "Bus. Like he's getting down there. You make it sound like a nigga got to travel a thousand miles by stagecoach or mule or some shit."

But I don't like the idea of it. It will be nighttime. It will be late. I think about him at some bus stop, waiting and waiting for a bus that will come later than the schedule promises. "He'll stay here with Massimo and me."

"I don't care. Maybe try and teach him something while you got him. Tell him to pull up those damn pants. Tell him to cut his hair, walking around with a afro looking crazy. He got two tattoos, now. I tell you that?"

"What are they of?"

"Please. I don't even know. Some Korean mess his mother taught him."

"God. You sound like Dad, complaining about his clothes, his looks. You want him to wear a suit and tie all the time?"

"It'd be better than what he's looking like now. And did I tell you? He surfing now."

"*Surfing*?"

"A black surfer," Owen says, and I can just see him shaking his head as though he's at a loss as to where to go for help with such a problem. "He started taking the bus to Huntingon Beach and learned how to do it."

I imagine Dae-Jung on a surfboard, riding high on a wave, beads of water nestled in his tight kinks like diamonds in a black crown. "Wow. Surfing. That's really something." Next to me is a pencil and a receipt from groceries that Massimo has left on the table. I turn it over on the blank side and with my free hand start sketching something of what I imagine. I envy this figure commanding the high precipice of a big gray wave, and yet I would never even try. "There are other black surfers, though. Not just Dae-Jung."

"And I bet they're laying on their mama and daddy's couches, too." Owen yawns in my ear and that tells me that he's getting off the phone. "He'll be out of the house in two years and then I don't care. If he puts a bone in his nose, cool. Long as I don't have to be paying for his grown ass." But he's lying, my brother. He and Mika will help in some way because they have a little bit of money. Not a lot, but more than Mom and Dad had.

When I hang up, Massimo says, "Dae-Jung? I like Dae-Jung."

"Yes. Just for the night."

"You didn't tell Owen about Keith," Massimo says, pulling on the gray stubble of his beard.

"No. Since he's not coming, I don't want him to worry."

"I hope you know what you are doing."

I go to the cabinet and pull out a package of strawberry Pop-Tarts to eat with my espresso.

"Really?" Massimo is plaintive. "We have so many good things to eat and you decide to open a plastic wrapper to eat the plastic that is inside?" He watches me break the Pop-Tart into four pieces and dip it in my espresso. "And you don't even heat it up. You are supposed to toast it," he says, suddenly the Pop-Tart purist.

I chew and stare at him, grinning. He throws an orange kitchen towel over his shoulder and wipes his hands on it. "You are ridiculous," he says with uncharacteristic admiration. He will give in and let me and my tragic food choices be. "My beautiful boy eating your 7-Eleven trash. You know what you look like? You look like a delinquent hoodlum."

"That's redundant, Massimo. A delinquent is a hoodlum."

"No it's not. A hoodlum is more dangerous, no?"

This question, I have to think about. "I suppose it depends on what you've done."

On the counter in front of me is a Manny Ramirez bobble-head that Massimo somehow acquired for me because a few years back, I had missed Manny Ramirez bobblehead day at Dodger Stadium. That day he hit pinch hit a grand slam. Now, Manny taunts me with his wagging head, as if to say, *Now what? What do you think of me now?* I had whined while walking around the house. "I wanted a Manny Ramirez bobblehead," I had repeated mournfully. How did I not get tickets for that game? For seats in Mannywood? And one day, there was Manny, in my kitchen, nodding his head at me in affirmation, Massimo saying, "Now you will stop whining, yes?" But soon after, there was a mess with Manny. Cheating. Steroids and laziness, letting what should have been easy fly balls land in front of him. The outrage of it all. For that kind of money? Who did he think he was? The disappointment in the multimillion-dollar cheater. With women's fertility drugs, no less. That was particularly confusing, this unlikely intrusion of women's wombs into the world of baseball.

"Hello? What are you thinking?" Massimo waves a palm in front of me. "You are still in love with that silly toy," he says, and it sounds like see-ly. "And that cheater. How much you care about that silly game." He turns to load the dishwasher, clanking things loudly. I almost get into our tired argument, about how much he loves soccer, and why is that more reasonable, but we never get anywhere with that. He loops the dishrag through the oven handle, and looks around his clean kitchen. More than anything, he loves this kitchen, its smooth surfaces, the stainless steel, the myriad colorful dishes that lend an air of festivity, no matter how dark the day. And the windows. Large windows that bathe everything in golden light. I love this kitchen too, whereas I did not love the kitchen I grew up with, after a while. I saw better kitchens in magazines and on television, and so the kitchen I grew up in became just a place where dishes got washed and where food was boiled and fried and where hair got pressed with hot combs. I wonder about Manny Ramirez's childhood kitchen in the Dominican Republic, wonder about how far he traveled away from this kitchen to play ball in America. Of course, one should not cheat. One should simply be good at what one does. The best. But what if, when he arrived to the game, everyone was already playing it differently, and he was simply playing the game in this new and different way that everyone else was playing it? But the outrage. The letters in the *Los Angeles Times* sports section. It was like people taking to the streets with torches, rope, and pitchforks. I had said this to my father. When the news broke, I was so disappointed in Manny, but somehow, saw his side. "Dad," I had said. "None of it's fair. Manny was just the one who got caught." "True," he had said. "But you don't cheat. Ever. Just because everybody else is doing it? That's the last thing the Dodgers got to worry about, anyway," he had said. "Those folks that own them are getting a divorce, and look at all the money they got that they ain't put back into the game. They are *not* baseball people. They just rich folks that bought themselves a team. Anybody that got money can buy something, but do they deserve it? How hard they working for it? What they doing with all that money, charging the people fifteen dollars to park and fifteen dollars for beer and they worth 835 million? How two people have 835 million? *Two. People*," he said, like curse words. At the time, I was only half listening. It seemed like he was getting off topic, since I was talking about Manny getting a lot of money that people didn't think he deserved.

But anyway, maybe none of that matters now. That was then. This is now. The McCourts are done, and there will be a brand-new ball game.

Massimo thumps me on the head. "I have been talking to you," he says. "Are you listening?"

❋ ❋ ❋

I'M HAPPY THAT I got a job. So glad I get to say Yes when Dad asks me for the fiftieth time have I gotten a job yet. School starts Monday. It's Friday. I got a job in a week, as ordered. I'm just answering phones in the art department, but still. The woman who interviewed me said I had a nice voice. She said I spoke clearly and articulately. When she says this, it makes me want to speak even more perfectly. She says this like it's amazing that I speak so well. The School of Fine Arts makes me happy. Just being here. In the main office, there are four walls and they all have prints of different paintings on them, Picasso, Monet, Dali, Warhol. Kids come in and they look different from the rest of the kids on campus. Sloppy, but cool. This one guy wears holey jeans covered in paint and a T-shirt with a tie. Fifties dresses that June Cleaver wore with pumps, this one girl wears with white Converse and tube socks. She looks crazy. It's pretty rad, actually. But the best is this black girl with a mohawk. A mohawk. Her head is completely shaved on the sides and then it's crazy spiky down the middle of her head, like seven inches high. I have never, ever seen a black girl like this before.

When I'm done with work, I like to walk through the student gallery. There's a nice painting on the wall. A black woman with a huge afro that has an eye in it. I keep stepping to the side and all these other positions, but the eye always follows me. Even when I'm almost out of the building.

When I'm done walking through the gallery, I'm in my own dream world, thinking about how pretty the campus is, all the brick and fountains and gargoyles, Tommy Trojan glistening in the sun, the bell tower's ringing like I think it would sound in a beautiful old church in Europe, when somebody talks to me.

Excuse me, miss, this voice says. But I'm not really paying attention.

Have you ever considered a MasterCard or a Visa? I stare at the person talking to me. A guy dressed nice in khakis and a white dress shirt. His hair is cut neatly and his ears stick out a little bit, all shiny and pink in the sun. His hair is blonde and curly, but the curls are lying down in waves. I keep my hands down at my side because I imagine myself doing something crazy like running my fingers through his hair.

Do you have to pay for it? The Visa or the MasterCard?

No. He smiles and he has deep dimples in his cheeks. Here, he says. Look. He holds up a paper. This is the application form and all you have to do is fill it out. Please, he says. Take a look.

I read it and it's easy to fill out and everybody around me, all these other kids, are filling out applications too. One question on the form is about my job and how much money I make.

Excuse me? Sir?

He smiles at me some more. Sir? We're practically the same age he says, and squints at me. You don't call your boyfriend Sir, do you? He laughs and winks at me.

That makes me nervous and I drop the pen he gave me to fill out the application. I take a deep breath. Um, I make nine dollars an hour at my work-study job answering phones. Is that enough?

You go here, don't you? He's not smiling as big when he asks me this, like he's worried about it.

Yeah, I say. Yes. I attend USC.

Then that's enough, he says.

I finish filling it out. I'm going to get a Visa and a MasterCard, I decide. Next to the Visa and MasterCard table is the American Express table. When I look at the application, the guy working that table smiles at me too. He's dressed exactly the same as the guy I just talked to. He says to somebody already filling out an application, Would you please step aside so this young lady can fill out her application?

So I do.

I DON'T KNOW where Anika is, and I want to watch her TV. Game six. National League Championship. They have to pull this one out or else it's over and St. Louis clinches it.

Usually, I only watch Anika's TV when she's here. What's hers is hers and what's mine is hers. It's not like she's dying for anything I have, but if she needs toothpaste because she's out, she uses mine like it's hers. But I have to ask to watch her television. I think about how stupid she's being and I think about how this is the last game of the series and then I turn on the game. It's the worst. I mean close. Middle of the seventh and Dodgers are tied with St. Louis four and four. I'm chewing on my nails. What are they *doing*? You guys! Pull it together!

Anika walks in carrying a stack of books and throws them on her bed without looking at me, without even Hi, and I know before she says anything that she's pissed about the television. I say, I hope you don't mind, but it's the last game of the Championship Series. You want to watch?

She kicks off her shoes and slips into her flip-flops. Anika takes her time answering me. My eyes go back and forth from the game to Anika. Lasorda's called in Niedenfuer because St. Louis has scored two singles already. Come on you guys. Come *on*. Where's your *heart*?

I want to watch something else, Anika says, and I look at her like she's high. I mean, is she serious? What else is there to watch?

Anika. This. Is. The. Last. Game. Of. The. Series.

She shrugs and shakes her head and looks around the room. When she does this, it looks like she's trying to tell me she's deaf and can't hear or something.

I don't want to fight about this. I hate fighting. It makes me sick, people screaming at each other. Hitting each other. Even just the yelling. And when I'm really mad, I'm sick. It's like I can't handle fighting or being real mad. And besides, there's got to be a way that we can both get our way.

Ozzie Smith is up and he sent the ball into the seats in the last game that Niedenfuer pitched, so Niedenfuers got to be real careful about what he throws.

Seriously, Anika says. She puts her hand on the knob and I don't even think about it. I push her hand away and stand up. Wait a minute. God. This is a crucial pitch, I say, and just then I hear the crowd roar and I see Ozzie Smith rounding second. Shit. It's a triple. A *triple*.

Anika says, It's *my* television.

But you don't understand how important this game is! I throw up my hands because I don't even know what else to do.

I *so* don't care, she says and turns the TV toward her. I turn it back to me.

And then she pushes me.

I forget about baseball. My mind is working very slowly. I can hit her. I can slap her. I can push her back. But then it will turn into a real fight and I will miss the game. I want to punch her face in for making me miss the game. From far away Vin Scully is saying that Niedenfuer has struck out Jack Clark to end the threat. All the things I want to say, I don't say. You fucking bitch. You cuntress. That's what the girls are always saying to each other. You idiot. Who turns off a championship game in the middle of a tie? I hold my hands down close to my sides. I want to bring them up to fight her so bad. Yank a big chunk of that straight hair out of her head. But none of that is really going to help me see the rest of the game. I say, Don't you ever touch me again or I will punch you in the face. I will. I swear. I can tell she doesn't believe me, though. She just turns up her lip like something smells bad. She pulls the TV closer to her and sits on the edge of her bed, changing channels. I feel like a scream is right behind my eyes, my nose, inside my mouth. There is nowhere else to go because I don't know anyone else who would be watching the game. So I sit on my bed and draw. I draw until I can't feel the screams behind my eyes and nose and mouth. I draw the Dodgers logo, the L going through the A. I draw a television around it, so that the letters are in the TV. Then I draw all kinds of TVs around that big one, medium ones and small ones. Old-fashioned huge ones that are solid pieces of furniture, big as a table or bookshelf. My neighbor Joan had one of those a long time ago. I put a smaller, more modern television on top of the old big one and I draw images inside of those. One is just the outline of a staircase slanting down with six kids standing, one on each stair, in line, biggest to smallest. Another is a girl on a surfboard with her ponytail flying out behind her. I draw a bubble coming out of her mouth with the words Moondoggie! Another one has a covered wagon and horses. There's no people in it, only a bubble with the word Pa! And more televisions after that so that the whole page is crowded with televisions, except I keep a space on the very bottom. On the bottom, I draw a baseball player with the number 34, his leg is up and his eyes are rolled up like Valenzuela always does, like he's looking up at heaven, but in this drawing, he's looking up at all those TVs. It takes me two hours to do all this. But I don't even know how all the time has passed. I don't even feel like I'm on my bed, in a dorm, across from someone I wanted to smash in the face. I didn't even hear the television this whole time, I swear. And when did Anika turn it off? She's listening to the radio now, doing her homework. Two hours. That's what my Mickey Mouse watch says. The game is over then. I take the phone off the desk and pull the extension cord all the way across the room and out the door. I close the door behind me and sit in the hallway and call my dad.

Someone in a room somewhere is saying, Oh. My. God. No fucking way, dude. Random!

Hello?

Dad, I say. Who won?

You didn't watch the game?

No. Not all of it.

Why not?

Anika wanted to watch something else. It's her TV. So.

Yeah, Dad says. Her TV.

Who won the game?

You sound tired. You tired?

No. I'm not tired. I pull on the phone cord to straighten all the tight curls and then I watch it spring back.

She ought to let you watch that game. You not asking her all the time, are you?

No. I never, ever do. That's the thing. She makes me sick.

Uh huh. Stay in school, you can buy all the TVs you want. Won't need to ask nobody.

They lost, didn't they?

Yeah. Jack Clark hit a home run off of Niedenfuer.

Dang.

All you can do is start thinking about next season, now. That's the end of that.

Anika cracks open the door. She needs to use the phone. I make her wait for two seconds before I let her know I'm going to get off. Now I know something I never knew before. There are some people who have never had to wait. Or even ask. Like Anika. It makes you an asshole. A bitch, like Brenna said. I'm getting tired of always asking and waiting. I say, I have to go, Dad.

All right then, he says. Hey. In two days you gone be eighteen years old. You a old woman now.

That makes me laugh. No, I say. I'm not old yet. Wait till I'm forty. That's going to be old. Old and wise.

If you lucky, Dad says. If you lucky.

So far, I say. But I don't even know if I've been lucky or not.

Dad says, Next season. They'll be all right next season. That's the beginning of something new.

All right, Dad. Next season, I say. And I believe it.

THESE GIRLS ACROSS the hallway, I think I like them. I hang out with them lately in the dorm. One is the daughter of some senator in Virginia. Her name is Adelaide Randolph. She's tall and skinny like all the girls who still call themselves cows even though I'm like thirty pounds heavier than they are. Adelaide has brown hair and green cat eyes. Long nails with French tips. She dresses like Michael Jackson. Completely. The black hat, the black and red leather jacket. The black pants white socks black loafers. She even has the glove. Crazy. And she pulls it off, that's the thing. I'd look like I was smoking something if I walked around USC like that. Even though I'm the black one, she totally owns the look. Some people can get away with anything.

Her roommate is this super cool girl named Lavendar. Her actual name. Dar for short. But everybody calls her Nurse, because of her major. Her parents were hippies or something, and now they're loaded and living in Berkeley. Nurse always wears her hair in two long braids and a baseball cap. San Francisco Giants. Jesus. But I like Nurse, so we don't talk about baseball.

It's Spring Break and they want me to go to Palm Springs with them. I don't have any money, though.

You got credit cards, don't you? Nurse says.

Yeah, Adelaide says. I got my Dad's Amex, so we're totally there. You're going. Don't *even*.

So I'm going to Palm Springs with them.

I can't believe you've never been to Palm Springs, Adelaide

keeps saying. I'm not even from here and I've been like, *so* many times.

I know, I say. I don't know.

Adelaide drives her black Jag and plays Michael Jackson over and over again. All Michael. "Thriller." "We Are the World." "Pretty Young Thing."

Ugh, Nurse says. Something else, please, but Adelaide says, My car, dude. Shut the fuck up. She turns up the music and then yells, We're going to scam on some dudes! Two for me, one for you, Nurse.

Hey, I say. What about me? I'm sitting in the back seat and I pat Adelaide on the back of her head.

We'll see if there's some hot brothers for you in Palm Springs, Virgin. She always calls me that because she thinks it's funny. She keeps saying, There is no Santa Claus, Virgin. Or Easter Bunny or Tooth Fairy. That's what holding out's like. Like you're waiting for one of those lame things to come along and make you happy.

Yeah, Nurse says. Her foot is sticking out the window. She moves her feet to "Beat It" and points her big toe every time on the word It. After a while, nobody talks anymore and we just look out the window. I have never seen this before. Not even on TV, that I can remember. Miles and miles of sand and dirt and weeds and mountains the color of three different kinds of mustard. Dark yellow, almost brown, bright yellow like French's mustard, and a yellow with lavender going straight through it. The rocks on the hills look like Mars and the windmills look like giant white men with the arms waving at me like crazy. Over here. Over here.

I want to get out of this car and run as fast as I can, up the mountains. The sky is blue, like swimming pool water, and the air is hot in our faces and smells good like a shirt that just came out of the dryer, warm and soft against my cheek. And the light. How to explain the light on the mountains? We are still in

California, but the light doesn't seem real, it feels like a different planet, Mars on a movie set, spotlights on the rocks, ten times stronger than the sun. Like somebody is yelling Action, flashing gold all around. How would I make this color if I tried? This is Palm Springs, California.

Before we get to the hotel, Adelaide stops at a liquor store so we can get some alcohol with her fake ID. She comes to the counter with vodka and beer and Bartles and Jaymes peach wine coolers for me because that's the only thing I can think of. I don't drink. But I will this week. Mom and Dad don't have to know about it. Adelaide says, Get this, will you? I'll get the next round.

Uh, I say. Sure. But when the sunburned guy at the cash register adds it all up, it's like thirty bucks, which seems like a lot of money to me. Plus the hotel that we're going to have to split for 150 bucks apiece. Miss? the guy says. And I guess it's okay, since Adelaide and Nurse will get some of the other stuff. Adelaide uses her dad's credit card, and Nurse doesn't have to work because her parents pay for everything, but still.

When we get to the hotel, it's all totally worth it. Gorgeous. A view of the hills and green all around the pool with huge palm trees that look like they're sparkling whenever there's a breeze. White deck chairs are on all four sides of the pool and there are four bungalows facing each other. Sliding glass doors let us out to the pool and first thing, Adelaide and Nurse are practically naked. Bikinis, even though they're supposed to be cows. I wear shorts and a long white T-shirt that covers the shorts. Grandma, Nurse says. Shit. You don't have a swimsuit?

Damn. Wear some more clothes, Laura Ingalls, Adelaide says. Where's your fucking bonnet?

No, I say. No swimsuit. Not since the fifth grade.

But don't you want to get in the water? Nurse says.

Yeah, Adelaide says.

No. I'm not getting in the water. I don't really like it, I say. Why do they like the water so much? It's good if it's hot but after that. But they won't shut up about it. Even if I wanted to, there's my hair. If it gets wet I have to put all the Jheri Curl spray in it to moisturize it all over again, and I just don't want to be thinking of hair. So I just tune them out. I put on my Walkman headphones and listen to Squeeze, humming, Tempted by the fruit of another, tempted but the truth is discovered, feeling the hot air blow across my body like somebody's hot breath in my face and on my neck and across my legs. I close my eyes and dream and sweat runs down the sides of my face and into my T-shirt. I think, I am on Spring Break in Palm Springs, like a regular college girl. The heat takes me in and out of sleep. I keep my eyes shut, seeing the black, the red of my eyelids, smears of yellow, music in my ears, feeling like rubber from the vodka and wine coolers. It seems like hours and hours pass. And then, my eyelids go completely black. Someone is blocking the sun.

Ladies, this guy says. He's got two beers in his hands. Coronas with lime. He holds them out to Nurse and Adelaide. They look at each other and roll their eyes. But if they don't want the beer, I'll take it. I'll take a beer from this guy.

My name is Tad, he says. He puts the beer down on the pavement and crouches down. He balances himself perfectly on his feet, his hands on his knees. His hair is sticking straight up and is white in places, like he streaked it. Or the sun bleached it. His face is peeling a little bit, but he still looks good to me, even though his eyes are covered by Ray-Bans. But then he pushes them up over his head. His eyes are gray and his eyebrows are bleached too. He looks like he surfs, like you'd see him in a Gidget movie. Some '50s guy, that's what he looks like.

He goes, You guys party?

No, Nurse says. We don't.

Look at me, I'm thinking. Look at me. Look at me. Ask.

I'll just leave these here, then, Tad says. Just in case.

Uh huh, Nurse says.

Thanks, Adelaide says, and flicks her hand at his back when he turns away. Like, Shoo. You bother me.

You guys, I say. You guys are cold. Why'd you shine him like that?

He talked to us wearing sunglasses, Adelaide says. I couldn't even see his face at first. She sits up and splits her ponytail in two pieces to tighten the rubber band. She lies back down. She says, I'm supposed to take a beer from some dude who doesn't even know that he's supposed to take off his sunglasses when he's talking to people? Please. And then he brings two beers? There's three of us. Asshole. No class whatsoever.

He was cute, though, Nurse says. She shields her eyes and looks over at the group of people he's with. All dudes.

Yeah, I say. I liked his eyes.

Adelaide sits up again and looks at me. She gets up and stretches and the lines from the chair make a pattern all over her butt and back. She's wearing a black bikini that's sagging in the ass. But she won't eat anything. Ever. She puts her hands on her hips and points her chin at Tad's group. Too bad they don't have any brothers for you, Ave. We need to find you a brother on this trip. If I was a black dude, I would totally go for you.

Why?

Because, Adelaide says. She squirts some Bain de Soleil in her hands and rubs it all over her stomach and legs. She pulls her sunglasses down over her face and I can't see her eyes. She says, You're cute. Nice eyes. Nice smile. Totally mellow. She stops talking and then she says, You know.

But I don't know. Only black guys like nice smiles and nice eyes and mellow girls? I drink some more vodka and orange juice.

Another cooler. I keep my sunglasses on and look at everybody lying around and swimming and drinking. There are no black guys. There are no black girls. There's only me.

I just keep sleeping and drinking and listening to music. Joy Division, The Smiths, Elvis Costello, Nik Kershaw. Time goes by fast and it goes by slow. The sun is going down and there's the breeze and I want to stay out here all night. I can just stay out here in this chair.

But there aren't that many people out anymore. The ones out here are quiet and cooling off from cooking all day. And where are Nurse and Adelaide? Nothing in their chairs but damp towels, like they used to be there but melted away. Evaporated. Like I imagined them. Imaginary friends, I say, laughing. That's so funny. I get up and get another wine cooler out of the Igloo next to Adelaide's chair.

I take it with me because I'm going to do something.

A guy is sitting on the edge of the pool, drinking a beer, so I get up and go to him. I feel good, like I'm floating. I can feel the hot concrete come up through my feet, travel up my legs and then my face. I sit next to the guy. Close. Put my legs in the water.

Look, I say. Isn't that trippy how your leg looks like it's almost in two pieces when you put it in the water?

He looks at my legs and then at me. He smiles, but just a little. He's dark. Super tan. Black curly hair and thick fingers that have hair all over them. What is he? Is he Italian or Greek or Mexican or something else I don't even know? He's not black. That, I can tell.

I put my hand in the water. I pull my hand out of the water and just stare at it. It looks like an old person's hand.

I put my hand in the water again and when I take it out, I dribble water up his leg. He looks at me funny, with squinty eyes and his head turned like James Dean does in *Rebel Without a Cause*.

I'm Costas, he says. He looks at me hard, like he's studying me.

I'm Avery.

You feeling good, Avery?

Yes, I say. I am. I am, Costas.

He nods at my T-shirt. It says Trojans. What year? he asks.

Freshman.

Senior.

Go Trojans, I say, and punch my fist in the air.

He laughs. I *guess*, he says. He peels a little bit of the label off his beer. Drinks some. Puts it back down.

I like Costas. He's golden, I swear to God, and his hair is making these tight waves all over his head, little shiny brown bows all over. I lean into him and smell coconut. I kiss him on the cheek. He leans away from me.

Man, he says. Avery. You're wasted, girl.

Yes, I say. I like it though! He shakes his head, and I put my hand on his thigh and he looks at my hand for a long, long time. I move my hand up a little bit, just to see what he will do. There's nothing bad he can do to me. Maybe say stop and that's not going to kill me. I'm not wondering if he thinks I'm cute because I think he's cute. That's all that counts right now. He doesn't take my hand off. He stares straight ahead at the hills all rocky and orange. I say, The sun's going down, and move my hand up some more. The tip of my finger is underneath his shorts.

Check out my boy Costas, someone yells behind us. Getting him some chocolate! He turns to yell at the guy, and when he does, my hand falls off his leg. You idiot, he says over his shoulder. You fool. He stands up, and then he gets up and walks off toward my bungalow, but then he disappears. I don't want to sit at the pool by myself with those jerks behind me, so I get up too. I walk toward my room. I'm about to pull on the sliding glass door when I hear someone behind me.

Come here, Costas says, and pulls me to the side of the bungalow where it's dark and nobody can see us. He puts my face in his hands and kisses me. He says, You got nice lips. What were you trying to do back there?

I don't know. I rub the front of his shorts.

Shit, he says. Okay.

He sticks his hand underneath my T-shirt. He feels my boob and I slide down the wall. My legs won't let me stand up again. I think for two seconds. I hear Mom telling me to keep my legs closed. But my legs want to be wide open. Let's do it, I say. Let's do it.

Slow down, girl. He kneels down and holds my face again. He stares into my eyes. Fuck, he says. You're just too drunk. I'm not doing that. That'd be fucked up.

I'm not that drunk, I say. He's hard and I touch him. He takes a deep breath. I say, I swear I'm not that drunk.

Okay, he says. He looks around. You can suck my dick, but that's it. Here, he says, and lies down on his back. He pulls down his shorts. I kneel over him, thinking after this he'll be so into me, after this, even though I don't know what I'm doing. He talks to me the whole time. Don't just lick it, he says. Move your head up and down. Watch the teeth, though. Use your hands, too. Not that hard, though. No, that's too gentle. A little hard. Yeah, like that. He's moaning. He's saying yes and he's coming and I don't know what to do, so I swallow.

I'm still kneeling over him and I smile. He puts his fist to his forehead and stares up at me. He says, You didn't know what you were doing, did you?

No, I say. I never did that before.

He sits up, pulls up his shorts. Looks at me like he's almost mad at me. Don't tell me you're some kind of virgin or some crazy thing.

I am, I say.

What are you, crazy? That's what you want? Some guy you don't know? On the side of a hotel room? Drunk?

I don't care about that, I say.

He shakes his head. Then I'm glad. I'm glad we didn't do that. And be glad I'm not a grade A asshole, either.

You're nice, I say. I like you.

He smiles at me. He slaps my face soft like those Italians in *The Godfather* and then he strokes it. You're a trippy girl, he says. Let's get you to your room.

We walk around the corner, but when I pull on the sliding glass door it's locked. I pound on it and Nurse pulls it open. She looks at me and frowns at Costas.

She's better now, Costas says. But she was kind of trashed.

I'm fine, I say. Fine, fine, fine.

Thanks, Nurse says, and pulls me in. Peace out, she says to Costas. But she doesn't smile and she slides the door so hard the glass wobbles.

There's some guy in bed with Adelaide, passed out. I can't believe they didn't wake up when Nurse slammed the door. Who's that? I walk closer to the bed so I can see his face. Cute. He's cute. It's the surfer dude from earlier.

I whisper, I thought he was an idiot. I thought he didn't have class.

Nurse cracks open a 7UP and sits cross-legged in a chair. His dad? Knows her dad, it turns out. Fraternity brothers at USC from a million years ago. He's loaded too. His dad is, anyway.

But what about him not having class? What about the two beers instead of three?

That was before, I guess, Nurse says, and rolls her eyes. True love. Who was that dude? She slurps her 7UP loud and Adelaide turns over. She turns over for the slurping sound but not the door. Nurse says, Please don't tell me you did it with him.

No. I didn't.

Good. Thank God.

It was just a blow job, I say.

Nurse slaps her forehead. You're not even going to remember it in the morning. Trust me.

Yes I will, I say. I'm going to remember this for a long time. He liked me, I say. And he wasn't a brother.

Yeah, but what *was* he? Like Turkish or something? A Jew?

Turkish? I don't know what that is. I shrug. He looks white to me.

Yeah, Nurse says. But not *white*, white.

What's the difference?

I don't know, Nurse says. But still. Maybe he's Italian or Greek or something.

But that's white, no?

Nurse turns up her palms, like, What do you want me to do about it? Okay, she says. Congratulations. He's white. I'm going outside.

She slams the door behind her, trying to wake up Adelaide, I'm sure. But they're totally dead. They look like a little prince and princess sleeping in those sheets, like in one of those Hans Christian Andersen stories I loved when I was a kid. They're in their own special little world. They're a fairy tale.

PALM SPRINGS WAS totally worth it, even though I've spent so much money. I've already maxed out my credit card. It's the only one I have left—don't even ask me about the other ones—and I don't even know how I'm going to pay it all back. First we split the room, and then Adelaide and Nurse wanted to go to these places and eat food I've never even heard of before. And even if I've heard of some of this stuff, why would you want to eat it? They order mussels, which look like snot on a seashell. They order paté, which looks like a big square piece of baloney, which would have tasted good if it was baloney. But for twenty bucks. They order three different desserts, just to try them. Who orders extra food just to try it and leave it sitting on the table? And appetizers too. How much food do you need? I order the same thing every time because I don't like spending money on something I'm not going to want to eat. So it's burgers and fries and chicken for me. Stuff that actually makes you feel full when you eat it. They always want to split everything three ways because it's easier. And it is easier, I guess. I don't want to sit there counting who has what and how much it costs and I don't want to look like the cheap one. It's all on credit, anyway. I just don't want to even know what my balance is.

But it's the end of the week and Nurse and I have screwed ourselves because we haven't even tried to write papers that are due when we get back. Ugh, Nurse says. I'll get it done. Me too, I say. Me too.

Mine's done, Adelaide says.

What? we say. When?

She turns up Diana Ross singing Ain't no mountain high enough. I got it before we left, she says.

What does she mean? I ask. What do you mean, you *got*?

I got it, Adelaide says. She points. It's so pretty here. I don't want to leave. She keeps one hand on the steering wheel and rolls down the window to make waves in the air with her other hand, even though the air coming in is so hot we can barely breathe. Cost me just a hundred bucks, she says. Chaucer. Wife of Bath. Like I'm going to say something new about that. I got better things to do.

Ad, Nurse says, shaking her head. But she's smiling.

She *bought* a paper? I have never heard of anybody buying a paper before. Even stupid Anika with all her money never bought a paper. She was always working. But I think about this. I think of Adelaide taking something that is not hers and putting her name on it. Now it's hers. People can buy that. So is it just stupid for me to do the work? But I *have* to do the work. It's not stupid if you *have* to do something and you do it. But what if I didn't have to? What if I could just spend a hundred bucks and get a paper? If I really, really wanted to, I could charge a paper on my credit card, I guess. But no. I can just see myself getting caught and kicked out of school. Mom and Dad. Oh my God. I can just hear it. You mean to tell me you gone get into USC and then not do no work? You gone *buy* a paper and get kicked out when all you had to do is sit your ass down and write a paper? Ain't got to do no real work. Ain't got to punch no time clock. No kids to feed. All you need to do is go to class and pay attention. Write a paper and be one step closer to being better off than anybody we ever knew? Is that what you mean to tell me? That instead of doing that, you decided to go on ahead and get kicked out?

Jesus. Forget it. No way. And anyway, I just don't see myself doing that. It's not fair work for a fair grade.

Adelaide keeps looking at me while she's driving. Why are you staring at me, she says. What the hell are you looking at?

Nothing, I say. I don't know. But I do know. I don't think it's fair that she gets to do whatever she wants. She gets to fuck the surfer dude, be skinny, buy a paper, and look like Michael Jackson.

I say, I'm sick of Diana Ross and the Supremes and all that. Why don't you put on some Depeche Mode. I dig through my bag and pull out my cassette.

That shit? She makes a face. What kind of sister are you anyway? British white boys? This is Miss *Ross*. She says. You hear me? *Miss Ross.*

I'M JUST TRYING to get through school. I just want to focus on graduating and enjoy being in school. I feel like, being on campus, even though it sometimes is crappy and I feel like I don't really get along with hardly anybody, I'm protected here. Campus feels better than the rest of the world.

But my mother is always calling me with bad news. Every time she calls me, I swear. I always say, What's wrong? after she asks me how I'm doing. And then she tells me. Your cousin Layla back home pregnant again. Already got five babies. What she need another one for? Your aunt Janice finna lose her house. She done fell six months behind on her house note. Your uncle Cesar, don't nobody know what's wrong with him. Back home, they say he talking to hisself, tried to strangle somebody down the hill and the police had to come get him. The house falling in, too. Gone have to get them a trailer or something. And Keith, Lord have mercy. That boy. Arrested *again*. They gone keep him for a long time, this time. Running around with that white boy. That white boy always seem to come up all right. But where Keith at? Uh huh, Mom says. Uh huh. Acting like he can afford to run around.

I listen, but I can't stand to listen, because it's always something. Always sad. Babies. Money. Sickness. Bad news from Tennessee and the old neighborhood about people and things I can't do anything about. I can only think, Thank God it isn't me. I'm glad I don't have a baby. I'm glad I'm in school. I'm glad I'm not sick. And I'm not crazy. I'll graduate. I'll get a job and I'll live by myself. Get a boyfriend. Finally.

I say, How are you doing, Mom? Fine?

You know, Mom says. Fair to middling. She breathes into the phone. You got any change on you?

I think for a moment. I just got paid. My check is four hundred dollars. I have to make it stretch the whole month, every month. I live off campus now, so for rent, one hundred dollars. Bus pass, fifteen dollars. Food, eighty dollars. Credit card payments, two hundred. I don't have any student loan money left over this semester. Once I paid my tuition and books, it was all gone. I can't afford anything else.

Do you? Mom says. I got an extension on my phone bill and my trash bill, but I got to get them paid.

It's been like this since she and Dad split up. The way Dad left wasn't dramatic, like on TV when parents sit kids down. He just came home less and less and then I was in school. It was happening all along and then it was done. He pays the house note, but there is all this other stuff. I say, I can give you fifty dollars, Mom. Would that help?

Yeah, Mom says.

I don't hear anything else for what seems like a long time. Thank you, she says.

Why did she have to say that?

You're welcome, I say. I wipe my eyes and sniff because my nose is running.

You got a cold?

No, I say. Well, maybe a little.

Get you some Vicks salve if you stopped up and get you some NyQuil too. And vitamin C.

I will, Mom.

Now do it soon. Don't try and wait. Do, it'll get worse. And wrap that money up real good before you mail it so won't nobody take it.

Okay, I say. But I wish I could tell her the truth. That I didn't have a cold. That her Thank You was the worst thing she could have said to me. It makes me feel like a cheater, like I'm taking credit for hard work that somebody else did.

ON MY WAY to work at the School of Fine Arts, I keep thinking about my budget. I can see there's something going on in front of Bovard. There are all these American flags and red, white, and blue balloons. And TVs. I want to stop, but if I stop for too long I'll be late for work, and I can't afford to mess up in any way with that job. The money comes first, no matter what. But I stop because there's shouting. USA! USA! U.S. out of Africa! U.S. out of Africa! I ask this redheaded boy, What's going on? These idiots, he says. He points to a group of guys in dress shirts and ties. They're Young Americans for Freedom. They're pissed because we're protesting on Ronald Reagan's birthday. He's in there.

Who? *Reagan*? In *Bovard*?

Yeah.

I look up at my favorite building.

Well who are you guys?

U.S. out of Africa! He yells with his fists in the air. This is a disgrace, he says. We are one of the last major universities to divest from South Africa. It's sickening.

His face is pink from yelling. I barely know what he's talking about. I know about apartheid, but I don't know about schools and divestment or anything like that. There's this black man touching my shoulder. You are with this group? Students for Peace and Justice?

Oh, I say. No. *No*.

Come, he says. He takes my hand and pulls me into the crowd. I'm trying to pull my hand out of his, but he won't let go. Listen, he says loud. He yells, Everybody! People crowd around him. Whites, blacks, Asians, and people I can't even tell what they are. Everybody, he says. This is what we do in Soweto. He dances. Marches in place with his fists in the air. And he sings. I look at his smooth face, cheeks that are sharp like carved wood. But I just stand in one place. I'm not even supposed to be here. I'm not going to sing and dance and look stupid. Everybody else is doing it, though. I can't do it. I believe in sanctions, of course.

Who wouldn't? I'm totally on their side. But it seems crazy to risk being so late for work, for people I don't even know so far away. And it looks like it could turn into something wild. People could get arrested even, and I don't want to make those kinds of waves. Like I need that in my life, getting arrested. And what's marching going to do? Besides, I'm only one person. They can do all of this without me. I keep trying to get away from the guy but he's got me. Hey, he says. What are you doing? You cannot protest and stand still. That is not protest.

This time I really yank my arm away. I have to go to work, I say. I'm late.

He looks at me with a funny expression. Like he is enter-tained by me. Of course, he says. There is something more impor-tant. Making money. Perhaps your money will trickle down to us all standing here and standing in South Africa? He turns up the corner of his mouth. It's supposed to be a smile but his eyes—he keeps his eyes down like he's looking at my feet. He makes me look down too. He makes me think there is something wrong with my feet, my dirty white Converse. And then he turns his back like I'm not even here. When I get out of the crowd, there is a guy in my way. One of those guys in a shirt and tie. A Young American for Freedom. All I see is a big gap in his front teeth. And a big nose. It's none of your business, he screams at me. This is *America*. You worry about *America*.

I push him on the shoulder. Get out of my way. He's so close to my face, some of his spit lands on my lip. I'm mad, and I'm thinking, You don't know who I am. How can you talk to me like you know something about me and what I think? But he's looking at me like he hates me, like he knows exactly who I am. He hates me so much and he doesn't even know me. I try to get past him but he blocks my way and keeps yelling. You don't even belong here, he says. You better thank God for affirmative action. I can't get around him and he won't do anything but yell. I'm trapped. I can't say anything and he won't let me get away. I start to shake. I tell myself, Don't cry. Don't you fucking cry. When I finally push past him, I say something stupid. I say, You're supposed to be for freedom, and I end up crying anyway. I'm late for work on top of that. Dad's always going on and on about Reagan this and Reagan that, anti-union, anti–civil rights, and don't care nothing about black folks, about poor folks. Those white folks love him. They *love* him, Dad's always saying, but I don't care about any of that right now. All I'm trying to do is work. I got enough problems worrying about myself.

The phone doesn't ring that much when I get to work and I'm glad because I'm still shaking and I don't think I can make my voice, my words, sound the way they're supposed to sound. I draw because it makes me stop wanting to cry. I draw Bovard, with the vines coming down and out, the tips of the vines like fingers tapping people on the shoulders or wrapping themselves around people's necks. I draw the vines popping the balloons that I saw, but I'm drawing in pencil, so they're not red, white, and blue. It's all gray from my pencil. Everything is all gray. I draw a man dancing. I draw him hopping up and down with dots and arrows to show he's moving. Then I draw myself lying down next to the dancing man. Just lying down like I want to do right now. This isn't enough, though. I feel like there's so much more I could do, so many ways to say what I'm feeling, all mixed up, but I don't know how.

April walks by my desk. Still, after three years, she has the mohawk. It's straighter than ever. She's still wearing her Dr. Martens and torn fishnets and shorts with a T-shirt. She hikes her backpack on her shoulder because it keeps sliding down. I go, Why don't you just put it on both shoulders?

She shrugs. Because I'd look like a dork? She sits on the corner of my desk and plays with a hole in her fishnets. What's all that?

Nothing, I say. Nothing. I pull it to me because I don't like her seeing what I draw. She's always trying to see but it's crap, so why show it to anybody? It doesn't even make any sense. Besides, I'm not in art school. She is. I'm answering phones.

April looks around the office like she's bored and then she jerks the paper away from me. She rips the corner but there's nothing there but white space anyway.

What the fuck? She turns the paper sideways, upside down. Holds it out in front of her as far as her arms let her. That *Bovard*? Who are the people in ties?

Young Americans for Freedom.

Those assholes. What's the business with the vines? She squints at the paper and pulls it closer to her face.

I think about it, but I'm not sure. I don't know, I say. I take the picture back and look at it like I've never seen it before. Maybe, I say. Maybe they're tapping everybody and saying, You've been looking at us all this time, but now we're going to really make you look.

Yeah? So? April says. After looking, then what?

I stare into space. I shrug. I don't know. I have no idea.

April nods. She takes the paper back. It's pretty good, though. I like it. Oh! Wait a minute, she says. Check this shit out. She pulls out a book. The cover says Rauschenberg in big letters. This dude is the shit, April says. I fucking love him.

She pushes the book at me and her hand is holding down the page of something he did called *Minutiae*. I don't know what I'm looking at, except I see what looks like three room dividers covered in newspaper clippings, comic strips, photographs, and pieces of posters. There is paint, dripping down and coloring all of this. And fabric. Wood, metal, plastic. The colors. Red, yellow, blue, green. And plants are painted, too. Something growing in the middle of all of this. I have never seen anything like this before in my life. This is just the picture of this amazing thing. What does it look like for reals? In person?

I've never seen this before, I say.

Why are you whispering?

I'm not.

Yes you are. You're whispering. He's bad, huh?

People can do this?

Where have you been?

Where is he?

I don't know. Boston?

Can I borrow it?

For how long?

One day. Just give me one day.

April shrugs. She stands up. Sure. Avery's in love, she sings.

But after a while, all I hear is a sound like eee, eee, eee. I'm not listening, really. I'm looking. I didn't know you could do this, put a whole bunch of stuff together that seems like junk and tell a story about people. That's what this Rauschenberg is. A story. I'm looking and I want to do it too. Tell a story.

APRIL DOES IT again. Blows my mind. She takes me underground. She's all, You're going! Don't even. But I have a lot of schoolwork to do. Papers. Tests coming up. So I try to get out of it but she's not hearing me. She's in my room and I'm throwing clothes together and then she's driving me away from school in her Honda. Turns out that underground is just five minutes from school. This club that moves around. You just have to know somehow. I'm thinking that we're seriously going underground, underneath the street, but no. Just down some gross, wet alley with rats and pee smell and garbage and into some old building that used to be something else and I'm practically deaf the minute I'm in and it feels like the whole building is throbbing with music. Just beats and beats. It's full of people and so beautiful, I have to tell you. Marble. Ceilings so high that in the dark with the strobe light you can't see where the limit ends, where the walls stop. Long, long red velvet curtains with gold ropes pulling them aside. Like a castle. People everywhere. Boys in makeup and skirts and girls in suits or practically naked. So many people pierced in the lips and eyes. I'm trying to see everything at once, but my eyes can only see one thing at a time. Then I see her. A black girl with a bald head dancing in the corner all by herself and that's the weirdest to me, the bald head on a girl. Why did you do it, I want to ask her. You could be pretty, but no. She's the light color brown that you know her hair would be curly or wavy with no nap at all, and that's what she does. What do people think? I want to ask her. Your mother? Your father? Your teacher? Your boss? What does everybody think about that bald head?

Tourist! April yells in my ear so hard that it hurts, like she stuck a needle in it. She's got to yell so I can hear her, but it still hurts. I left and you didn't even know it, she says and she hands me a clear plastic cup with something in it. Your mouth is open, I swear to God it is, she says.

I hold it up to my nose and smell it. It's orange juice and something else. What's this? I yell. I don't drink!

Yeah you do! Tonight you do! April says. She taps my cup. Cheers! She tugs on her torn fishnets and pulls her cutoff Levi's up on her hips. Her uniform, I swear. But she looks good. Tonight her mohawk is slicked down on one side of her head. At least she left some hair on her head, not like that other crazy girl. April looks like something. I've tried to look like something tonight, with my striped tights and loafers and pink Day-Glo shirt. A black beret to cover my crazy hair that's half straight and half nappy because I haven't had anything done to it in a while. Why does everybody look like something and I look like nothing? I pull at my clothes and beret. I look dumb, I yell over

New Order. I look confused! No dude! April says. You look eclectic! Eclectic man!

And then I get scared because there's a roar out of nowhere and then this guitar that sounds like blues and rock and funk all at the same time and then this mohawked black guy wearing a brown suit and red bowtie is running on the stage screaming, Hello motherfuckers! The whole band starts to play and then this dude just has a fit on stage. A serious fit like a seizure, singing his song. The crowd is moving all together but wild in different directions like ants that got stomped by some invisible giant's foot. I'm being pushed and slammed and bumped and kicked and the singer jumps from the stage into the crowd like a crazy person because how does he know that anybody is going to catch him? And I get kicked in the face somehow and the crowd is roaring Fishbone! Fishbone! Angelo! Angelo! And my face hurts and I smell like the alcohol that I spilled all over myself and I don't know where April is and the singer has stopped singing and is asking everybody, Who don't give a fuck, y'all? Who don't give a fuck!

This is mostly what I remember. The longest night of my life. I'm so glad to get back to my room and I don't think the underground is for me, except I keep hearing that dude asking me if I don't give a fuck, but I don't know what he means, exactly. About what? About who? Because I might answer, Yes. I do give a fuck, too much of a fuck. Or I might have to answer, Not enough. I don't give enough of one. And anyway it's a weird question coming from a weird black dude in a suit and a bowtie and crazy hair sticking up like he's being electrocuted. Keith would have liked it, all the noise and the fits and the chaos, and he would have yelled straight out, Me! Me! I don't give a fuck, motherfucker! Ain't nothing in my way!

You wouldn't be confused about how he meant it, either.

23

MASSIMO IS LEANING in the doorway of the bedroom. He says nothing. He hangs his head, as if staring at his crossed arms. He is thinking and thinking. My eyes glide over him, the graying hair, the white oxford, still crisp after travel and lying down with me. His bare feet are crossed over each other. He clears his throat and lifts his head, levels his eyes at me. "So?"

"He might come tonight."

"What? Ma-donna," he says. I hear his accent, his way of speaking, acutely in this moment. It sounds like Ma-done-na, a long O in the middle. When we first met, I thought he was talking about our iconic Madonna. Madonna from Detroit, who now sounds as though she is from England. I had said, "Why do you keep saying *her* name?" He had looked at me with the same bewildered eyes as now.

When I say nothing, he asks me again. "Why? How did that happen?"

But I don't know why. It's an impossible question, the real why. Massimo scratches underneath his arm. "No," he says slowly. "This is all very bad. This is a bad idea, Avery. You need to tell him to stay away. You need to tell him, the next time he comes into my fucking house?" Massimo brushes his hands together, and then holds them up, clean of imaginary debris. "He will see," he says.

I go to Massimo in the doorway. Pull his arms apart and hold his hands in mine. "You love me."

"Yes," Massimo says, frowning, as though I am asking him a trick question.

"You have been good to me, even when I have not been good to you."

He says nothing, but does not allow his eyes to meet mine. He's trying to decide between angry and impassive, the two emotions that have enabled him to cope with me throughout the years.

"You have to let me deal with this the best way for me." I put his arms around me and let them go after he holds me without my help. But now, I say again, "I don't need your help."

"No?" Massimo is finally smiling. He laughs. "You need my help often."

We have been talking in the dark, save for the sliver of light that has traveled down the hallway into the bedroom. "I'm tired," I say, pulling Massimo to the bed again. "You are up, you are down. You're trying to sleep, and then you're not. You are already dressed to go. Decide what you want. You are running out of time." He rubs the back of my head. I smell lemon and the spicy scent of his deodorant. Cigarette smoke. In the muted light, I watch him undress. This is what we do. He holds my gaze while he unbuttons his shirt. He pulls on his belt and it jangles. He lets his jeans fall to the floor and then he steps out of them. Then his underwear. Black underwear that clings to his thighs. He never looks away. He stands in front of me, naked, waiting for me to do the same. First my white tank top. Then my jeans. My bra. My underwear that looks like the kind worn by little boys. He does not look at my body all this time. Only my eyes. *I see you,* we say to each other with our eyes. *I see you.* And when Massimo is on top of me, I can hear his sounds, murmurs and heavy breath. My name. God's name. The slickness of sweat is between us, but I don't know if it has come from me or from him, from his hard work. When we were together for the first time, I could not look at him and I did not want him to look at me. Yet, I wondered. What is he looking at? What does he see? What kind of woman? Please, I thought. Let me be the thing that he wants to see. "Please," he said. "Please look at me, Avery."

24

ON THE WAY to the gallery, Massimo cuts his eyes back and forth from me to the road, as if checking my temperature with his eyes. "Are you nervous?" he keeps asking. "You don't look nervous."

"Do you think I should be?"

"Don't you?" he asks, frowning. "I do."

"About the show or about Keith?"

He doesn't answer. He turns up the Levon Helm he's letting me play because it's my night. He usually makes fun of Helm, singing in an exaggerated twang, "The poor old dirt farmer he's lost all his corn-orn-orn." He yodels until I tell him to stop ruining such beautiful music. I was going to call Brenna on the way to the gallery, but now the phone rings and it's her—not the first time we have been thinking of each other. I turn down the music and tell Brenna that much is the same. She is uneasy that nothing, absolutely nothing, has changed since she left earlier this afternoon. "What's going to happen," she wants to know. "He must be the worst he's ever been, breaking into houses and stealing from people. What are we supposed to do?" None of us knows the answer. All Brenna knows is that she's glad that she will not be there to see him.

When we were just children, Brenna gave up her baby the way she told me she was going to have it. As if it were nothing. At least, this is how I thought about it when I was that girl in high school. "I'm knocked up," she'd said. "My ass is grass." And I was furious, as if I truly understood what was at stake. "We've been watching those lame cartoon sex ed things since the fifth grade," I hollered. "It's not that hard. Just don't let any sperm get any- where near you. The end." But, of course. Now I know that there is, sometimes, an extraordinary difference between how someone appears, how they may act, and what is truly the matter, the per- son, at hand.

"Are you really glad that you won't be seeing him? You could have come. You could have seen him and talked to him."

"For what?" There's a muffled sound and coughing. She's tilt- ed the phone away from her mouth so that she doesn't cough into my ear. I can see her doing that. "Plus I'm already home. I'd have to drive all the way back."

Stores and restaurants speed past my passenger window in a blur of colors, shapes, and light. "What do you mean for what? Just to see him, of course."

"It wouldn't be him, though. I don't know who that would be. And it's weird, him there with all those people we don't know. If I ever see him again, I want it to be some place where we both can be ourselves and not be worried about the people around us."

I almost say that she doesn't have to worry about that, but I'm not certain of it, myself. She keeps talking, asking me if I'm sure I don't mind that she's not coming, and I don't. I see her all the time, she has always seen my work, and so I don't need her to stand in a room with me if she doesn't want to. This is just letting Brenna be who she is, what everyone around her has done all her life.

My mind wanders as Brenna talks. I imagine her and Keith in a simple white room, talking quietly, middle-aged people with a binding history. She and Keith were never friends again, not af- ter he was sent away and she had the baby. When the baby came, a girl, Brenna simply wasn't at school one day, and the next day, my mother told me she'd had her baby, and just like that it wasn't hers anymore. I felt sad for Brenna and for Keith and for the baby, I thought. But I had so much catching up to do. It was as if when Brenna had her baby, she and Keith went somewhere I could never go. There was no way for me to get to this place, and so for a long time, I pretended this place did not exist. Sad is not the word for this condition. Lost and looking seem to be better words.

"Honest to God, Ave," Brenna says, suddenly very loud on the other end. "I'm pissed. I'm pissed at him, that's why I don't want to see him. I'll want to slap him. He just fucking gave up. Why'd he have to give up? We fucked up. We were kids. But pull it together. He could have gotten his shit together. He has to believe whatever people say about him? He's got to go turn into an addict? What a waste. It's such a waste, man. If he could have just pulled it together we could have done something different. Both of us. But no, you guys were always believing some shit somebody said about you."

I know better than to get into it with Brenna when she's on a roll. And anyway, I understand everything she's saying and not saying. Keith and I were the same. She's right. And yes, Keith did quit, as if what he was fighting for was already over. But she doesn't understand that she had a luxury, as little as she and her family had. She had the luxury of not having to listen to all the voices Keith and I had to. I didn't think I could afford to ignore the voices. They were everywhere, all the time, but I found help, a place to put the voices, a way to turn them into something I was saying back. Maybe Keith tried to ignore the voices but couldn't. He needed help from something stronger.

When we hang up, Massimo says nothing. He just looks at me and turns up Levon Helm. He hums quietly and sounds good, actually, now that he's respecting the song and the story being told. Brenna stays with me. She said that she and Keith could have done something different. She means that they could have been together, still, even without that baby. They could have made new ones. I remember once, when Brenna visited me at USC, she teased me about being there. "I need to come in here and fuck up this place," she had said, rolling around on Anika's bed and messing up her expensive cloudlike comforter.

I see her smooth face. It's raining outside. She pulls on the sweatshirt I loan her. It's red with "Trojans" blazed across it in deep yellow. "Oh my God you guys," she says. "Oh my total God. This makes me look so fat! What's Doogie going to say? Will he give me his pin now that I'm such a fat fucking cow? Oh, I hate my mother!"

"That's what I need to do," Brenna says. She turns to face the mirror. She stares at herself for a long time. She says, "I need to marry one of these rich fuckers around here. Move to Orange County or Malibu and have some kids and sit on my ass."

"You'd last two seconds," I say.

"You're right." Brenna raises an eyebrow at herself in the mirror like, *You joker.* And then her eyes settle into the wide, expectant gaze of someone listening and waiting, already anticipating someone or something that she can't yet see.

From the car, I survey people on the street or in cars passing us by. Strangers I will never meet, who I nevertheless wonder about. Every day, I know that she and Keith imagine their child out walking the world somewhere, an endless possibility. But what if she ever meets them? What will her eyes tell her? Her father's qualities will be impossible to discern, so faint they will be invisible. She won't know he was funny and tough like her mother. Smart. That when he was a child he was on his way to being anything. There was nothing in his way. At least, none of us saw anything at the time.

Massimo and I have arrived at the gallery. It's a lovely space. Simple white walls and the exhibit name in black on glass. From the car, I look around, outside and through the glass into the gallery, but don't see the one person we all have been looking over our shoulders for.

I'M JUST THINKING commencement is synonymous with graduation. I think graduation ceremonies mean the same as commencement ceremonies while I'm standing around with everybody. Mom, Dad, Dad's girlfriend Theresa. Owen, Brenna. They're all so proud of me, asking me, What's next? What are you going to do with your life? And I still don't know. I have a degree in business and I don't care about business. After graduation, I'll quit my work-study job answering phones in the art department and work as an administrative assistant at an educational testing service, grading tests. It was the first job I saw advertised and I applied, just to be making some kind of money.

Dad holds my graduation cap in his hands and fingers the tassels. I shift my weight, negotiating black pumps that Dad bought me for interviews and an eventual job. Underneath my black graduation robe is a black suit, a skirt and blazer with shoulder pads that remind me of the made-for-TV Frankenstein, Herman Munster. This is the last fight I have with my father that I really want to win, a fight over what I need to be wearing. You have to dress the part, he had said, nodding and pleased with the way I looked coming out of the dressing room. Very professional, he said. But I felt strange in the clothes. I was in costume. Instead I wanted something loose, something that I could turn into my own with accessories, jewelry, shoes. No, he said, no. You need at least one suit. But it wasn't even a real suit. It was made out of some kind of polyester that didn't look too tacky because it was black. But still, in four years at USC, I had learned the difference between items of worth and items that signified one's worth. My father was trying to help me signify to the world how valuable, how worthy I was. I watched him pull out his wallet and carefully count four ten-dollar bills and saw that there was only twenty dollars left in the wallet. The saddest twenty-dollar bill I have ever seen. And that is why he won, why I am wearing a black polyester suit under a heavy black robe with black hose and black pumps in eighty degrees.

Who died, Brenna asks. She hugs me and her voice tickles my ear. Or is it you who's dead, dude? She steps back and takes a picture but I don't smile, I just stare back at the eye of the camera. Jeez, she says, at least look happy. It's commencement. She points at the program and grins. Mom and Dad knew that Brenna would be here and have tolerated her after polite hellos and how have you beens, but she reminds them of something that they don't want to be reminded of, of mistakes and decisions made that may have been the wrong thing to do. This is their happy day. Brenna doesn't care, though. She jokes with Owen and both of them make fun of the way I speak. She sounds like she writes it down in her head before she says it, Brenna says. Doesn't she? Sound like one of them shrinks on TV, don't she? Owen says, laughing. Still, no matter who's not talking to whom, and who is making fun of whom, everyone is here for me. Proud.

In the crowd of robes and tassels and leis around necks, I see a mohawk walking toward me. April. Still. She hasn't changed after these years. I've taken off my robe because I can't take the heat anymore. I drape it over my arm, like a waiter holding a long, black napkin. Hey, she says, and hugs me. Her nose ring glistens in the sun when she pulls back to look at me. Whoa, she says. Who died? And Brenna laughs. Brenna keeps staring at April with a big grin on her face. I can tell she gets a kick out of her. She winks at me and says, Hey. Let me take everybody's picture. All of you together. My family looks at April as if they could look at her forever and still not be able to name what in the world she is. Hi, she says, thrusting her hand out to Mom and Dad. You must be Ave's parents. I'm April. Where do you want me to stand? Mom and Dad look at her as if she's not quite speaking English. Mom's face says, Now I know this crazy-looking girl is not getting ready to mess up our picture with that hair, looking like some Indian, a earring hanging from her nose like some kind a African.

Closer, Brenna says. Stand next to Avery, April. Get in tighter. Everybody does, and I can't wait to see that picture when Brenna gets it developed, April standing next to me like some sister separated at birth, raised by somebody crazy. When April leaves, Mom stares after her and then shakes her head. Why she mess up her head like that? What she supposed to be doing?

She's an artist, I say. She has an art degree now.

An art degree? Mom says. That don't spell nothing. She gone eat her art?

Do, and she'll be hungry, Dad says.

Need to spend some money on getting her head done right, Owen says.

It's the only thing my parents agree on, after hello and how you doing, since they no longer are together. And they would agree, too, that they're both doing so much worse for money, now that they aren't working, together, on that progress we started when we moved to the suburbs, into that nice house with the yard I loved, a million years ago. But today, they agree. It is a great day, the beginning of a good life.

They don't know that my job has nothing to do with my degree, that education and business are far apart. We stand around and they linger, as if they don't want the day to be over, when I want it to be over so that I can stop feeling like a liar. How much money you gone be making, Dad asks me.

Um. Not that much to start, around thirty, I lie. But then the longer I'm there, the more I make. I don't need a lot of money anyway.

Don't need a lot of money? My father and mother and Owen trade looks.

I say, School is more about the education you get, not the job.

Uh huh, Dad says.

And I look down at my shiny black pumps because I only half believe that. I remember how much I wanted my own television freshman year. A nice downy comforter and not to worry about money at all in Palm Springs. And all the reminders of the importance of money since then. I don't dare tell my parents that my credit is already ruined because of money I spent that wasn't mine. I tell Dad that I don't owe that much in student loans, which is a lie. I owe a lot. For me. For us.

That's all right, Owen says, slapping me on the back. You one of them educated negroes now, he says, laughing. And I try not to think he is somehow making fun of me, because he refused to go to school and he and his family are absolutely fine because they have done what all my family has done since the beginning of who we have ever been in America. Work. None of us disagree about the success of this strategy, for the most part. We only disagree on what work is, and whether or not everyone gets equal pay for equal work.

Everyone wants to see the degree in my hand, the one they handed to everyone when they called our names. Let me see, Brenna says. Open it up, Dad says. Hurry up, Owen says. Let's see this thing. I pull off the red satin ribbon to keep it in a tight scroll. I unroll it and we all look at it. The bright sun glares off the white paper. It's blank. Nothing is on it.

Bogus! Brenna says. That sucks. Mom frowns and Dad puts my cap under his arm and leans in to look closer at the blank paper.

Mom says, Anyway, I don't care. Brenna, take our picture with Avery and her degree. So Brenna does. Mom and Dad stand with me in the middle, holding my blank piece of paper.

Be sure to get that to me, Brenna, Mom says. I bet it's a good picture. I bet it look like we all going somewhere in that picture, she says and squeezes my arm tight. We proud of you Avery,

Mom says. She nods like she's agreeing with herself, as though a question has been confirmed.

I roll up my fake degree. I say, Don't worry, you guys. It's not supposed to be the real one. The real one comes in the mail.

25

MY DEGREE CAME in the mail about two months after I dragged Brenna to the Formosa for a night of escape and Hollywood glamour, a place from which she fled and drove the whole forty minutes back home to West Covina that very night. But that night changed my life, the night I met Massimo at the Formosa, Massimo who looked at me as though he understood my worth, who lived in such a beautiful house, very much like homes I had seen elsewhere all my life on television. Lovely, his house is lovely, and living in it feels so good and comfortable when I forget a lot of things, try to forget a lot of things, like how tenuous it all is, a shiny mirage in the desert, just within reach, if all the circumstances of one's journey are just right. I told my therapist this. I said, "The people who think they know Keith now, I wish they could have seen him when he was younger. We were exactly the same. Exactly. Except I didn't have any courage and he didn't have any fear and we never could even it all out so that everything would be equal and fair, no matter what life threw at us."

26

ALREADY, THE TINY gallery is full of people. There are three other people who are showing too, and most of the people are here for them. The stark white walls and the lights illuminate everything sharply. All the voices together in this small room fill my ears like a distant roar. My eyes fall on important-looking people with severe eyeglasses that look like art in and of themselves. Smart, crisp suits and billowy feminine dresses draped over bodies completely covered in tattoos. Black. So much black, and hats of all kinds. I remember a time when I would have been completely absorbed by all of this, wanting to look the part, but now, I just put on my Dodgers cap. I had it in my purse, not thinking I'd have the guts to show up at my own show as if I had just wandered off the street or from some hike, down from the hills. But I have the guts. It's just a baseball hat, but still. For the only other real showing I had, two years ago, I dressed down. I was embarrassed. It was art, after all. Not a real job like the ones my mother, father, and brother have always had. "Not a real job," my brother Owen always reminds me. So I dressed down to show people that I didn't think too highly of myself, did not think I was better than anybody else, even though I lived in a big house on a hill with a European. My art and I were no big deal. But I forgot the nuances of the situation, thought my family would approve because I'd be showing them that I did not think I was better than anybody else. But the guests kept asking, "Where is Avery Arlington?" No one could seem to find me.

At the end of the evening, my father asked me, "Why in the world did you wear *jeans* to something like this, Ave. Looking like you just walked in off the street. I thought you knew better than that." He straightened his tie, which was much too formal for my hole-in-the-wall show. I can imagine what his expression will be when he sees I am wearing a cap. Disappointment. So no, it's not merely a baseball hat.

I stand against a wall, watching people, and occasionally glance at my corner of the gallery. I only have four pieces, and if you listen carefully when you stand in my corner, you can hear two things: the crack of a baseball bat followed by the roar of a crowd, and, afterwards, the strains of a young Elton John singing about being young, gifted, and black, the most ironic version of a song ever recorded. And yet, ultimately, knowing that it is not meant to be ironic makes it even more a treasure. British, white, male, gay, to be young, gifted, and black, and that's a fact. It loops over and over as you linger at my art. First, placed on the table, is a white, crisp oxford shirt, so white that it's got a hue of blue. A red tie encircles the neck. The tie is extra long and extends with wire so that it resembles a noose. On one side of the shirt is a hole that looks like a bullet could have made it, and on the other side of the shirt is a red lipstick print. One painting is a portrait of myself, Keith, and Brenna, as I imagined our alter egos, in some other world of opposites, the world in which Elton John is young, gifted, and black. I've combined myself with an image of Shirley Temple, with brown skin my exact match and her trademark dimples just below either side of her bottom lip. Instead of my closely cropped hair, I have blonde ringlets on the sides and a tiny mohawk in the middle of my head. Next to me is Brenna, wearing a white three-piece suit just like Pam Grier did in her most famous blaxploitation, *Foxy Brown*. Brenna's afro is just as high, but looks like a bright red fireball. Her gun is pointed directly at the viewer. Next to Brenna is Keith, who is wearing a white letter-man's sweater. He has red Richie Cunningham hair and carries books under his arms. My other piece is a mountain fashioned out of wire and clay. I glued on all kinds of images that I drew on thin vellum paper, which make up a collage. There are all my *Teen Beat* and *Tiger Beat* idols, foods like greens and ham hocks and pigs feet and baloney and artichokes, houses like shacks and mansions and apartment buildings and Victorians. And on top of the mountain, I made a baseball stadium out of Popsicle sticks and toothpicks. I painted it blue and called that installation *Three Strikes*. The last is a self-portrait. Just my plain face from the shoulders up, with a background of white. No smile. No expression at all. I'm just looking at you so that you can look at me.

I see Massimo in the very back of the gallery, distracted by a friend. This friend, Justina, I have never liked. I see Massimo laughing, his head thrown back, already with a plastic cup of wine in his hand. The first time I met her, she was a new transplant from the Midwest, a new lawyer in Massimo's firm. He had invited her over, and from the moment she opened her mouth, I disliked her. She had come from the office, came through the door wearing an ill-fitting, dated suit that looked like something from the '80s. It even had shoulder pads. Her shoes were old, too. Slightly worn. Square at the toes with a block heel. That kind of shoe was no longer in style. She gave me a big hug, and I felt the cold bottle of wine she was holding touch the base of my neck. For a moment, it brought to mind Brenna and her Slurpee cups placed on my neck years ago. "Hey, girl," she said. "I've heard so much about you. Massimo been telling me 'bout you and I feel like we old friends, girl." I stared at her, wondering if I was being put on by the voice coming out of this white woman, wondering just what Massimo had told her about me. She seemed confused about me, which made me confused about her. Was this how she

talked at the firm? With clients? As I endured the rest of the evening, ignoring her cues, her voice began to change, the more wine
she drank. No more sentences punctuated with "girl" and "child
please." She was back to being a white woman from the Midwest
by the end of the evening, complaining about how fake Los Angeles was. By the time she left, in spite of Massimo's protests that
she might be too drunk to drive home, she was positively bel-
ligerent. "Well, you probably wouldn't know," she had said, complaining about student loans and how impossible hers would be
to pay back. "You obviously come from some place where you
didn't have to worry about all that. The way you speak," she said.
"The way you carry yourself. You probably went to private school,
didn't you? A pool in your backyard? Like everyone in L.A.? A
car the minute you turned sixteen? Summer vacations in Europe?
Must be nice," she had said, pushing around the asparagus that
Massimo had roasted on the grill. Massimo had frowned. "Avery
did not grow up that way, Justina," he had said. "Tell her, Ave."

But I agreed and disagreed with her. She was confused about
where I came from. She imagined her California, but couldn't
imagine mine. She didn't understand anything about space, distance, and time. I said, "Yes. There was a pool when I was growing
up. But I'm born and raised here, grown in California, as organic
as this orange," I said, tossing the fruit that served as a table setting. "If that's fake," I said. Then, Justina was brunette and chunky.
Now she is blonde and sleek, hair extensions, shoes that are up to
date. It took her about six months to transform into the quintes-
sential California girl, worthy of a Beach Boys song.

I look for someone else I know—who knows something of
me. My father, my nephew. I scan the room, and there it is. Dae-
Jung's afro. Huge, with the pick nestled in it that drives my brother
crazy. I walk to him and see he's wearing his uniform: pants hanging way too low, his plain white T-shirt tucked in only partway.

Black Converse sneakers shredded, just the way he likes them. Skateboard in hand, he's bent over something, studying it. From the back, he looks like what some people think of when they think they know what an African-American is. There is nothing of his mother and all her people who came before her. Only his eyes, the color and shape of them, insist that one sees a hint of that distance, space, and time. I weave through the crowd, eager to get to him. I'm so glad he's made it here, safe. I won't tell him about my relief, because he'll think I'm treating him like a child. At every age, he's reminded me: "Auntie Ave, I'm nine." "I'm thirteen, Auntie Ave." "I'm fifteen." "I'm sixteen." But I've always had morbid thoughts. I wonder. How old will he get? How old will he get *before*? Before something happens to him or nothing happens for him? If I were a betting woman, how would I bet on the odds? The chances? Why this feeling of needing to bet in the first place?

I stand behind him for a moment, watching him study another artist's installation, four sharp prongs coming up from the floor like the tines of a pitchfork.

"Careful. That looks sharp."

Dae-Jung turns at the sound of my voice, smiling, and he hugs me, mindful of my baseball cap. "Things are looking up," he says and pulls on the bill.

"Way up. Goodbye. Good riddance McCourts. This is our town."

Dae-Jung grins, amused by my fandom. It's not something that middle-aged aunts are supposed to take seriously. But that's the thing about being in one's forties. I'm older and wiser. At eighteen, I told my father I would be wise when I was forty. If you're a baseball fan long enough, you know: It's not *just* a game. Ask anybody who cares. Look what happens when you don't pay attention to the game. Some people come in and make you think that what is happening is the best thing for everybody, when really it's only the best thing for the people making the money. America's team. Bankrupt. Until some unimaginable person comes out of nowhere to take us where we need to be. A Jackie. A Fernando. A Gibson. A Chan Ho Park.

"What's this supposed to be doing?" Dae-Jung asks. He reaches out as though he's going to touch the pitchfork, and I slap his arm down.

I don't know what it is, exactly. All I know is that it looks dangerous. Thinking of danger, I'm reminded of Keith, who I forgot about briefly. I still don't see him, and yet I swear I can almost feel him, close by, the warmth of a hand just about to touch my face.

"You tell me. You were studying it."

He pulls on the pick in his hair. Pulls it out and shows me. "Maybe it's one of these," he says. "Symbolic of all the afros of the nation." He caresses his chin and nods with mock satisfaction.

"That's quite the interpretation. I thought it was a pitchfork-type thing."

"Why?" Dae-Jung frowns. He looks again. "I don't see it."

Someone touches my arm and I jump, but it's only an acquaintance saying hello. Frannie, a student at LACC who works at The Bourgeoisie Pig, the coffee shop down the road from our house. Her blonde dreadlocks are pulled up in a dramatic, hefty bun, but the only jewelry she has on is the gold hoop in her nose. She's got her son Levi hanging on her hip, and when I hug her, he grabs my cap.

"Dodger fan. Yes!" When he holds his little hand up, I give him a gentle high-five. His hair is dark and straight, not blonde like his mother's at all, but it's sticking up all over his little head as though it's caught up in static electricity. "How great is this?" I ask him, pulling on his wispy hair.

"It's crazy," Frannie says. "Don't ask me why it's doing that. The air must be really dry or something." She surveys the gallery and hikes her sliding boy higher up on her narrow hip. "There's some kooky stuff in here. Not yours, though," she says, color breaking out on her neck and cheeks. "It's good to see what you do. Also," she says, grinning, "I'm glad it's free. I can stay a while and it won't cost me anything." Levi screeches for no reason, it seems. Only for the pleasure of the sound of it.

I think of school, the days of tight budgets and maxed-out credit cards. And I didn't even have a baby. I don't want to think about how things might turn out for Frannie, but I do. Everything could be so hard that she gives up. Or, everything could be so hard, but she keeps going. Levi will have to be the one to tell that story. When Frannie leaves, there are others greeting me so that by the time I turn back to Dae-Jung, he's across the room, in the corner that holds my work, neck craned and looking at my portraits. What does he think? Above everyone else's opinion, I want to know his, no doubt something beyond my imagination. His catching the bus from the San Gabriel Valley to the beach, for example, who knows how many times. Such love of the beach and the water is beyond me, but this kid gets on a board, paddles out to vastness with the fearlessness of someone who takes for granted that he will be coming back. Me, I'm still afraid of drowning. And ghosts.

Again, someone is touching me, and again, it's not Keith. It's a man, surprised to see that I'm not a man, when I turn to face him. He recovers, though, and asks if I have seen his wife's purse. I stare into his face, bespectacled with heavy black frames, deeply lined and tan, with unruly gray hair. He looks to be the age of Massimo, late fifties, but dressed young in jeans and Converse like Dae-Jung's, only his are newer and cleaner. Because the ceiling is so high and the space is so small, I don't think I have heard correctly. I lean toward him and cup my ear.

"I'm sorry?"

"My wife's purse," he says more firmly, and his eyes assess me from my cap to my Vans.

"Your wife's purse? Why would I know where your wife's purse is?"

"She just put it down for a minute. She's frantic," he says, already walking away without answering my question. But then I see the doughy, unnecessary security guard hired for the evening making his way across the room. Thinking about chances and odds, I know before he gets to his destination that he's going to Dae-Jung. I get to them at the same time as the man with the careless wife.

"What are you doing? He didn't take anybody's purse."

"Ma'am, I'm handling this." He puts one hand on his gun, which looks like a prop. He holds the other one out, palm up and flat, telling me to stop. He has the face of a baby. Dimpled and smooth, even though he towers over all of us.

"Take somebody's purse," Dae-Jung says. "*What?*"

At first, I do what the security guard says. I stop. I wait. But momentarily, this strikes me as absurd. I'm one of the artists here. This is my show. My nephew stands before me, those startling eyes making demands. *You need to tell this man that I didn't steal anybody's purse.*

"This is *my* show," I say loudly. "*Mine.* This is my nephew. He is a guest. *My* guest."

But the louder I speak, it seems the less this person who is supposed to bring me security is listening. More eyes fall on us, people causing a scene in an exhibit. With all those eyes, I feel as though we're an exhibit: Me, looking like a boy in jeans and a T-shirt, Dae-Jung with his afro and pick buried in it, the guard, seemingly the voice of reason—unless you look very closely—and a respectable older man seeking justice. Part of me goes somewhere else, goes numb. I can hardly feel my legs beneath me. Somebody else, a voice from somewhere in the crowd, says, "Do we need to call the police?"

"It's under control," Massimo says. "We know each other. We're family," he says, by my side suddenly, grabbing me by the elbow. "Do I need to do something?" He stands with his hands at his sides and his fists clenched. Ready to raise them. "What's happened to Dae-Jung? What's going on?"

"This motherfucker says I stole somebody's purse." Dae-Jung, for some reason, puts his skateboard flat on the floor, as if he is about the skate out of the gallery.

And then, the guard puts a hand on Dae-Jung, saying, "Calm down, young man."

"Calm down? You need to calm down," Dae-Jung says. He yanks his shoulder back. "You don't even know who I am and you over here asking me about a purse. Why me? Why are you asking me?"

But the guard tries to do it again. Touch Dae-Jung, perhaps to calm him. A stranger's hand on my nephew, a stranger in uniform, is something that I thought I would never see. "Don't you touch him," I say. "He's a *boy*. He hasn't done anything." But Dae-Jung resists, not so gently this time. He tries to jerk his hand away, and then, I see the security guard jerk him back. Hard. He says to my nephew, "Do you want me to throw you down on this floor?" The sound accompanying my pieces is ending Elton John's song, and the crowd is cheering again.

I don't know everything that happens next. I get between Dae-Jung and the guard and push him. I push and push again. He pushes me back and tries to grab me, but in the scuffle, I fall on the floor and split my lip on the edge of Dae-Jung's skateboard. I jump up as though I have springs in my shoes. Massimo shoves the guard and raises both hands as if he means to punch him but gets an elbow in the eye when the guard raises an arm to protect himself, and Dae-Jung picks up his skateboard as if he's about to swing it against the guard's head.

"What are you doing?" I scream, holding my T-shirt to my lip. "Stop it! You're a surfer for God's sake." Both Massimo and Dae-Jung look at me as if I've gone crazy. We all stand together breathing heavily. It seems very quiet. But I haven't gone crazy. I have a vision of fierce clarity. I'm simply reminding my nephew of all the beautiful vastness, wherever it may take him, that lies ahead.

27

MASSIMO, DAE-JUNG, and I are sitting side-by-side on a curb outside the gallery while Dae-Jung shakes and wipes his hands on his jeans over and over as if to cleanse his hands of what they almost did. My lip is still bleeding, blood smeared on the front of my shirt, and Massimo's palms are bloodied, torn open somehow in the scuffle, and one of his eyes is turning black and blue. Massimo keeps asking me, while gently patting my lip with his own shirt, "What did you think you were doing? Are you crazy? Are you trying to get yourself killed, pushing the guard like that? Why did you have to do anything at all?" But he was doing something, and even Dae-Jung was about to do something, and finally, I was tired of not doing something, except for in the safety of my home studio. I shake my head, and Massimo asks, "No? No? What do you mean, No?"

The security guard has been relieved of his duties and the crowd inside has thinned, presumably because we ruined the nice time everyone was having.

"You're a surfer, for God's sake!" Dae-Jung cries abruptly, and we all laugh. "Stop, Dae-Jung," Massimo says, "My eye!" "My lip," I say. "It hurts to laugh." But we all keep laughing because what happened hurts a little. Massimo is alternately cursing and laughing. "I'm going to sue their asses," he says, shaking his fist into the air. "They will see why they do not fuck with us."

"Sue them?" I lick my lip, liking the metallic, salty taste of the blood. "For what? For being a clueless guard and some idiotic purse losers?"

"I wonder if they found the purse," Dae-Jung says. His feet are still on his skateboard, and he slides it back and forth as he sits.

"Who cares?" Massimo says, leaning forward a little so Dae-Jung can see his face. "Worry about your own purse." Dae-Jung pantomimes modeling a purse for us, exaggerating his gestures to make us laugh. But I can see it, the skateboard and the surfboard and the tattoos and his afro, pick high in his head. Everything complemented by his big purse, glittery and resplendent as stardust, bursting with all kinds of currency, turning it all into his latest look. Stellar. The next step beyond.

I wrap my arm around Dae-Jung briefly, before letting him go. "Massimo's right. She'll get another. You worry about your own." Such a simple thing to finally know, that there's always going to be another fight for another purse and for another work of art. You just have to show up ready to fight. And you can't sleep or lie down. You put one foot down and then the other until you get to where you're going, until you're there.

The night is warm, and I smell eucalyptus in the breeze. When I take deep breaths, the feeling in my lungs is so clean and refreshing, I feel it in my brain, in my eyes, in my heart. Overhead, the palm trees loom like guardians, fronds gently rustling, sounding like the faint roar of a distant ocean. I think of my father arriving. He still hasn't made it yet. Neither has Keith. Maybe Keith won't come at all tonight. Or maybe when he gets here, we'll be long gone. But none of us in the family are out of the woods yet. Keith will always be here, in some way, a haunting voice on the other end of the phone. Strange disturbances in the home as if someone has been there, but has vanished into thin air. A memory. But my father will be here. In the flesh. How to explain the three of us sitting here in bad shape, looking as though someone has gotten the best of us, except they didn't. We all fought for what was right. We didn't take what was happening. We won.

Still, I can just see my father's face as he walks up to the gallery in a nice suit and maybe cufflinks, seeing me sitting there with Massimo and Dae-Jung. He'll see Dae-Jung's big hair first, but then return to the bigger problem of all of us sitting on a curb collectively looking rough. He'll walk up, slowly recognizing faces that are familiar to him. His arm will reach out, and his face will have a look of resigned horror as though witnessing someone's inevitable tumble and slide down some rocky, jagged mountaintop. He'll ask me, "What are you doing sitting on a curb, bloody? Isn't this your night? You. Of all people. This is a mess," he'll say.

But I'll say, "No. No. It's good that it's come to this. Sink or swim. This is the beginning of something. A new season, right? We're all going to get up off this curb. Let's go inside. Look, in the corner, at all the things I have put together. All that stuff tells a story. Trust me. Please don't think, 'I see all of this stuff, but it's just junk. What value is it to anyone, Shirley Temple, letterman sweaters, artichokes, sugar toast, white girls with afros, Leif Garrett, our old neighbor Joan, a baseball stadium made out of flimsy sticks, a black Richie Cunningham? Mohawks and a brown-skinned cholo wearing a Dodgers cap? Remnants of people and things that are memories.' Please look at it," I'll say to my father when he gets here.

But I'm not just telling him. I'm telling everybody. Come in. Look at everything. Take in the show. Ask yourself, what kind of story does this tell? What, in the world, does all of this stuff have to do with us?

ACKNOWLEDGEMENTS

I have received support from many people since the conception of this book many years ago. I would especially like to thank the following people whose help was essential to my completing this book and getting it out in the world: My deep gratitude goes to Rosalie Siegel, my first agent. I thank her for her patience, stamina and generosity. I thank my current agent, Jennifer Lyons, whose faith in the book and all that I am trying to accomplish through it has sustained me. My heartfelt thanks to Dan Smetanka, for his vision and thoughtful edits. For their support, insight, and expertise, I must thank Veronica Gonzalez, Victoria Patterson, Danzy Senna, Michelle Latiolais, Michelle Huneven, Jane Ingram, Linda Sims, Tom Ingram, Aimee Bender, Leah Mirakhor, Alison Umminger, Karen Tongson, Tania Modleski, Walton Muyumba, Amos Mogliocco, William Handley, Zohreh Partovi, Ellie Partovi, Sabrina Williams, Mimi Lind, Bruce Smith, Gordon Davis, Chris Freeman, Michelle Gordon, Jeffrey Johnson, Dyeann Johnson and Wynell Burroughs Schamel. Much thanks to everyone at Counterpoint; how lucky I am to have landed there. My deepest thanks and appreciation goes to my husband, Kerry Brian Ingram, the writer and scholar I most admire.

ABOUT THE AUTHOR

photo © Ellie Partovi

Dana Johnson is the author of *Break Any Woman Down*, which won the Flannery O'Connor Award for Short Fiction and was a finalist for the Hurston/Wright Legacy Award. Born and raised in and around Los Angeles, California, she is an associate professor of English at the University of Southern California.